Rosie Harris was born in Cardiff and grew up there and in the West Country. After her marriage she resided for some years on Merseyside before moving to Buckinghamshire where she still lives. She has three grown-up children, and six grand-children, and writes full time.

Also by Rosie Harris

Troubled Waters
Patsy of Paradise Place
One Step Forward
Looking for Love
Pins & Needles
Winnie of the Waterfront
At Sixes & Sevens
The Cobbler's Kids
Sunshine and Showers

Turn of the Tide

ROSIE HARRIS

arrow books

Reissued by Arrow Books in 2005

10

Copyright © Rosie Harris 2002

First published in the United Kingdom in 2002 by
William Heinemann
First published in Arrow Books in 2002

Arrow Books
The Random House Group Limited
20 Vauxhall Bridge Road, London SW1V 2SA

www.randomhouse.co.uk

Addresses for companies within
The Random House Group Limited can be found at:
www.randomhouse.co.uk/offices.htm

The Random House Group Limited Reg. No. 954009

A CIP catalogue record for this book
is available from the British Library

ISBN 9780099421290

The Rand   hip
Council (F   ation.
Our book   aper.
FSC is   ing
en

Prin

To all my family and friends on Merseyside,
or who have ever lived there, and Liverpudlians
everywhere.

Acknowledgements

I would like to thank Nicola Sak, and Frank and Hilda Hunter, for their help with background information.

My thanks also to Lynne Drew, Anna Dalton-Knott, Mary Chamberlain and Caroline Sheldon for all their help and support.

Chapter One

The long, narrow road of drab, dilapidated houses had an air of broken-down despair hanging over it like a grey cloud even though it was a bright morning in late spring.

A small child, little more than a baby, barefoot, a rubber dummy stuck full square in its mouth, its soiled nappy hanging between its bandy legs like a small hammock, waddled out from one of the half-open doors. It squatted down at the edge of the pavement and began poking around in the black slimy dirt that oozed along the gutter.

Two women, who were sweeping away the debris from outside their own front doors, watched curiously as a trim young girl, carrying a brown fibre suitcase, came tripping along the street, the heels of her white T-strap shoes clicking like castanets. She was dressed in a blue-and-white dress that skimmed her trim figure and barely reached her knees. Her cropped dark hair was half hidden under a white cloche hat, she wore no make-up and her heart-shaped face was fresh and pretty.

Lips pursed, she peered anxiously at each house, a frown puckering the wing-shaped brows over her dark brown eyes.

'Whose house yer lookin' for, luv?' one of the

women called out, leaning on her broom and openly studying the stranger.

The girl paused, resting her suitcase on the pavement. 'Mrs Flanagan's. Do you know which one it is?'

'Know it!' The younger of the two women gave a raucous laugh. 'Give over, chuck, everyone in Bootle, let alone in Anfield Road, knows the Flanagans.'

'What do you want with them, then, luv?' asked the older woman, lifting the front of her grubby pinafore to wipe her nose.

'I . . . I'm going to live with them.'

'Live with the Flanagans!' The woman laughed in disbelief. 'Their house is bursting at the seams as it is. Six of them holed up in there already. No room to swing a cat, let alone take in a lodger!'

Lucy looked uncomfortable. She had tried to imagine what it would be like meeting Aunt Flo and her family for the first time. She knew nothing at all about them. Her mother had never even mentioned her aunt's existence until a couple of weeks ago, only days before she died, when a letter had arrived with a Liverpool postmark.

She would never forget how when she had taken the letter up to the bedroom her mother had given such a deep sigh of relief that it had sent a shiver right through her frail body.

'This will be from your Aunt Florence, your father's sister,' she'd murmured weakly as she struggled to open it.

'Dad's sister? I never knew he had one,' Lucy

2

said in surprise as she plumped up the pillows behind her mother so that they were supporting her in a more comfortable position.

'Oh, yes. She's a couple of years younger than he was.'

'And she lives in Liverpool?' Lucy was taken aback.

Her mother nodded.

'So why has she never been to see us?'

Her mother shook her head, a troubled look in her faded eyes. 'It's a long story, dear.'

Lucy perched on the side of her mother's bed. 'Aren't you going to tell me about her and why we've never met?'

'Later, my dear, when I'm feeling stronger.' She reached out and took Lucy's hand. 'It's enough for now that you know about her. Put this letter somewhere safe so that you know where she lives and where to go when the time comes.'

Lucy frowned. 'When the time comes? I don't understand. What do you mean?'

'Promise me, Lucy . . . ' Her mother reached out and took her hand, holding it tightly. 'Swear to me that you'll do as I ask no matter who tries to persuade you to do otherwise,' she begged, a faint sheen of perspiration on her upper lip.

Lucy leaned forward and kissed her on the brow. 'Of course I will, Mother. Haven't I always done what you wanted?'

'Yes, yes, my dear.' The pressure on Lucy's hand increased. It felt like the talons of a bird clinging on. 'This is different. It's your whole future . . .' A spasm of coughing racked Maude

3

Patterson's thin frame. Exhausted, she lay back against the pillows.

Lucy dabbed the beads of perspiration from her mother's brow and sunken cheeks. 'Try not to talk, Mother. It only makes you worse!'

'There is something I must say, my darling. Something you must promise me. I won't be able to rest until you do.'

'I've already promised to do whatever you want me to do,' Lucy reminded her. 'Tell me what it is and then try and rest. Should I make you a nice cup of tea first?'

Her mother shook her head impatiently. 'Lucy,' her voice was surprisingly strong, 'promise me that you will go to your Aunt Florence in Liverpool as soon as anything happens to me. You mustn't stay here in this house no matter how much Stanley tries to persuade you to do so. I've protected you all these years, but it wouldn't be right for you to stay on here. You must get away. Do you understand? You mustn't be alone here with him.'

Two vivid red spots burned on the sunken cheeks like angry boils, and the harsh noise of her breathing filled the bedroom like the rasp of a saw going through wood. Lucy held her close, smoothing her hair, trying to calm her as she began to shake uncontrollably.

'Promise me, Lucy,' she whispered hysterically. 'Swear to me that you will do as I ask.'

'I promise, Mother,' Lucy told her solemnly. 'I'll leave here and go to live with Aunt Florence Flanagan in Liverpool when ... when ...' Tears

4

choked her. 'I know what you mean, Mother, and I do promise, only don't make me say those terrible words.' Tenderly she pressed her lips to her mother's brow. 'Now, lie back and rest and I'll go and make that pot of tea,' she told her.

When she returned with the tray holding two cups of tea and a plate of biscuits, the alarming flush had drained from her mother's cheeks. She appeared to be much calmer, almost serene. She smiled gratefully as Lucy put the tray down on the bedside table. Then her eyelids drooped, and her breathing became so shallow that her sunken chest barely moved. Every vestige of colour drained from her face, leaving her skin translucent, her lips bloodless and her nose white and pinched.

The end had come quickly after that. There was no time to get help. By the time Stanley Jones returned home from the Cotton Exchange in Liverpool, where he worked as an accountant, his housekeeper Maude Patterson was dead.

Tears pricked at Lucy's eyes as she recalled those traumatic events. She brushed them away and gave a tremulous smile as she brought her thoughts back to the present, aware that the two women were waiting for her to explain why she was going to live with the Flanagans.

'They invited me to come here ...' Her voice trailed off as she saw the disbelief on their faces.

'Invited you?' the older woman mimicked. 'Not one of Frank's floozies that the bastard's got into trouble, are you?'

'Shut yer gob, Fanny. Does she look like a slapper?'

Lucy coloured up with embarrassment. 'My name is Lucy Patterson and Mrs Flanagan is my aunt,' she told them primly.

'Flo's your aunt!' The two women looked at each other as if mystified.

'That's right. She's my father's sister.'

'Well, that's a turn-up!' The younger of the two women ran her tongue over her lips as if physically enjoying this titbit of juicy gossip. 'I'm Sal Hicks, by the way, and this is Fanny Nelson.'

The older woman lifted her cotton apron and wiped her face again. 'Flo's niece, you say, chuck. Never knew she had any family, other than her old man and her kids, of course. Does Fred know you're coming?'

'Fred?' Lucy frowned. 'Who is Fred?'

'Who is Fred!' The older woman cackled. 'She'll soon find out, won't she, Sal! We all know the old bugger and we all keep out of his way. Nasty old sod, even when he's sober.'

'Fred is your uncle, luv, and you want to watch out for him,' Sal warned. 'Nasty old devil, like Fanny says. Wicked temper and too free with his hands, if you get my drift.'

'No, I don't think I do,' Lucy admitted. Her heart was thudding. It sounded frightening. 'Do you mean he hits people?'

'He doesn't just hit 'em,' Fanny sniffed, 'he does a damn sight more than that. He'll thump you black and blue even if you're a woman. Keep well out of his way if you're going to live with the

6

Flanagans. And you'll find your cousin Frank is even worse than his old man. Nothing in skirts is safe when he's around. There, I've told you, luv! Warned you! So watch your step with both of them.'

Lucy looked bewildered. 'And my Aunt Flo, doesn't she say anything, or do something about the way they carry on?'

'Flo Flanagan? Poor old cow! She has a hard time of it and no maybe with that lot,' sighed Fanny.

'She's had her share of trouble like the rest of us,' Sal added quickly, 'but Fred's a grafter, I'll say that for him. Works down the docks, rain or shine. And if the ganger don't take him on then he'll mooch round and see if he can get some other job, anything to make a bob or two. Frank's a docker as well but he's a right idle bounder. I think he enjoys being laid off. He's been trouble ever since the day he was born. Even as a kid at school he was always brawling. And their Selina is even worse. Right slapper she is, I can tell yer, for all her airs and graces. I shouldn't think they're your type at all, luv.'

'It's young Karen I feel sorry for,' sniffed Fanny. 'She used to be such a pretty little thing, but now she looks so frail that a puff of wind would blow her over.'

Lucy felt a tingle of fear. She wondered if she'd been rather too hasty in leaving the house in Wallasey, that had been her home for as long as she could remember, for this unknown destination in Liverpool. The more she heard about her

Aunt Flo's family the more she wished that her mother hadn't made her promise to come and live with them.

'They say that Karen is epileptic,' Sal went on. 'It's a terrible sight when she has one of her fits. She foams at the mouth and her body twitches all over and then she falls down.'

'She still goes on twitching, even when she's on the ground,' Fanny added lugubriously. 'Wets herself, too. Sick all over the place, sometimes, as well.'

'The funny thing is, she never seems to really hurt herself,' Sal said in a puzzled voice.

'Oh, yes she does,' Fanny argued. 'She bruises herself! I've seen some terrible cuts on her legs, too, when she's been thrashing about and caught them against something.'

'She's never broken any bones though!'

'No, you're right about that, chuck! I read somewhere that it's because when people have fits they goes all floppy like and when they fall that cushions them. If she stiffened up and tried to save herself then she probably would break an arm or leg.'

'Can't something be done for her? Haven't they taken her to see a doctor?' Lucy asked in a shocked voice.

'Nothing any of them can do, is there,' Fanny said sagely. 'It's one of them afflictions you read about in the Bible. A sort of punishment for being wicked.'

'How can you say a thing like that!' Sal exploded. 'Wicked? Young Karen? That's a load

8

of old nonsense if ever I heard it. Blasphemous, too! She goes to Mass as regular as clockwork, same as the rest of them Flanagans.'

'Keep your hair on! I didn't mean *she* had been wicked. I was thinking of the others. Frank and that Selina. And old Fred, if it comes to that.'

Sal looked mollified. 'That's all right then. I think Karen is a little angel, and if their young Shirley takes after her it will be a blessing, just so long as she doesn't start getting them fits.'

'Shirley?' Lucy looked apprehensive. How many more were there in the Flanagan family, she wondered. The terraced houses looked pitifully small to accommodate so many people, especially when four of them seemed to be adults and one of the others was so sickly. Where on earth did they all sleep?

'Shirley's about eleven and still at school, only a kid. Cheeky little brat, though, got too much to say for herself by half.'

'How come you didn't know any of this then, luv, seeing that Flo Flanagan was your dad's sister?' Fanny asked.

'He ... he's been dead for a long time,' Lucy explained.

'And your mam wasn't on visiting terms, I take it, even though you only lived across the water?'

Lucy shook her head.

'Well, it's a right turn-up, that's all I can say,' Fanny muttered. 'It's the first we've heard of you and the first you've heard of them! You'd best be getting along and meeting them, hadn't you?'

9

Lucy gave a nervous smile. 'Yes, I suppose so,' she admitted.

'D'you want one of us to go with you? I'll come if you like,' Sal said eagerly.

Lucy hesitated, then shook her head. She would have liked nothing better than to turn round and take the tram back down to the pier head and catch the next ferry boat back to Wallasey. Tears welled up in her eyes because she knew she couldn't do that. She'd promised her mother that she wouldn't stay with Stanley, but would go to her Aunt Flo's in Liverpool, and that was what she had to do whether she liked the idea or not.

Lucy smiled tremulously at the two women, then squared her slim shoulders. 'Thank you, it's very kind of you to offer, but I think it's something I ought to do on my own.' She picked up her suitcase. 'If you would tell me which house it is, then I'll be on my way.'

Chapter Two

When she heard the knock on her front door, Flo Flanagan rose from where she was kneeling in front of the shrine she'd arranged on a clothes chest in her bedroom, wondering who it could be.

With a puzzled frown, she looked at the alarm clock on the rickety little table that stood alongside the double bed she shared with her husband Fred. It was too early in the afternoon for Shirley to be home from school, and it certainly couldn't be Fred or Frank, or even Selina, home from work this early. Not unless they were ill. And if that was the case then they wouldn't knock on the front door. They'd come round to the back door. And if she was out and that was locked, then they all knew the key was on a piece of string, and that all they had to do was put a hand through the letter-box to reach it.

Laying down her rosary, she took a last lingering look at the little altar that she'd arranged as her tribute to the Holy Mother. On the white pillowcase there was a jamjar of flowers standing between two candles, in front of a framed picture of the Virgin. Her head was covered by a blue cloth, and she was holding the body of Christ in her arms after he'd been taken down from the Cross. Flo made the shrine every year, and said

11

special prayers to the Virgin Mary throughout the month of May.

Fred laughed at her. He said that was the trouble with converts, they were more religious that those born Catholic. Even though Flo insisted that the rest of the family went regularly to Mass every Sunday come rain, hail or shine, he rarely went to church himself, except to confession and Holy Communion at Easter.

He didn't celebrate the saints' days either.

'I can't remember when they all are,' he would say with a shrug of his massive shoulders. 'There's one for every day of the bloody year according to Father O'Reilly, but the only one I can remember is St Patrick's.'

Father O'Reilly would nod sagely whenever he heard Fred say this. A tolerant man, he recognised that some members of his flock took their religion less seriously than others. He approved of Flo Flanagan and her devout attitude, and the way she made sure that the rest of her family were regular at Mass, and that they went to confession and Holy Communion at least once a month.

In his eyes she was a good woman. Every year he visited her on the first day of May to bless the shrine she created to the honour of the Virgin. For the rest of the year he was always on hand to listen to her worries and offer words of comfort when she was at her wits' end over Fred's boozing and Frank's philandering, and Selina's many slips from grace.

Above all, he was always ready to offer comfort and to pray with her when Karen had one of her epileptic fits. At such times, he would always assure her that God wasn't punishing the child, or her, only testing the strength of their beliefs.

Perhaps this interruption was also one of God's ways of testing her faith, Flo thought wryly as she made her way downstairs. She so looked forward to the quiet half-hour she spent praying each afternoon during May. It calmed her, soothed her and, at the same time, made her feel thankful for the blessings she had.

Praying to the Virgin was better than talking to a friend. There were no interruptions, no one putting forward their views, or telling you how they thought you should deal with your problems, or making a comparison between your life and theirs.

The Holy Mother neither criticised, nor praised, nor indeed said anything at all. Her serene look, though sad, had such a calm forgiving air that at the end of her afternoon session Flo always felt much more confident about facing any problems that lay ahead of her.

She sensed a special affinity between herself and the Virgin Mary. As a mother whose son had known trouble, even though it was not of His own making like it was with her Frank, Flo believed the Virgin Mary understood the grief and foreboding that she so often encountered because of Frank's behaviour.

As the knocking was repeated, Flo hurried down the stairs. She opened the front door, and then stared blankly at the young girl standing on the doorstep.

For a moment the two of them stood there in silence, weighing each other up. Lucy saw a plump, stocky, middle-aged woman with lank grey hair and sharp dark eyes, dressed in a shapeless dark blue dress. Flo saw a pert young girl, who in spite of her smart clothes looked very young and very nervous.

'If you're selling I don't want any, and if you're collecting I haven't anything for you, so you're floggin' a dead horse,' Flo told her as she caught sight of the suitcase.

'I'm not doing either, Aunt Florence.'

'Aunt Florence?' Flo Flanagan stared open-mouthed.

'That's right. I'm Lucy Patterson . . . your niece.'

'Niece?' Flo didn't know whether to be relieved or dismayed. For one frightening moment as she opened the door she'd thought it was one of Frank's discarded girlfriends, and wondered what trouble there was in the offing this time. 'You mean you're my brother John's daughter?'

The girl smiled wistfully. 'I've never heard him called by his name before. He died such a long time ago . . .' her voice trailed off.

'Did yer mam, Maude, write me a letter a few weeks ago?'

'Yes, that's right.' Lucy nodded her head. 'My mother died last week so I've come to live with you, like you agreed.'

Flo took a deep breath. 'She said she was ill, but I had no idea she was dying,' she said slowly. 'I thought . . . well, I don't really know what I thought.' She shook her head from side to side in bewilderment. 'I never thought it would ever come to this, girl! Not to you moving in . . . not so soon, anyway.'

Tears sprang into Lucy's dark eyes and she bit down on her lower lip. 'You did agree . . . my mother showed me the letter.'

'Well, yes, like I say. I've got kids of me own so I know that when a body's not well they get anxious about who's going to take care of them if the worst should happen. And you having no dad alive, well, naturally I said you could come to me if anything happened to her but . . .'

'She died last week,' Lucy repeated quietly. 'The funeral was yesterday.'

'Oh, my dear!' Flo crossed herself. 'I'd no idea she was that ill. I gathered she was going through a bad patch, and feeling anxious about your future. I thought she needed a reassuring word . . .' Flo paused and looked helplessly at Lucy. 'Well, since you're here, luv, you'd better come in.' She turned and led the way, leaving Lucy to follow.

Lucy felt unnerved by the lack of warmth in her aunt's greeting, and not for the first time that day she wondered if she should have come to Liverpool after all. If only her mother hadn't made her promise to do so, she thought miserably. She'd always been so happy in Belgrave Road, which had been her home ever since her father died and her mother became housekeeper to Stanley Jones.

The large, comfortable house was close enough to the town centre, and to the park, for her to walk there whenever she wished. And the seaside resort of New Brighton was only a short bus ride away.

Stanley Jones was a senior clerk at the Cotton Exchange in Liverpool. He left at eight thirty each morning, a thin dapper figure, always neatly dressed in a dark suit, white shirt with stiff collar and a sombre tie. He had sparse light brown hair that was receding slightly at the front, and his grey eyes were hidden by horn-rimmed glasses. He always wore a black trilby and carried a rolled black umbrella.

A shy, studious man, he'd only been in his early twenties when his parents died and he inherited the house in Belgrave Road. Outside work, his whole life seemed to revolve around his books and music.

Lucy had never been able to understand the reasoning behind her mother's concern about her being in the house alone with Stanley Jones. She could never remember him being cross with her or even raising his voice in anger. The day she'd broken his precious Spode vase, when she'd been helping her mother by doing some dusting, he'd looked sad, but he said he quite understood that it was an accident and that she was not to worry about it.

He was more concerned about the fact that a piece of the vase had cut her arm when she'd tried to save it. He'd wanted her to go to the hospital, because he was sure her arm needed a stitch in it, but her mother had bathed the cut and put a bandage on it and said it would soon heal up.

Her mother had been the one who'd been cross

and had scolded her for days. The vase had belonged to Stanley's family and he'd prized it very highly and, as her mother had pointed out, it was completely irreplaceable.

For as long as she could remember, Stanley had been kindness itself. At Christmas, and on her birthday, he always gave her a lovely present, and at Easter time he always bought her an enormous chocolate egg.

When she'd been at school he'd taken as much interest in what she was doing as her mother did, and was forever telling her how important it was to take her mother's advice and study hard so that she could pass exams. He'd often helped her with her homework, explaining things much more clearly than the teachers did at school – which was probably why she was always near the top of the class and why she'd managed to pass the exam to go to Wallasey High School when she was eleven.

For some reason that Lucy had never been able to understand, her mother didn't seem to approve of Stanley helping her with her studying. She would hover in the room, pretending to be dusting or tidying up, as if she was afraid of leaving them together.

She never actually said anything, Lucy mused. Probably because she knew Stanley was able to help with my homework and she couldn't, and she was very anxious for me to get my School Certificate and eventually go to college and become a teacher.

Lucy blinked away a tear. That had all been a

pipe dream. When her mother had become seriously ill, she'd had to leave Wallasey High before she was fifteen to look after her so she'd never sat for any of her important exams.

Stanley had looked quite dismayed when, after the funeral, she told him that she was going to her aunt's in Liverpool. She tried to explain that she didn't really want to do so, but she'd promised her mother that she would.

His face clouded. 'I thought you'd be staying here, Lucy, and completing your education to become a teacher. You wouldn't have to run the house. I'd employ someone to do that,' he told her, taking off his spectacles and polishing them agitatedly.

She knew he was hurt by her decision, but she couldn't ignore her promise to her mother. She tried to make Stanley understand this, but for once he didn't agree with her.

When she'd come downstairs about an hour later, after packing the things she thought she was likely to need, Stanley had refused to say goodbye, or to wish her well. Instead he stayed seated at his desk in the dining-room with his back towards her, shuffling through a pile of papers as though totally absorbed.

'I'll come back for the rest of my clothes some time next week if that is all right,' she said.

'Very well. You've got a door key so you can let yourself in if I'm not here,' he said without even turning round.

His tone had been stiff and cold. It was as though they were strangers, or he was dismissing

18

a servant. She'd had to fight back the tears. It seemed awful to be leaving on such a harsh note after all the happy times she'd known there.

On the bus that took her from Belgrave Road to the ferry, and on the boat all the way over to Liverpool, she could think of nothing else. The hardness of his voice rang in her ears. She found she couldn't sit still in the inside cabin so she went up the gangway to the top deck and walked around. At least there she could blame the keen wind that was blowing in from the sea for the tears in her eyes.

As she got off the boat, and trudged up the steep slope from the landing stage to the roadway, she felt as if she was climbing into a different world. Looking back across the Mersey she could see Wallasey town hall and from there right along the coastline to Egremont ferry. Further on still, she could even see the tower at New Brighton soaring up into the sky, and not far from it, New Brighton pier jutting out into the greyness of the River Mersey. Beyond that was the open sea, with the shadowy outlines of the Welsh mountains in the far distance.

Squaring her shoulders as she went in search of a tram that would take her to Aunt Florence and her new home, she was acutely aware that she was leaving not only Wallasey, but also her childhood, behind her. What lay ahead she had no idea.

Now that she was here, and having listened to what the two women she'd met in the road outside had had to say, all her doubts flared up anew. It was obvious her Aunt Florence wasn't expecting her, and, what was more to the point, didn't really want her there. Probably because she has quite enough to do with looking after the family she already has, Lucy thought despondently.

The house wasn't very inviting either, Lucy decided, as she looked round the room her aunt had taken her into. It was a long, dismal room that seemed to run almost the full length of the house. At one end was the narrow window that looked out on to the street and at the other end a coal-burning range. There was a door beside the grate that led down two steps into what seemed to be a scullery because she could see a sink and the edge of the wooden roller of a mangle.

On top of the range was a huge black kettle and a couple of smoke-grimed cast-iron saucepans. The mantelpiece over it was crammed with bric-à-brac, letters and tins. In the middle of the room was a scrubbed wooden table with a long bench seat on one side of it, and an assortment of wooden chairs. Two were pushed underneath it on the opposite side to the bench, and there was one at each end. Against one wall was a sideboard and the shelves above it were stacked with an assortment of plates, cups, saucers and dishes of every kind.

The atmosphere was stuffy. There was an overpowering smell of onions and grease from frying. The sash window was covered by a piece of net curtain to screen out the view of the street outside. The window looked as though it had never been opened in its life judging from the screws of newspaper stuck in all the way along the edges to keep out the drafts.

'Put your suitcase down then, chuck,' Flo told Lucy, 'and I'll make us a cuppa and we can try and sort things out before the others get home from work.' She opened up the top of the range and pushed the blackened kettle over the glowing coals. 'You took me a bit by surprise, luv,' she went on as if trying to explain her rather cool reception.

'Yes, I'm sorry, Aunt Florence. I should have written to you the minute my mother died in case you wanted to come to the funeral. I . . . I just didn't think, I was so upset. Stanley Jones, the man my mother kept house for, arranged the funeral and everything. It was all so quick in the end.'

'So why come over here to me?' Flo ran a hand through her grey hair, pushing it back from her forehead. 'Couldn't you have stayed on where you were, chuck?'

'That's what Stanley would've liked me to do,' Lucy admitted. 'He said he'd get a woman in to do all the cleaning and so on, and I could finish my education.'

'Sounds cushy enough to me, so why didn't you stay there?'

'My mother made me promise not to do so. When your letter came, and I took it up to her, she told me she'd written to you and that I was to go and live with you if anything happened to her.

21

She said I wasn't to stay there with Stanley Jones a day longer than I had to.'

'I see!' Flo studied Lucy shrewdly. 'Fancied you did he, this Stanley Jones?'

'Fancied me?' Lucy's face flamed. 'What do you mean?'

'Came on a bit strong, like. Tried to touch you up, that sort of thing?'

Lucy looked perplexed. 'Stanley was always very kind to me. He bought me presents at Christmas and always something special for my birthday.'

'And what did he expect in return, luv? A bit of kissing and hugging?'

Lucy shook her head. 'He seemed to be quite happy to see how pleased I was with his present.'

Flo turned away as the kettle began to splutter to the boil. She reached up on to the mantelpiece and took down a tin caddy, then spooned tea from it into a cracked brown pot and filled the pot with boiling water.

Lucy watched her walk across to the sideboard. There was a rattle of china as she picked up two odd cups and saucers and set them down on the scrubbed table. On the flat top of the sideboard was a white jug covered by a piece of gauze with beads sewn to the corners to weight it down. From this, Flo poured milk into the two cups and followed it with tea from the brown pot. She replaced the gauze on the milk jug, put the jug back on the sideboard and brought a bowl of sugar over to the table.

She handed Lucy a teaspoon. 'Help yourself,

luv. Now, do you want something to eat? A cheese-and-pickle sarnie to go with that? I'll be cooking a proper meal later on. They're all home around six and as hungry as horses the lot of them.'

'No, thank you, Aunt Florence.' Lucy carefully measured a spoonful of sugar into her cup and concentrated on stirring it. Her aunt's questioning had left her feeling confused. Perhaps she should have stayed in Wallasey and not come rushing across to Liverpool. If only her mother hadn't made her promise to do so. If she had simply said it might be a good idea, then Lucy felt she would have been free to stay on at Stanley's place.

'I never knew my father had a sister or that you lived in Liverpool, not until your letter arrived,' Lucy said, smiling across at her aunt.

'You didn't! Well, it doesn't surprise me, not really, chuck. I only ever met your mother once and that was before she and John were married. Your father never approved of me marrying Fred. Didn't think he was good enough for me. Right riled up he was, and wouldn't even speak to me afterwards. I never heard a word from him after I got married, and it broke my heart at the time. Mind you,' she stirred her tea reflectively, 'I'd probably do the same thing again if I had to live my life over.'

Flo drained her cup and poured herself another. 'I'm warning you, you'll find living here a damn sight different from your posh place in Wallasey,' she said bluntly. 'You won't be getting a room all to yourself for one thing, and there'll be no one running round after you. As well as having my eldest, Frank, and my husband to wash and cook and clean for, I've got three girls, and one of them is on the sickly side, so you'll be expected to help out and pull your weight.'

'I do understand, Aunt Florence, and I'll try my best to fit in and do whatever I can to help,' Lucy assured her earnestly.

'Right, luv! Then for a start call me Aunt Flo. Aunt Florence is too highfalutin for around here, chuck.'

Lucy smiled contritely. 'Yes of course, Aunt Flor ... Aunt Flo, I'll try and remember that.'

'Orright, luv!' Flo's plump face softened into a smile. 'You're very like your dad, you know. He spoke all posh like you do! You can't have been very old when he died?'

'I was only four. I can barely remember him.'

'And it's been just you and your mam since then? Poor cow! It must have been tough going for her,' Flo sighed.

'Yes, I believe it was at first,' Lucy agreed. 'She had no money and nowhere to live until she got the job as housekeeper to Stanley Jones. After that her worries were more or less over, so she said. Except for worrying about me, of course. She was always on at me to study so that I could pass exams and get a good job when I left school.'

'No new husband, though?' Flo probed. 'This Stanley Jones didn't want to marry her, then?'

'Marry her!' Lucy gave a peal of laughter. 'Stanley was only in his early twenties when Mum moved into his house in Belgrave Road. His parents were both killed in a train crash and he was left the house. He wanted to go on living there so he needed someone to take their place.'

Flo drained the last of the tea from the pot into her cup and stood up. 'And she'd be turned thirty and she had you to bring up. You're right, luv, too much for such a young man to take on.'

Flo picked up their two cups and saucers and carried them through into the scullery. 'Bring the teapot, will you, Lucy,' she called back over her shoulder. 'It's time I got started on the evening meal.'

'Can I help you?' Lucy offered as she followed her.

'Empty the pot and then run some water into that enamel bowl and you can peel the spuds ready for the chips, while I start frying some onions and the sausages.'

'And will you tell me all about my cousins?' Lucy asked shyly.

'No need, chuck, they'll all be home before long so you'll be able to meet them for yourself,' her aunt told her.

Chapter Three

Squashed in between her cousins, Karen and
Shirley Flanagan, Lucy tried to make herself as
small as possible. She kept her dark brown eyes
fixed firmly on the plate of sausages and chips in
front of her while her Aunt Flo said grace, and
then picked up her knife and fork without even
looking up.

Sitting directly opposite her was her cousin
Frank, a big handsome man in his mid-twenties
with broad powerful shoulders and thick dark
hair brushed back from his wide forehead. He
kept staring at her, his vivid blue eyes sharp with
curiosity, and it filled her with confusion.

From her place at the head of the table, her
Aunt Flo seemed to be keeping a wary eye on
them all. Lucy could tell by the way her aunt's
brows drew together in a frown, whenever she
looked in her direction, and saw the barely
touched food on her plate, that her aunt was
concerned by the lack of enthusiasm she was
showing for her meal.

She wanted to eat. She'd had nothing since
breakfast time and she was desperately hungry,
but there was a painful lump in her throat that
was stopping her from swallowing. It was partly
nervousness because she'd never sat down to eat

with so many strangers before, and partly unhappiness.

The six other people around the table were all so very different from any she'd ever known. She felt, too, that they didn't want her there. She was an outsider, an intruder, and each one of them in their own way, and for their own reason, resented her presence.

None of them had been remotely pleased to see her when they'd arrived home that evening. Her Uncle Fred, a huge, corpulent, intimidating man, had merely grunted when told who she was. He'd stared at her from beneath heavy brows and then ignored her.

Her cousin Selina had been the most frightening. Lucy had been overawed by her glamorous looks and flamboyant clothes. She'd wished the ground would open and swallow her up as Selina looked her up and down disdainfully, as though silently criticising her dress, her shoes and her appearance generally before asking her mother very pointedly, 'Where's she sleeping, then?'

Frank's eyes had narrowed to hard blue slits as he eyed her up, but his attention was immediately diverted as his mother plonked down a plate piled high with sausages and chips on the table and told him to 'get stuck in and leave the questions until afterwards'.

Shirley and Karen were the only ones who had shown a companionable interest. Shirley had come bursting in from school, a plump giggly girl, in a gymslip and white blouse, her cheeks pink and shiny, her hair all over the place. She was bright with chatter about her day, but she'd gone quiet when her mother had introduced them. Her cheeky grin was replaced by a questioning look when her mother told her that this was her cousin Lucy and that she had come to live with them.

The only one who had really given her a welcoming smile was Karen. Fragile looking, with mousy hair and enormous pale grey eyes, Karen looked so frail in her shapeless, washed-out cotton dress that Lucy's heart went out to her. The thin bloodless lips and bony frame brought the last few weeks of her own mother's illness vividly back to Lucy's mind. She remembered what the women she'd spoken to in the street had told her about Karen, and recalled that her Aunt Flo had also said something about her being sickly.

Her thoughts in turmoil, and aware of the uneasy atmosphere in the room, Lucy struggled to eat the food in front of her. The others had already finished, and her Uncle Fred was running a piece of bread around his plate, wiping up the last of the onion gravy with a hearty slurping sound.

Frank leaned across the table, his fork poised above Lucy's plate. 'Are you going to eat those sausages or not?' he demanded.

She shook her head, too embarrassed to answer. She felt even more mortified when without another word he stabbed at two of them and transferred them on to his own plate. Then he leaned forward again and speared up a forkful of her chips, sticking them straight into his mouth.

'Bloody pig!' bellowed his father. 'You're not the only bugger bringing in a wage packet, you know.' He leaned forward, picked up the remaining sausage from Lucy's plate and stuffed it into his own mouth, licking the grease and gravy from his thumb and fingers.

Frowning, Aunt Flo stood up and began collecting the plates. She stacked them in a pile and told Shirley to take them through to the scullery. Then she collected cups and saucers from the shelves above the sideboard and brought the pot of tea that she'd made earlier and left standing on top of the range to keep warm, to the table. She poured it out, dark and stewed, and Lucy's stomach turned over when her aunt pushed a cupful towards her. She added plenty of milk and a heaped spoonful of sugar to try and make it more palatable.

Fred Flanagan took a noisy slurp from his cup, wiped the back of his hand across his mouth, belched and stared fiercely at Lucy.

'Well, girl, what you doing here in my house, then?' he asked, scratching his chest.

Nervously, Lucy cleared her throat to answer, but before she could speak her Aunt Flo looked round at them all fiercely. 'She's my brother John's girl, her mam died last week so she's coming to live with us. Now shurrup the lot of you. If you've finished eating move out of the way so that I can get finished for the day.'

'Keep your hair on, woman,' Fred snarled. He pulled a crushed packet of Woodbines from his jacket pocket and lit one. 'I've a right to know who's living in me own house, and eating the grub I slog me guts out to provide, haven't I?' he asked, taking a deep drag on his cigarette.

Lucy looked from one to the other of them in fright. She didn't want to start a row and she wondered what she ought to do. Then she saw Frank was grinning as if he was enjoying the spectacle, and she relaxed a little.

'Where's she sleeping? That's what I want to know,' Selina demanded.

'She can share my bed if she likes,' Frank offered, leering at Lucy.

'We'll have none of that talk, so shut it,' Flo snapped. 'Time you were off down the pub, isn't it,' she added. 'Not like you to sit around jawing once you've had your grub.'

'We don't usually have anyone here worth chatting up,' Frank grinned, pushing his thick dark hair back from his forehead. 'Anyway, where's she going to sleep?'

'In with the girls, of course. Where else is there?'

'We can't get another bed in there, we can't move as it is,' grumbled Selina. 'Those two are always in my way when I'm trying to get dressed,' she added, glaring at Karen and Shirley.

'Then the sooner you move out the better,' Frank told her.

'Put a sock in it, Frank. No one asked your opinion. It's all right for you with a room of your own.'

'Room you call it! Coffin more like. If I stretch my arms out I can touch the walls on either side.'

'That's what comes of being built like a brick shit house on a Welsh hillside,' his sister told him nastily.

'No fairy yourself, girl. Got an arse on you like a barrel and a pair of tits like . . .'

'That'll do,' Flo warned. 'Get out in that scullery and get yourself washed before I start on the dishes. There's hot water in the kettle if you want to shave and there's a clean shirt up on the rail.'

'Is it ironed?'

'Iron it yourself, you lazy sod,' snapped Selina. 'Why should our mam wait on you, tell me that?'

'Because I bring home twice the money you do. And ironing is women's work. If you don't want our mam to do it then you do it for me.'

'Like hell! I've been working my fingers to the bone in a factory all day so I don't intend coming home and ironing shirts for you. If I want to iron a man's shirt then I'll get married.'

'If you can find anyone who'd marry a tart like you! One that isn't already shacked up, that is.'

'That'll do, that'll do.' Aunt Flo held up her hand to stop them squabbling. 'I've put the flat-iron on the range to heat up and I'll iron your shirt, Frank, while you get yourself washed and cleaned up.'

'I'll do it if you like, Aunt Flo, I'm quite good at ironing,' Lucy volunteered.

'Give me your sausages and now offering to iron my shirt,' teased Frank. 'What you after then, chuck?'

'I'm not after anything,' Lucy told him primly. 'I'm sure Aunt Flo is tired and I thought it would help her.'

'Did you now!' Frank ruffled her short hair.

31

'Right little creep, aren't you! Make sure you make a good job of my shirt then.'

Flo fetched out an old blanket from one of the cupboards in the sideboard, folded it up and laid it across one end of the table. 'There you are, Lucy, and here's a pad to hold the iron. Mind you don't burn yourself.'

'Don't kid yourself that you can hang around the house doing odd jobs for our mam,' Selina sneered. 'If you're going to live here then it's only fair that you find some work and pay your way the same as the rest of us. Karen's here to do jobs like ironing and cleaning and helping Mam around the house. It's about all she's capable of because she's a bit sickly, see,' she added by way of explanation.

'Oh, poor girl! That must be terrible for her!'

'Oh, poor girlie,' Shirley tittered, kneeling up on one of the chairs, her elbows on the table, watching Lucy struggle to smooth the creases from the shirt Frank had pulled down from the airing rack and tossed across to her.

'Shut up, you cheeky little brat!' Selina swiped a hand towards Shirley's head, but her young sister dodged out of the way.

'Missed!' Shirley yelled with an impudent grin. 'So whose bed is Lucy going to sleep in?'

'It will have to be Karen's, won't it,' her mother answered. 'She's got the biggest bed of the three of you. That all right with you, Lucy?'

Lucy's dark eyes widened. She'd never shared a bed with anyone in her life. She hadn't even shared a room. Her mother had often said that if

Stanley ever wanted anyone to come and stay then she would have to move into her bedroom and sleep on the sofa while they were there, but it had never happened. Stanley didn't have many visitors. He liked to spend his evenings reading, listening to music, or helping her with her homework. He hated any change in his regular routine so he'd never dream of asking anyone to stay the night.

Lucy was aware that they were waiting for her answer. The very idea of what was being suggested made her cringe. She'd never even undressed in front of anyone before, and now she was not only going to be in a room with her three cousins, but she was going to have to sleep in the same bed as one of them. She'd never felt so disconcerted in her life. She knew Frank was watching her, a humorous sneer on his face, so she took a deep breath and managed to smile and nod in agreement.

'Our Karen's got the biggest bed because she has fits and some nights she kicks and screams and wets the bed,' Shirley whispered.

'Karen can't help it and it only happens once in a blue moon,' Aunt Flo said briskly, putting her arm round Karen.

'And that's once too often as far as I'm concerned when I have to get up at six for work,' Selina muttered.

'Can you lot stop gabbing and leave a man to read his paper in peace before I belt one of you,' growled Fred from where he sat in the battered armchair by the side of the range. He rustled the pages of the *Liverpool Echo* angrily.

'I'll finish off Frank's shirt, Lucy, and Shirley can take you upstairs and show you where you'll be sleeping,' Flo told them. 'Take Lucy's case up with you,' she called after them as they went out into the hallway.

Upstairs was even more congested than it was down below. Lucy couldn't believe her eyes when she followed Shirley into their bedroom and saw how cramped it was. The three iron bedsteads in the room were practically touching. The slightly larger one was pushed tight up against the wall under the narrow window; the other two, which were side by side against an adjacent wall, were so close together that it was impossible even to walk sideways between them.

'That's Karen's bed,' Shirley pronounced, indicating the one under the window.

Lucy looked round at the drab walls, and at the skimpy striped cotton curtains hanging at the narrow window, and thought of the bedroom she'd had in Belgrave Road. It had been nearly twice the size of this one. There had been pretty sprigged blue-and-white paper on the walls, blue damask curtains and a white honeycomb bedspread trimmed with blue satin piping around the edges.

It had been well furnished; a mahogany dressing-table, a matching wardrobe, a chest of drawers and a comfortable armchair. There had also been a table by the side of the bed covered

34

with a blue cloth embroidered with flowers and edged with white lace.

She looked round again in dismay. There wasn't anywhere to hang their clothes, and hardly enough room to get undressed. No wonder Karen was able to disturb them if she was taken ill. It would be a job not to do so, Lucy reflected.

She wondered if there was a bathroom.

As if reading her thoughts, Shirley said, 'We always wash in the sink down in the scullery. And the lavvy's outside, round the corner from the back door.' She giggled. 'Remember to put your foot against the door because there's no lock on it, only a latch and that's broken. If our Frank knows you're out there he'll walk in on you just for the hell of it. Our Selina goes mad if he catches her with her knickers down. Bet you would, too.'

Lucy looked shocked. 'Of course I would! What about you? Don't you mind?'

'I don't use it if I can help it, except for a pee. I wait until I go to school where there are locks on the door.'

'And what do you do about having a bath?' Lucy asked.

Shirley wrinkled her nose and giggled again. 'That's a Saturday-night special for me and Karen.'

'What do you mean?'

'Dad always goes to the pub, and Frank either goes with him or out on the town. Mam stokes up the range so that there's plenty of hot water, and brings in the tin bath that's hanging on the wall out in the scullery, the one that she uses to rinse things in on washday. She fills it up so that Karen and me can have our bath in it. I usually have mine first in case Karen has a fit, and then the water would go cold while we were seeing to her.'

Lucy shivered. 'Does that happen very often? Karen having a fit, I mean.'

Shirley shrugged. 'Varies! Depends on her mood and who's been yelling at her and,' she shrugged again only more expressively, 'a whole lot of things. You'll see.'

'And what about the others? When do they have their baths?'

Lucy shook her head and shrugged again. 'Any time. I don't know. Our Frank might be having one right now.'

'Now!'

'Perhaps not. Anyway, he's having a shave so I suppose he's going out boozing so he probably won't bother.' She gave Lucy a wide smile. 'Aren't you going to unpack your case?'

Lucy looked round the cramped room. Two nails had been knocked in behind the door and from these hung an assortment of clothes which, from their size and style, Lucy judged belonged to Selina. There were also piles of clothes over the metal rails at the bottom of all three beds.

'I don't think there's any room for my things,' she said hesitantly.

'Oh go on, shove Karen's things to one end and put your stuff on the bed rail as well. Go on, Lucy, I'm longing to see your other clothes,' urged Shirley.

'I haven't brought many with me, only enough to last me for two or three days.'

Shirley looked puzzled. 'Are you going away again then?'

'No! No, of course not, but it seemed silly to bring everything until I found where you lived. I can always go back and collect the rest.'

As she spoke, Lucy opened up her case and took out a pink-and-white spotted voile dress, a pair of navy shoes, a dark-blue cotton skirt and a short-sleeved blue flowered blouse.

'Coo, they're pretty!' Shirley stared at them enviously. She leaned forward and peered into the case. 'What else you got in there then?'

'Not much! Only my nightie and knicks and washing things,' laughed Lucy.

'Have you brought your own towel and flannel and soap?' Shirley said in surprise.

'Of course I have! You don't use anyone else's, do you?'

'We all use the same one,' Shirley giggled. 'Our flannel is a piece from an old towel, not a posh one like yours. Bet our Selina pinches yours if she can.'

'She jolly well won't, there will be a row if she even tries,' Lucy told her heatedly. 'Why doesn't she buy her own, anyway?'

'Buy her own! She tips up her wage packet to our mam and after she's paid her tram fares every day out of what Mam gives her as pocket money, she's only got enough left to keep her in lipstick and fags. Or so she tells me whenever I try to get a penny out of her for gobstoppers.'

'Why doesn't she get a better job and earn more money?'

Shirley shrugged. 'Dunno. She always says "better the devil you know" and she's worked there ever since she left school.'

'Where's there?

'H & Y Foods. It's a factory and it stinks something awful when you walk past it.'

'And where do Uncle Fred and Frank work?'

'Both of them work down the docks unloading the boats. That's if there's any work going. When there isn't they hang around the house, or go to the pub if they've any money, or just mooch around the streets. Frank does, anyway.' She picked up Lucy's voile dress. 'Can I try this on?'

Lucy hesitated. She wasn't used to sharing her clothes or her possessions. The look on Shirley's round face was so eager, and her voice so pleading, that she hadn't the heart to refuse.

Shirley wriggled out of her gymslip and Lucy shuddered as she saw the grimy line round the collar of her school blouse, but she unfastened the buttons on the bodice of the dress and handed it to her.

Eagerly, Shirley squeezed her plump little body into it, but it was so tight that she was unable to do it up. With a sigh of despair she let Lucy help her out of it again.

'It's so pretty,' she said wistfully. 'I wish it had fitted me so that I could have borrowed it.' She picked up the blue flowered blouse, held it up against her and looked questioningly at Lucy.

'That won't fit you, either,' Lucy told her firmly. 'Come on, let's go back downstairs.'

'You go, I've got to get dressed,' Shirley told her.

'It's all right. I'll wait for you.'

'You needn't.'

'Very well, then.' Lucy picked up the clothes she'd put on the rail at the foot of the bed she was to share with Karen, and folding them up put them back in her suitcase. 'See you downstairs then.'

Shirley nodded but didn't meet her eyes.

Lucy suspected that Shirley would open the case once she was out of the room. She knew there was nothing she could do to stop her, not without making a scene, and she didn't think it was a good idea to do that on her very first night.

As she went back downstairs, Lucy's mind was still in turmoil about what it was going to be like trying to sleep in such a crowded room, and wondering how often Karen did have fits. She was already in the living-room before she realised that Frank was coming through the doorway that separated it from the scullery. She gasped in shock when she saw he had nothing but a towel around his hips.

'I ... I'm sorry! I didn't know you were still getting ready to go out.'

He walked over to her, picked up her hand and ran the palm of it over his chin. 'Smooth as a baby's bum?' he asked, his sharp blue eyes twinkling at her discomfort.

She pulled her hand away sharply, her face flaming with confusion.

'How about my hairy chest, then?' He grabbed at her hand again, and this time he rubbed it up and down over the dark wiry growth that covered his chest and the top of his stomach.

Outraged by the intimacy of his action, she pulled back with a little scream. There was an angry rustle from the chair in the corner as Fred lowered his *Liverpool Echo* and glared at them.

'Stop your bloody larking about, you two,' he bawled. 'If you're going out on the tiles, Frank, then piss off – and you, you silly bint, stop squealing like a bloody cat about to have kittens.'

Frank grinned good-humouredly. 'What's the matter with you, then? Jealous, or just found out you've lost a packet on the gee-gees?'

'Bugger off!' his father snarled, rustling his newspaper angrily.

Lucy held her lower lip between her teeth to keep from crying. She felt trapped. She didn't know what to do for the best. If she ran back upstairs and found Shirley peeping inside her case, or trying on her blouse, then she'd think she was spying on her.

Yet it was equally distasteful to stay where she was and listen to the unpleasant exchanges between her uncle and her cousin Frank. She wondered where Selina and Karen were as there seemed to be no sign of either of them, or of her Aunt Flo.

She moved towards the scullery, calling out to her aunt as she did so.

'No bleedin' good yelling for her, she's gone to church and taken Karen with her.'

'To church! At this time of night?'

'Gone to confession.' Fred looked up, blowing a cloud of tobacco smoke in her direction. 'Yer not a Cat'lick, are you?' he said accusingly.

Chapter Four

Lucy found the continuous jibes and jeers from her uncle and her cousins reduced her to tears during the first few days she was at Anfield Road. Their sense of humour was so different from her own, or what she was used to. She often took them seriously when, in fact, they were jesting; or laughed because she thought they were teasing her when they said something that was intended to be serious.

She thought her Uncle Fred was teasing, on her third day at Anfield Road, while she was helping her Aunt Flo to serve out the evening meal. As she put a plate of scouse on the table for him, he looked at her from under his dark beetling brows and said, 'Is this all you're going to do for the rest of your life, girl?'

Instead of answering him she'd merely smiled and taken her place on the bench on the window side of the table, squeezed in between Karen and Shirley.

'Not bloody providing you with free bed and board for the rest of your life, while you skive around the house all day, you know,' he snarled.

'I'm trying to do my fair share. I've helped Aunt Flo get the meal ready and I did some shopping for her,' Lucy told him indignantly.

Fred slurped up a mound of food. 'That's not work. Karen can do that much and she's supposed to be sick.'

'Dad means you ought to get a job. Do some proper work and pay your way like the rest of us,' smirked Selina.

Lucy looked across at her aunt for support, but Flo avoided her eyes.

Lucy felt humiliated. She kept her head down so that they wouldn't see the scalding tears that had filled her eyes. She concentrated on separating a lump of translucent white fat from a chunk of grey stringy meat on her plate.

She didn't expect them to keep her. She knew she would have to find work, but she had wanted to settle into her new surroundings first. It was all so strange, so very different from what she was used to that most of the time she felt completely disorientated. She'd resigned herself to the fact that she'd never be able to be a schoolteacher, but she still wanted a career of some kind.

More and more she wished her mother had never made her promise to leave Belgrave Road. Living with Stanley Jones would be heaven compared to being here with this rough bunch of people.

They might be relatives, but she was quite sure that if her mother had ever met them she wouldn't have even wanted her to know them, let alone live with them. Aunt Flo was all right, she'd tried to be kind, and to help her settle in. The others, though, except Karen, not only resented her being there, but they were positively hostile.

Especially Selina. She went out of her way to sneer at Lucy and be as unpleasant as possible.

'Get off your backside then, girl, and bloody well start looking tomorrow,' her uncle told her. 'I'll give you a shout at six when I leave the house.'

'There's no need to call me, you make enough noise as it is when you get up. I shall be awake.'

'Forgive us for breathing,' jibed Selina, pulling a mocking face, which made the others all laugh. 'If you'd mentioned it before we would have tiptoed around the place.'

'You might have heard us, but you didn't bloody well come down to see if there was anything we wanted before we went off,' her uncle snarled.

'No, because I thought it was best for me to keep out of your way,' Lucy answered spiritedly.

'Or you thought you might be expected to make our sarnies and fill up our flasks.'

'Probably didn't want to bump into us while we were still only half-dressed,' guffawed Frank. 'Don't like seeing people without their clothes on, do you, Luce.'

'My name is Lucy, not Luce. And no, I don't like invading your privacy and I don't like you invading mine.'

'Flippin' 'eck, listen to her!' He laughed at her discomfort. 'I'll catch you in the lavvy yet, so you'd better watch out.'

'That will do, all of you. Leave Lucy alone,' her aunt intervened. 'She's done her bit round the house. She knows she'll have to get a job, don't

44

you, luv? Go and have a look round tomorrow, eh?'

'No bloody good wandering round the streets. She won't find work that way. With dresses that barely cover her backside she'll get taken for a floozie and get picked up.' Fred ran the back of his hand across his mouth. 'You want to try looking through the "Wanted" columns of the bloody *Echo* when you've finished your meal or get down to the dole hole in the morning and sign on there and see if they can find you anything.'

Lying in bed that night, listening to the heavy breathing from Selina and Shirley, and the muted sighs from Karen as she tossed and turned restlessly beside her, Lucy wept with frustration.

She hadn't been out of the house on her own since she'd arrived at Anfield Road. Tomorrow though, she resolved, instead of looking for work she'd go back to Wallasey, collect her belongings from Belgrave Road and perhaps go and see her old school friend, Brenda.

She felt she needed a sympathetic ear, someone who would understand her plight. Brenda Green, who'd been her best friend at Wallasey High, had left at fifteen and had been at work ever since, so she might even be able to suggest what sort of job she should look for, and tell her how to go about getting it.

She had no experience or training whatsoever so she couldn't just walk into a shop or office and ask for work. Her Uncle Fred had said to go to the Labour Exchange, and sign on for the dole, but she didn't even know where it was. And what did

45

you say to them when you got there, she wondered.

Lucy found it surprisingly easy to carry out her plan. As he'd threatened, Fred Flanagan banged on her door before he made his way noisily downstairs, hawking and coughing as he usually did at six in the morning.

Not to be outdone, Frank repeated the awake call by coming into their bedroom, grabbing at the blanket on the bed she was sharing with Karen and pulling it off them. Karen merely curled into a ball, but Lucy reached out, trying to snatch it back, feeling both humiliated and indignant.

She also felt a frisson of fear as she became aware that her nightdress had rucked up, and that Frank was staring fascinated at the expanse of white thigh that was revealed.

'Get out!' she hissed, her face flaming. Quickly she pulled the hem down to her knees, but she knew it was too late to distract his interest, and she was scared stiff of what his next move would be.

He grinned down at her. 'Nice legs! Not that I'm seeing anything I haven't seen before. In that dress you had on yesterday you show most of them when you bend over.'

Before she could think of a reply, Lucy heard her Aunt Flo calling out to Frank that if he didn't get a move on he was going to be late for work.

Frank ran a calloused forefinger from her ankle slowly up to her thigh. 'You're safe this time,' he leered, 'but you'd better watch your step when I'm around.'

Lucy felt herself trembling with feelings she couldn't identify. No one had ever touched her like that, or even seen her in a state of undress before today. Her mother had always been very strict about modesty at all times, even though there had only ever been Stanley in the house.

She dressed hurriedly, putting on the dark blue skirt and the blue flowered blouse she'd brought with her. She felt reassured that the skirt was a bit longer than her dress and that it came down to her knees. She didn't think she'd have the courage to wear really short skirts ever again, not after what Frank had said. She felt the colour rising in her cheeks as she remembered the touch of his hand on her leg. Her mother would have been shocked by such impropriety.

As she sprinkled salt on to the slice of bread and dripping her Aunt Flo gave her for breakfast, she confided in her aunt that as well as going job-hunting she was going to collect some of her belongings from Belgrave Road.

Liverpool landing stage was a seething mass of people when she reached there just after eight o'clock. A ferry boat, the *Royal Daffodil*, had arrived only a few minutes earlier from Seacombe, bringing shop and office workers from their homes in Wallasey. Four abreast they surged up from the landing stage to where the green trams waited to take them to all parts of Liverpool. The sailings to New Brighton didn't start until later in the day so Lucy went on board the *Royal Daffodil* which was about to return to Seacombe.

Only a very few people were crossing in that

direction so she had no difficulty at all in finding a seat inside one of the covered decks where she was sheltered from the wind. Ten minutes later she was on one of the yellow Wallasey buses heading for New Brighton.

It wasn't quite nine o'clock when she reached there and most of the shops, amusement arcades and cafés were still shuttered, including the pub at the bottom of Victoria Road. Lucy felt a moment of panic and wondered what she'd do if Brenda no longer lived there and she didn't find her after all.

It was too cold to stand still so she decided to take a walk along the promenade. The Mersey looked grey and cold as she stared out across it to Liverpool on the far side. From the distance, it looked so inviting, another world, full of promise.

She fastened the buttons on her blazer and put her hands into the pockets for warmth. As she did so her fingers touched the door key that Stanley had insisted she should keep. If she didn't find Brenda then she'd go straight to Belgrave Road and collect the rest of her things and take them back to Anfield Road.

By the time Lucy returned to Victoria Road most of the shops were open and there were signs of activity everywhere. As she pushed open the door of the pub Lucy found the pungent smell of tobacco and stale beer overpowering. A woman wearing a sacking apron over a black dress, her hair covered by a headscarf, was cleaning the floor. 'You can't come in. We're not open for customers until eleven o'clock,' she told her.

48

'Oh!' For a moment Lucy was taken aback. 'I wanted to see Brenda Green, does she still live here?'

The woman studied her for a minute. 'You a friend of hers, luv?'

Lucy nodded. 'I wanted a quick word with her if that's possible.'

Propping her mop against the nearest table the woman went across to a door marked 'Staff Only' and called out Brenda's name.

'Lucy Patterson! What on earth are you doing here?' Brenda greeted her in astonishment, flinging her arms round her and hugging her enthusiastically.

'Hello, Brenda!' Lucy felt reassured by the warmth of Brenda's greeting, and also astonished by how much Brenda had changed since she'd last seen her. She'd always been pretty, and her red hair had made her stand out, but now she looked so very grown up that Lucy felt naive in comparison.

'I went round to your place a couple of days ago when I was shopping in Liscard,' Brenda told her. 'I heard your mother had died and I wondered how you were. The house was all shut up.'

'I expect Mr Jones was at work, and I'm living in Liverpool,' Lucy explained.

'Liverpool?' Brenda's green eyes widened. 'What are you doing there? I didn't know you even knew anyone in Liverpool. Aren't you the dark horse!'

'I'm living with my Aunt Flo. She's my father's sister,' Lucy explained. 'I didn't know anything

49

about her, or her family, until about a week before my mother died.' Tears filled her eyes. 'It's horrible there, Brenda. They're ever so rough and their house is dismal, and my eldest cousin, Frank, is awful.'

'Come on.' Brenda took her arm and led her behind the bar. 'Come on upstairs and have a cup of tea.' She gave a puzzled laugh. 'Why didn't you stay on in Belgrave Road? Stanley Jones didn't throw you out, did he?'

'Oh no,' Lucy looked startled. 'Nothing like that. He wanted me to stay.'

'I bet he did! He's always been sweet on you. I bet you could marry him if you played your cards right.'

'Brenda!' Lucy looked taken aback.

'Well, why not? Being an old man's darling is better than being a young man's slave! Better than working for a living and I should know, I've been working behind the bar ever since the day I left school.'

'But you're happy working here?'

Brenda stretched her arms above her head so that her blouse strained until it seemed the buttons would pop. 'It has its moments,' she grinned. 'Plenty of men to flirt with, and if they annoy me too much I know my dad will soon sort them out.'

Lucy said nothing. She found herself wondering what Brenda would have done if she had been in her place that morning when Frank had walked into her bedroom.

'Sit down. I'll make a pot of tea, and then you

can tell me what has been happening,' Brenda ordered.

'Are you sure no one will mind my being here?'

'Of course they won't. It's my home, isn't it?'

Brenda busied herself putting out cups and saucers and making the tea. Lucy looked round the warm comfortable room enviously. It reminded her so much of Belgrave Road that she wanted to weep.

'Here we are then.' Brenda poured out the tea and pushed a plate of doughnuts towards Lucy. 'Help yourself and now tell me everything,' she said with a big smile. 'I want all the gory details, especially about your cousin Frank. What is so awful about him?'

Lucy reddened. She felt too embarrassed to tell Brenda what had happened when Frank had come into the bedroom she shared with her cousins, but Brenda was so insistent that Lucy found herself telling her how awful she found it living in the same house as someone like Frank, who was always teasing and taunting her and making fun of everything she said or did.

Brenda looked amused.

'It's all very well for you to laugh, you've no idea what it's like,' Lucy told her. 'And when he's not making fun of me, he's making suggestive remarks.'

'Like what?'

Lucy avoided Brenda's eyes. 'Things I can't bring myself to repeat,' she mumbled.

'Couldn't you go back to Belgrave Road?'

Brenda asked. 'I'm sure your mother wouldn't want you to stay there if you are so unhappy.'

'I promised her,' Lucy said stubbornly.

'Of course you did, and you've kept your promise, but it hasn't worked out the way she thought it would, now has it?'

Lucy shook her head. 'I know, but she didn't want me to be in the house alone with Stanley Jones.'

'That's ridiculous! I'd give anything to be in your shoes. A home of my own, a man who can't do enough to please me, and never have to go out to work.'

Lucy shook her head. 'You don't understand, do you?'

'No, not really. Probably because we look at things differently.'

'I'm supposed to be out looking for a job today,' Lucy said morosely. 'I don't even know how to start or what sort of job to look for.'

'It's a pity we're not taking on staff or you could have come here and worked,' Brenda told her. 'Perhaps later on, in a few weeks' time when the trippers come and we're busy. You could move in and share my room,' she added generously.

Lucy shook her head. Although her mother had quite liked Brenda she had never approved of her background. Lucy knew that the thought of her working in a pub would make her mother turn in her grave.

'That's kind of you, Brenda, but I'd have to ask Aunt Flo for permission to do that,' she prevaricated.

'Well, suit yourself. The offer's there if you want to take it up. You won't be able to go on to college and become a teacher like your mother wanted you to do, though, will you?'

'No, I'll have to try and get a job in Liverpool. There must be plenty of shops and offices where I could work.'

'Go and ask, it's the only way you'll ever find out. You can always say you were going to college if your mother hadn't died, and that you've been looking after her since you've left school, and that's why you've never had a job.'

Lucy felt her spirits rise. She was glad she'd come to see Brenda, she made it all sound so easy. It had been the same when they were at school; Brenda had only ever seen the bright side of a problem when they were in trouble.

Lucy stood up. 'Thanks for the tea and chat, Brenda. I suppose I'd better go and collect some of my clothes from Belgrave Road so that I have something suitable to wear when I'm job-hunting.'

'Do you want me to come with you? I will if you like.'

'Don't you have to work?'

Brenda pulled a face. 'We're not all that busy, except in the evenings. Dad'll let me have the day off when I tell him it's an emergency.'

'Emergency?'

Brenda grinned. 'Helping a friend is an emergency, isn't it?'

Lucy found it quite eerie to be walking into her old home. She felt as though it was months, not days, since she'd left Belgrave Road. The sight of the little crocheted doilies her mother had placed under all the plant pots brought a lump to her throat, and the huge Staffordshire china dogs, that had belonged to Stanley's parents and always stood guard on either end of the mantelpiece, reminded her of how happy she'd been there.

She was glad Brenda was with her, it would have been even more unnerving if she'd been on her own. As she wandered round the large, comfortably furnished house, and mentally compared it with the cramped terraced house in Anfield Road, she felt choked. She'd been so contented growing up there and she wondered if she'd ever be as happy again.

Sensing her discomfort, Brenda said hardly a word as she rummaged through Lucy's wardrobe, picking out the things she thought were most suitable to take back to Liverpool.

'Are you sure you don't want to take everything?' Brenda asked.

Lucy shook her head. 'No, I'd like to have an excuse to come back again later on.'

A couple of hours later they were on the *Royal Iris* ferry boat from Seacombe heading back to Liverpool.

'It's awfully good of you, Brenda, to come all this way,' Lucy told her as they walked up from the ferry towards the tram terminal. They were each carrying a bag of clothes and Lucy knew she could never have managed on her own.

'Get away with you,' Brenda grinned. 'I'm

enjoying it. I could do with a cuppa and something to eat, though. Why don't we pop into the Lyons Corner House before you catch your tram to Anfield Road? Come on, my treat,' Brenda insisted when Lucy hesitated. 'You never know, you might be able to get a job there as a Nippy,' she grinned.

As she watched the spry young waitress in her neat black frock and fancy white apron, a crisp white cap perched on her head, deftly serving them with tea, sandwiches and fancy cakes, Lucy admitted that she quite liked the idea.

'Go on then, go and ask the supervisor if there are any jobs going,' Brenda urged.

'This minute?'

'Why not?'

'I ought to find out what Aunt Flo thinks of the idea.'

'She won't mind what sort of work you are doing as long as you're bringing in the money and she doesn't have to keep you.'

Lucy shook her head. 'I'd sooner talk to her first.'

'If that's how you feel then we'll go and ask her right now. I'll come with you to make sure you don't back down.'

'You might be wasting your time,' Lucy warned. 'She mightn't be there. She may have gone to the market with Karen.'

'Then we'll wait until she gets home. I mean it, Lucy. After coming all this way, and buying you a meal, I want to see some results.'

Lucy fumbled with her purse, her face flaming.

55

'I'll pay my share if that's how you feel,' she flared.

'Don't be daft. I was only teasing. Come on.' Brenda picked up the bag of clothes that she'd put down beside her chair. 'Let's get going.'

When they reached Anfield Road, Lucy was acutely aware of how drab it looked. The narrow houses with their smoke-grimed fronts, the mangy black-and-white dog sniffing at the lamp-post. She half hoped, as she knocked on the door of the Flanagans' house, there'd be no one in so that Brenda would give up and go back to New Brighton.

To her dismay the door was opened by Frank, a cigarette dangling from one corner of his mouth.

'What are you doing here at this time of day?' she asked in surprise.

'Got stood off.' He took a long drag at his cigarette. 'Anything else you want to know?'

He was in his working clothes, his shirt open at the neck, the sleeves rolled up showing a length of brawny arm. He looked at them questioningly. 'Not another one moving in, is there?' he asked mockingly. His eyes were fixed on Brenda, lecherously studying her ripe, rounded figure and her peaches-and-cream skin.

Frank turned to Lucy. 'Mam and Karen have gone to church. They should be back soon. Who's this then?'

'My friend, Brenda Green,' Lucy told him. 'She's helped me to bring some of my things over from Wallasey. Can we come in?' she asked pointedly and waited for him to move his bulk to one side in the narrow hallway.

'You must be Frank.' Brenda gave him an appraising look. 'Lucy's told me a lot about you,' she added with a warm smile as she squeezed past him.

'And none of it good, I'll bet,' he quipped.

'I like to judge a man for myself,' she parried, fluttering her eyelashes.

'And I bet you meet plenty of them!'

'I do, actually.' She patted her short red hair provocatively. 'I work behind the bar of my father's pub.'

Frank's blue eyes sharpened. 'Here in Liverpool?'

'No, in New Brighton. The pub on the corner of Victoria Road and the Prom. Do you know it?'

'I've been in there once or twice, but I've never seen you there?' He studied her appraisingly. 'There's usually a red-headed Lady Muck and a middle-aged geezer with a beer belly behind the bar.' His eyebrows lifted. 'They're your mam and dad?'

'Wow! You're quite a detective, aren't you,' Brenda said skittishly. 'Must be brains under all that curly black hair.'

Frank's eyes narrowed. 'Brains and more beside. I'll prove it to you if you like.'

'Come over to our pub some night and I might let you,' Brenda giggled.

'Is that an invitation?' Frank's hypnotic blue eyes challenged Brenda's green ones.

Brenda tossed her head. 'Take it whatever way

you like,' she said archly. 'You know where to find me.'

Lucy couldn't believe her ears. After all she'd told Brenda about Frank and his lecherous ways what on earth did she think she was doing flirting with him in such a brazen manner?

She tried to attract Brenda's attention, but her friend was far too engrossed in her banter with Frank to take any notice.

Chapter Five

Finding work was far harder than Lucy had anticipated. She signed on at the Labour Exchange as her Uncle Fred insisted, and felt humiliated by all the forms she had to fill in, and the personal details she had to disclose. At the end of it all, she was told that because she'd never had a job before, and therefore had no stamps on her card, she wasn't eligible for any dole.

They also told her that there wasn't much hope of her getting any work because of her lack of experience. When she told them she'd like to be a Nippy, they said all she was suitable for were cleaning jobs or factory work. Unfortunately, there weren't many of these about, and there were dozens of experienced people after every one of them.

'It was a waste of time going there,' she told the Flanagans gloomily several nights later when they were having their evening meal and, as usual, they started questioning her about whether she had been out looking for work.

'Didn't they bloody well send you anywhere at all then, girl?' glowered her uncle, his mouth full of food.

'Yes, to a factory in Bootle,' Lucy told him.

'So what happened?'

'The foreman told me I was wasting my time and his because I had no experience.'

Fred grunted, but made no comment.

'I would have thought they'd send you to Frisby Dykes,' Frank chipped in.

Lucy felt hot colour staining her cheeks as the others all laughed. 'I don't know what that is,' she said stiffly.

'It's the posh ladies' and gents' outfitters in Lord Street. They only employ people who talk highfalutin like you do,' Frank told her, riveting her with his hypnotic blue stare. 'You'd fit in there a treat,' he added, grinning broadly.

She felt mesmerised, like a rabbit facing a stoat, as he reached out and pinched a handful of chips from her plate. With work-grimed fingers he spread them over a piece of bread to make a chip butty, shook salt and sauce over them, and then folded them up and took a large bite. With his forefinger he pushed a chip that was dangling from his lips further into his mouth. One of his bright blue eyes closed in a huge wink as he ran his finger slowly up and down his cheek.

Lucy fought back a sour taste in her throat as his action brought back memories of the way his calloused finger had moved up and down her bare leg when he'd pulled the blankets off her. She looked away quickly, fighting back her feeling of revulsion, holding her lower lip steady between her teeth to stop herself from screaming.

It played on her mind, though. So much so that when Brenda turned up at Anfield Road unexpectedly one evening, saying she wanted to see how Lucy was getting on, and if she was more settled, she found herself telling her friend all about the incident.

Instead of sympathising, Brenda looked amused. When Lucy said she was thinking of telling her Aunt Flo about what had happened Brenda exploded into gales of laughter.

'He only meant it as a bit of fun,' Brenda told her. 'You should see what the men who come into the pub get up to. They think nothing of pinching my bum, or grabbing hold of me and trying to snog me.'

'Oh, Brenda, how terrible! What do you do when that happens?' Lucy asked aghast.

'Kiss them back usually,' Brenda grinned.

'Even if you don't know them?'

'That's even better. If they think they're in with a chance they leave me bigger tips.'

'Brenda!' Lucy's disapproval showed on her face.

'If you are coming to work at our pub you'd better get used to the idea of being touched up,' Brenda told her.

'I certainly don't want to work there if that's what goes on,' Lucy said primly.

'There's no need to come that "holier than thou" act with me, Lucy Patterson,' Brenda snapped. 'I bet you let Stanley Jones kiss and cuddle you on the quiet. That's why your mam was so worried about you staying there on your own with him. The best thing you can do is to go back to him and see if you can get him to marry you,' she added spitefully.

'You're telling lies, all lies,' Lucy glared. 'Stanley never laid a finger on me. He was too much of a gentleman.'

'Pure as the driven snow, are you?' Brenda said contemptuously. 'Well, I'm not, and I don't care who knows it. I don't want to end up a shrivelled old prune which you'll be if you don't alter your ways.'

'I think you'd better go,' Lucy told her.

'I'll go when I please. I didn't come all this way just to see you, Lucy Patterson.'

'So who did you come to see?'

When Brenda didn't answer realisation slowly dawned on Lucy. 'You came to see my cousin Frank,' she said accusingly.

'So what if I did? He's been over to see me. Came to the pub only last night, if you must know.'

Lucy stared at her in disbelief. 'How could you, Brenda? He's horrible! His hands are always grimy, and he'd flirt with anybody.'

'So will most men given half a chance,' Brenda laughed. 'Don't worry about it. Frank and I understand each other.'

Lucy cried herself to sleep that night. Perhaps Brenda was right and there was something wrong with the way she looked at things. Brenda had called her prissy, and said she'd been overprotected by her mother, and didn't know what went on in the real world. If only she could find a job, she thought miserably, she'd prove to all of them that she was able to stand on her own feet.

As day after day passed, and she had no luck at

all, she became more and more despondent. She even looked different. Her hair had grown out of its smart styling and looked greasy. The heels of her smart navy shoes were worn down by so much walking when she went after jobs. She longed for a bath, but was too frightened to have one in case Frank walked in and caught her.

'Take no notice of them, luv,' Aunt Flo told her mildly. 'You'll land a job one of these days. I've been praying to the Blessed Virgin to help you find one. If you come along to Mass with us on Sunday then Father O'Reilly has said he'll say a special prayer for you as well.'

Lucy felt uncomfortable. She didn't want to get involved with her aunt's religious fervour, yet she didn't know what to say without offending her.

She'd been embarrassed when she learned that her aunt had a shrine in her bedroom, and that she prayed in front of it, on her knees, for half an hour every day. Ever since she'd been there Aunt Flo had been trying to persuade her to accompany Karen to Mass.

'Karen goes every morning,' her aunt told her. 'I go with her when I can manage it, but she never misses, not unless she is too ill to go.'

'She won't find any bloody work there,' Fred glowered. He ran the back of his hand across his mouth, and Lucy watched, fascinated, as he licked off a smear of brown sauce from it afterwards.

Selina was the only one who made no comments about her not finding any work. Lucy kept wondering if this was because Selina was hoping that if she didn't, and couldn't pay her way, they'd throw her out.

Yet, in the end, it was Selina who offered to find Lucy a job.

She'd been living at Anfield Road for almost three weeks, and even had to ask her Aunt Flo for money for the tram so that she could go and sign on. She'd been after countless jobs, but it was always the same story, no one was interested in taking on someone of her age who had no experience.

'If you're prepared to work in a factory then I'll have a word with my foreman,' Selina offered.

'You will!' Lucy smiled gratefully. 'Oh Selina, that would be wonderful.' Then her smile faded as she remembered how many other jobs she'd been after and never met with any success.

It certainly wasn't the sort of work she really wanted to do. Factory work didn't sound any better than working in a pub. If only she could have stayed on at school, passed her exams and gone to college as she'd dreamed of doing, she thought wistfully.

Still, since she hadn't been able to do that she had no choice but to accept her cousin's offer of help.

'I don't suppose I will get it, I've no experience, remember,' she said tentatively.

'Oh you will,' Selina told her confidently.

Selina was right. Jack Carter interviewed her in a tiny box of an office that was partitioned off from the factory floor where about twenty women and girls were sticking labels on tins as they came off a production line. He didn't ask her any questions at all, except what her full name and age were.

Lucy waited patiently, staring down at his dark head as he rapidly filled in the form in front of him, and wondered what came next. This was usually the point when she was told there was nothing available, or that she wasn't suitable.

Then he looked up. He was smiling and she thought how handsome he was. He had eyes almost as blue as Frank's, but a much higher forehead, a leaner face, a more prominent nose, and a deep cleft right in the centre of his chin.

'There you are then. That's all sealed and settled. Pull your weight and you'll be happy here.'

'You mean I've got the job?' Lucy couldn't keep the surprise out of her voice.

'Of course you have!' He gave a roguish grin. 'I wouldn't break a promise to Selina, now would I?'

Before Lucy could think of an answer he pressed a buzzer and from nowhere a petite blonde girl appeared. Jack Carter looked down at the form he'd filled in. 'Emma, this is Lucy Patterson. Find her an overall and a cap, and put her to work alongside you. Look after her for a couple of days until she gets the hang of things. No playing pranks on her, she's Selina Flanagan's cousin. Understand?'

'Of course, Mr Carter.'

'Right!' He smiled at Lucy. 'You go along with

Emma then and she'll show you what to do.' His blue eyes bored into her. 'You understand?'

'Yes, of course. And thank you, Mr Carter. Thank you very much for giving me the job. I'm most grateful.'

'You should be chuffed,' Emma told her as they walked away from Jack Carter's office. 'I know of dozens of people who've been after jobs here for months and they've always been told there aren't any. Just shows what you can do with a bit of pull.'

'Bit of pull?' Lucy looked bewildered. 'I don't know what you mean, I've never had anything to do with Mr Carter in my life before.'

'You mightn't have done so, chuck, but your Selina certainly has,' Emma giggled.

'Selina told me he was her boss, that's all I know,' Lucy told her.

'Oh, he's her boss all right, but he's a lot more besides. Everyone in the factory knows he's her fancy man. Can't say I blame her.' She gave an exaggerated sigh. 'He's smashing looking, isn't he. Most of the women here wouldn't mind being his bit on the side, I can tell you. Especially when so many perks goes with it as well.'

'What sort of perks?'

Emma tapped the side of her nose with her finger. 'That's for me to know and for you to find out,' she smirked. 'Come on, let's go and get you kitted out. Bet you're dying to wear a jazzy overall like mine. You wanna wear yer old clothes at work. No one sees them because they're always covered up. It's not so bad when you think about it, because it means you can keep your smart stuff for going out in the evenings. There's just one thing,' she gabbled on, 'if you come to work in curlers make sure they're completely hidden under your cap or you'll get told off.'

Lucy's delight in finding a job dulled rapidly. She quickly discovered that factory work was monotonous. In addition, the banter from the other workers upset her. Half the time she wasn't sure if they were teasing her or telling her off. Her mute acceptance of everything they said brought bursts of cynical laughter from those she was working alongside and made her feel inadequate.

The work, too, was both boring and exacting. As the tins came off the assembly line the girl in front of her checked them and discarded any with dents. It was Lucy's job to coat each tin with a liquid glue ready for the next girl to wrap a label around it. The glue had an obnoxious smell that Lucy found made her feel queasy.

Also, it was so runny that because she was not used to handling it Lucy found her hands, arms and the front of her overall were soaked with it. She was so clumsy she soon found that there were tins piling up on one side of her, and the girl on the other side grumbled that she was too slow.

'Not used to a bit of graft, are you,' Emma commented. 'This is a doddle. Wait until you get moved to filling the tins with fish or with meat as it comes out of the grinders.' She pulled a face. 'Now that really does stink!'

'I'm sure I'll get used to it. It's all so new to me.'

'Where did you work before you came here then?'

'I didn't. This is my first job.'

Emma stared at her open-mouthed. 'Gerroff! How old are you then?'

'Almost eighteen.'

'So'm I, and I left school at fourteen and I've never had a day off since. And you've never worked! That's bloody lovely! Been lolling around like a lady while I've been grafting!'

'My mother was ill and I helped to look after her,' Lucy explained.

'She better now?'

Lucy shook her head, biting her lip to keep back the tears. 'No, she died almost a month ago.'

'That's tough, chooks! Is that why you're living with your cousin Selina?'

Lucy nodded.

'Bit of a looker, isn't she? Daft the way she runs after Jack Carter when she could have almost any man she fancied.'

'What's wrong with Jack Carter?'

'What's wrong with him!' Emma lowered her voice. 'Floggin' a dead horse, isn't she! He's married, for one thing. Got a wife and three kids and since he's a Cat'lick he'll never leave them to marry your cousin.'

Lucy looked shocked. Emma was right, Selina was stunning. As well as a figure most women would envy, she had lustrous, shoulder-length black hair, vivid blue eyes with thick dark lashes and heavy arched brows as well as a beautifully shaped mouth.

'That's how she managed to get you taken on here,' Emma went on. 'She can twist Jack Carter around her little finger and we all know how she does it! Giving you a job here will keep Jack Carter in nooky for weeks,' she smirked.

Lucy didn't know what to say. The subject haunted her all day. She even mentioned it that night when they were all eating their evening meal, but the words didn't come out as she intended. There was an uneasy silence when she looked across at Selina and said, 'Thank you for asking your friend Jack Carter to give me a job, he must think an awful lot of you to do that.'

The moment might have passed if Frank hadn't sniggered loudly. 'Don't try muscling in on our Selina's boyfriend, Luce, or she'll scratch your eyes out!' he warned.

'Do you like it at H & Y Foods, Lucy?' Aunt Flo asked quickly, concern on her plump face.

'I think I will when I get more used to it. I'm rather slow at the moment and it seems to make some of the girls rather cross. They say the most dreadful things to me!'

'Probably taking the piss out of you because you're so prissy,' Fred sneered. 'Remind me of your old man, you do. John Patterson was too highfalutin for words. Never thought I was good enough to marry his sister, did he, Flo?'

'That was all a long time ago, and you shouldn't speak ill of the dead,' Aunt Flo said quickly.

'They're probably only taking the mickey,'

Frank grinned. 'And you don't like people doing that, do you, kiddo?'

'You're cruel. You're always teasing people,' Shirley grumbled. 'Except for our Karen. You never tease her, do you?'

'That's because she's an angel and you're nothing but a cheeky little tyke.'

Shirley pulled a face. 'Is Lucy an angel, too?'

Lucy felt uncomfortable as Frank looked at her appraisingly, tilting his dark head on one side, his blue eyes glinting speculatively as they met hers. She was sure he was thinking back to the morning when he'd walked into their bedroom and she felt her face reddening.

'I think Lucy's an angel,' Karen murmured dreamily. 'She's kind and talks to me, and I love her being here with us.'

'Oh, Karen, that's really sweet of you!' Lucy smiled across the table at her, touched by Karen's generosity of spirit since she'd been the one most inconvenienced by her arrival. Never once had she grumbled or shown the slightest annoyance about having to share her bed.

'She's had time to natter, she's been loafing around the house all bloody day ever since she got here,' muttered Fred as he pushed back his chair and went over to sit in the battered old armchair by the range.

'Get off your backside, Shirley,' he ordered, 'bring my cuppa char over here and then give your mam and Karen a hand to clear away. Her ladyship'll be too soddin' tired to help after working so hard in a factory all day.'

70

Chapter Six

'Friday! The best day of the week.' Emma Roberts greeted Lucy with a beaming smile when she arrived for work on her first Friday at H & Y Foods.

Lucy looked questioningly at her new friend's happy face. 'Are you teasing me again?' she asked. 'I would have thought Saturday was the best because we finish at midday.'

'That's good, too,' Emma agreed, 'but Friday is even better, it's when we get paid, dummy!'

As the day dragged on, Emma and the women nearby swapped details of how they intended spending their wages. The bulk would be handed over for housekeeping, a portion put aside for tram fares, and what was left was theirs to spend on clothes and pleasure.

Emma confided that she loved to go dancing, or to the pictures. 'Which do you like best, Lucy?'

'I've never done either,' Lucy admitted. 'My mother didn't approve of cinemas and she wouldn't dream of letting me go to a dance.'

'Flippin' 'eck! You mean you've never in your life gone dancing?' Emma exclaimed in amazement.

'Well, only once, and that was to a tea dance.'

'That's not a proper dance,' Emma agreed. 'When was that?'

Lucy smiled as she recalled the incident. 'It was my last day at school. We finished early and instead of going straight home I went with my friend, Brenda, to a tea dance. Brenda used to go dancing at the Tower Ballroom every Saturday night and someone had given her tickets for this tea dance at the Floral Gardens in New Brighton.'

'And did you enjoy it?'

Lucy managed a faint grin. She'd not really enjoyed it because she had felt so clumsy and out of things.

'Almost the moment we arrived, a middle-aged man asked Brenda to dance,' she explained to her friend. 'Brenda was in her element being whisked round the dance floor, but it meant that I was left standing by the wall, and feeling so out of things that I wanted to run away. I'd have done so, only I felt frozen to the spot.'

'Didn't you go on the floor at all?'

'Well, yes. Brenda came back all flushed and giggly, and insisted on us dancing together. That was even worse. I'd no idea what to do. I kept treading on Brenda's toes, and falling over my own feet. Brenda was doubled up with laughter and told me I needed practice. After that I never went dancing again,' Lucy said evasively.

'Never!' Emma's eyebrows shot up in surprise. 'Why ever not?'

Lucy looked embarrassed. 'My mother was pretty strict and she didn't like the idea. She worried about me so much. She was happier if I stayed at home, where she could keep an eye on me. She was always afraid that I'd come to some harm if I went off anywhere on my own.'

'You could have gone with your friend Brenda.'

'We'd left school by then and I didn't see her very often after that. Anyway, my mother was sick so I didn't have time to go dancing, or to go out at all.'

'That's all changed now, though,' Emma said brightly. 'You'll be able to go out as much as you like and wherever you like.'

Lucy looked startled. 'I don't know about that. I'll have to ask my aunt.'

'I shouldn't think she'd stop you!' Emma gave a knowing grin. 'Your Selina does whatever she likes, doesn't she?'

Lucy didn't answer, but for the rest of the morning, as she painted tin after tin with a daub of evil-smelling glue, she thought about what had been said.

Emma was right, Selina must go out a lot. She seldom saw her in the evenings, and the house in Anfield Road was so cramped that there was nowhere to hide or even be alone. Frank also went out every evening, and very often her Uncle Fred did as well, and neither of them came home again until it was pub closing time.

She'd never thought about going out even though, now that the days were becoming warmer, and the evenings longer, it was unbearably stuffy in the house. Perhaps it was the answer to her problem of feeling she was in everyone's way. If she went for a walk once she'd

73

helped to do the washing-up after their evening meal, then she'd be out of the house while Frank and her Uncle Fred were having a wash in the scullery.

Twice now she'd walked in there while Frank was stripped off to the waist, and once she'd gone in when her Uncle Fred was standing there in his vest having a shave. He'd been so angry that she'd thought he was going to hit her.

She had to admit that she didn't much like the idea of walking alone in Liverpool. Even going from Anfield Road to the open market with Aunt Flo was scary. The streets were so bleak and unfriendly, there were mangy dogs everywhere, shabby old women with black shawls around their shoulders and gangs of boys playing rough games. Perhaps she could ask Karen or Shirley to go with her. After today, when she'd been paid and had some money of her own again, she could even take them to the cinema.

Throughout the rest of the day, Lucy kept letting her thoughts dwell on what she would do with the money from her very first pay packet. She wondered how much Aunt Flo would expect her to hand over for her keep. She knew the others, Frank, Selina and Uncle Fred, handed over their wage packets unopened and Aunt Flo handed them back some money for their own use. She didn't want to do that. She wanted to feel she was in charge of the money she earned.

She tried to imagine what her mother would have said about her bringing home her first pay packet. They'd never discussed the probability of her getting a job, but Lucy didn't think her mother would have approved of her working in a factory.

By the time Jack Carter came round with the pay packets Lucy was so keyed up with excitement that he'd gone back to his cubby-hole of an office before she realised he hadn't handed her one.

'Mr Carter hasn't given me mine and yet you've all got yours,' she said, her brown eyes wide with disappointment. 'Do you think he's forgotten it and has gone back to his office to get it?' she asked the woman working alongside her on the assembly line.

'No, chuck, he hasn't forgotten. You won't be getting one this week.'

Lucy couldn't believe her ears. 'I won't be getting any wages? Why ever not?' She turned to Emma on her other side. 'She's teasing me, isn't she?' she whispered, her lower lip trembling.

'Afraid not, kiddo! They hold a week in hand, see. You'll have to wait until next Friday.'

'You never told me that!' Lucy said accusingly. 'You let me think that I'd get my pay packet like the rest of you,' she added disconsolately.

Emma looked taken aback. 'I wasn't holding out on you, I thought you knew,' she defended.

'I still don't believe you,' Lucy said. 'I'm going to ask Mr Carter.'

Jack Carter confirmed what the other girls had already told her.

'Sorry, luv.' He patted her shoulder consolingly. 'Your Selina should have explained that to you.

Do you want me to lend you a couple of bob to tide you over?'

'Oh no!' Lucy looked shocked. 'It's very kind of you, but I can manage, thank you,' she mumbled.

Even as she said it she knew she couldn't, but pride wouldn't let her admit how much she had been relying on her pay packet: she had only a few coppers left to her name.

Her misery increased when she arrived back at Anfield Road that evening and watched the others hand over their wage packets to Aunt Flo.

'Where's yours then, girl?' Fred Flanagan demanded.

'I didn't get any wages!'

'Didn't get paid?' Fred paused with a forkful of fried cod halfway to his mouth. 'Gerroff! No one in their right mind works for nothing, girl. Didn't you have the sense to go to the boss and tell him he'd missed you out?'

'Oh, she did that all right, but you know they hold a week in hand, Dad,' Selina said quickly.

Lucy looked at her gratefully, hoping the explanation would satisfy her uncle.

'So we'll be getting bloody chip butties all next week, will we,' Fred grumbled. 'Frank's been off half the week and her ladyship, here, has brought home no ackers at all, so we won't be able to afford any bleeding meat.'

Lucy felt humiliated. It wasn't her fault she'd received no wages. She'd worked hard all week and she had broken nails and sore fingers to show for it.

'I suppose you'll be expecting one of us to dub

up the money for you to ride on the Green Goddesses all next week,' her uncle scowled.

'I'll give you the money for your tram fares, Lucy,' Frank offered, giving her a broad wink.

'I thought you'd been stood off?' his father growled vehemently. 'Come into a blasted fortune on the quiet, have you?'

'I have been laid off, but I've given Mam the money for me keep.'

'How d'ye bloody well manage to do that?'

'Doing bar work at night,' Frank said laconically.

His father looked surprised. 'Kept bloody quiet about it. What's up, afraid I might expect you to pull me a pint for free?'

'No! I didn't think you'd give a damn. New Brighton is hardly your local, is it?' Frank grinned.

Lucy felt a sense of unease. Frank working in a pub at New Brighton. Did he mean the pub where Brenda lived, she wondered? She felt hot and cold all over at the thought that they were seeing each other. Brenda must be mad. She'd told her what sort of man Frank was, but she'd obviously ignored her warning.

And now Frank was offering to give her the money for her tram fares. She didn't know what to say. There didn't seem to be any alternative. She needed the money to get to work, but at the same time, she certainly didn't want to be under an obligation to Frank.

'Thank you, Frank. I'll pay you back the moment I get my wages next week,' she said stiffly.

'And what about the bleedin' ackers for your keep this week? When will you be paying that back?' her uncle asked querulously.

Lucy hesitated, her cheeks burning. 'Next week, I hope,' she promised, 'but I'm not sure how much my wages will be, and you haven't told me how much I have to pay you each week.'

'How much! Bloody hell! What do you think this is, a sodding hotel?' he exploded. 'You'll hand over your pay packet unopened, the same as the rest of us do, and you'll get back some pocket money.'

'I'd sooner know how much I have to pay for my keep, so that I know exactly how much I will have left,' Lucy said stubbornly. 'I'd like to be able to budget my spending and perhaps be able to save some.'

For the first time since she'd been at Anfield Road, Lucy heard her uncle laugh. Long and loud, his blue eyes popping, his enormous belly shaking, he roared and belched until she thought he might have a seizure.

Then his mood changed. His fist came crashing down on the table, setting the crockery and cutlery jangling. His face contorted. His eyes still bulged, but the laughter had gone out of them. Now they were dark with anger. His face was mottled with fury, the sinews in his thick neck stood out like strands of rope, and saliva frothed at the corners of his mouth.

Lucy cowered back in her chair. She felt terrified, he looked like some kind of monster. She didn't know what to say or do. The silence all around her only increased her feeling of panic.

Frank pushed back his chair and stood up, breaking the tension. 'If that clock's right then I'd better be going or I'll be late for my shift at the pub.'

Suddenly they were all moving. Aunt Flo began stacking the empty plates, and telling Karen to carry them through to the scullery. Lucy made her escape, and followed Selina upstairs to their bedroom. She knew she ought to be helping with the washing-up, but she thought it was better if she kept as far away from her uncle as possible until he calmed down.

Selina was sitting on her bed, combing her long dark hair. She looked up as Lucy came into the room. 'I can get you some money if you're desperate,' Selina told her.

'That's very kind of you, but like I told Mr Carter, I don't want to borrow money if I can help it.'

'I wasn't talking about borrowing,' Selina told her as she fished a lipstick out of her handbag. 'You've got far more clothes than you need so why not sell some of them?' she suggested as she began to carefully outline her lips.

Lucy looked at her in amazement. 'My clothes would never fit you,' she exclaimed. Not only was Selina at least two stone heavier than her, but she also had a much more voluptuous shape. Her curvaceous figure was eye-catching, and she flaunted her ample cleavage in tight-fitting blouses and dresses that had low-cut necklines.

'They're not for me!' Selina laughed contemptuously. 'I wouldn't be seen dead in most of the things you wear even if they would fit me. I have friends about your size, though, who might buy them if they're going cheap.'

'I see. I'll think about it,' Lucy murmured, playing for time.

She didn't like the idea of selling her clothes, but neither did she feel happy about Frank lending her money, so it seemed to be the lesser of the two evils.

'Yes or no?' Selina persisted, her blue eyes glinting. 'I'm doing you the favour, remember.'

'Yes, I suppose I could,' Lucy agreed reluctantly.

'Good! My mother doesn't need to know about this!' Selina warned.

Lucy looked puzzled. 'Why not?'

'Well, for one thing she'll expect you to give any clothes you don't want to Karen or Shirley. And for another, if she knows you've got any money then she'll expect you to hand it over for your keep.'

'Oh, dear!' Lucy looked confused. She felt guilty about doing something underhand.

'It's up to you,' Selina shrugged expressively. 'I know you need money and I thought this would be a way of helping you out.'

'Yes, I do,' Lucy agreed. 'And it's kind of you to try and help but . . .'

'You don't want to part with any of your stuff? Surely there must be some things you've had for ages that you're fed up wearing? Or what about your mother's clothes. I bet she had some nice things, even some jewellery you don't want.'

Lucy bit her lip, wondering what on earth her mother would have thought of such an idea.

'Your mam would probably tell you to go ahead,' Selina said, as if reading her mind. 'After all, there's not much point in leaving them hanging in a cupboard when you could be using the money you'd get for them.'

'You're right, I suppose,' Lucy agreed reluctantly. 'I'd have to go over to Wallasey to get them.'

'Why don't you go tomorrow, straight from work. We finish at one o'clock on a Saturday.'

'Won't Aunt Flo ask questions?'

'If you don't tell her she won't know anything about it, will she.'

'She'll wonder where I've gone and she might see me bringing them in.'

'Not if you get back here just after six o'clock. We always go to church at that time on a Saturday night to go to confession. Mam always waits for me and Karen and Shirley so that we can walk back together. I'll make sure we aren't home again until seven. Here.' Selina handed her a half-crown. 'That's enough for your fares to Wallasey and for you to buy yourself a sandwich.'

Lucy stared down at the money in her hand. It seemed all wrong to sell her mother's clothes, but Selina was right, there was no point leaving them hanging up in a wardrobe in Stanley Jones's house. If Selina could sell them there wouldn't be any need for her to borrow any money from Frank.

She found it hard to believe that he was working at Brenda's pub, yet from what he had said it certainly sounded like it. With the money Selina had given her, if she left work at one, and she didn't have to be back in Liverpool until after six, she'd have time to go and see Brenda, and find out if it was true.

It would mean going without a sandwich, because she'd need the money for her bus fare to New Brighton, but it would be worth it to know the truth about what was going on.

For a long time, Lucy couldn't get to sleep for thinking about her trip and all the things that could go wrong. Supposing she missed a boat, or the tram took longer than she thought it would, and she was walking into the house as they all arrived home from church. Or supposing her uncle saw her coming in with a suitcase, he was bound to ask where she'd been and what she'd got there.

In the morning, in order to clear her conscience, she told her aunt that she was going to Wallasey, to collect the rest of her belongings, when she finished work.

'You'd best take a sarnie to work with you then, luv, or you'll be famished. I'll make it for you while you eat your breakfast. Cheese and a bit of pickle, do you?'

Her aunt didn't ask how she was going to pay her fare so Lucy didn't tell her that Selina had loaned her the money. She intended to repay it as soon as Selina sold some of the clothes. She didn't want to be indebted to any of them.

The morning seemed to drag on for ever. She hardly said a word to anyone, and after teasing her about not getting any pay the day before the others gave up talking to her.

'Silly to be so sulky,' one woman pronounced. 'You've got to get used to knocks in this world. You can't go on being featherbedded all your life. You don't know what hardship is, my girl.'

The moment the one-o'clock hooter sounded Lucy made for the door. She tore off her cap and overall and hung them on her peg. It was a really hot day so she didn't bother to put on her jacket, but was out of the building and down the road to the tram stop as fast as she could run.

At the pier head, as she made her way down to the ferry, she saw that both the *Royal Daffodil* and the *Royal Iris* were berthed side by side.

Lucy felt luck was on her side as she made her way on to the one sailing direct to New Brighton. She went up on top deck, revelling in the tang of salty fresh air. The sun was warm on her bare arms and the sky was a deep blue with puffy cream clouds swirling high above her head.

There were several large liners berthed at the dockside and the Isle of Man boat was steaming up ready to leave. She felt as though she, too, was on holiday as they moved down river. The water was smooth and there was a glint of golden sands in the far distance.

Although it was too early in the season for

holidaymakers, a number of trippers from Liverpool were taking advantage of the glorious weather to have a day out and when she arrived at New Brighton she found it was crowded.

Going into the busy pub was something of an ordeal, but having come this far Lucy was determined not to go away without seeing Brenda.

She spotted her the moment she went in. Brenda was wearing an emerald-green dress that made her hair look even more red than usual. She was carrying a tray of pint glasses to a table in the far corner. Lucy waited near the door until Brenda had handed round the beers and then stepped forward and stopped her as she made her way back to the bar.

'Can you spare a minute, Brenda?'

'What on earth are you doing here?' She stared at Lucy in surprise. 'And what have you done to your hair! Are you trying to grow it?'

Self-consciously, Lucy scraped her hair back from her face with one hand. 'It needs cutting,' she mumbled.

'Well, it doesn't suit you like that!' Brenda told her. 'Anyway, what are you doing here?'

'I wanted a word with you.'

'Right now? Can't it wait until I finish at three o'clock?'

'Not really. I'm on my way to Belgrave Road to collect the rest of my things, and I have to be back in Liverpool by six.'

Brenda looked nervously towards the bar where both of her parents were serving.

'It's not a good time, we're awfully busy!'

'Five minutes, Brenda. That's all it will take.'

Brenda looked thoughtful. 'Go outside and wait, then. I'll be out in a minute.'

It was almost ten minutes before Brenda appeared. 'This is our busiest time, are you sure it can't wait, Lucy? My dad will be hopping mad if he finds me hanging about out here. I've told him I'm popping out to collect up the dirty glasses that have been left on the window-sills.'

'What I want to ask you won't take a minute,' Lucy insisted. 'I want to know if you're seeing my cousin Frank?'

Brenda's eyebrows shot up. 'What if I am?' she said flippantly.

'After all I told you about him, you must be mad.'

Brenda looked indignant. 'That's my affair, isn't it?'

Lucy looked at her in despair. 'He says he's working in a pub at New Brighton, so is he working here?'

'I don't see that it's any of your business.'

'But is he?' Lucy persisted.

'Yes, he is,' Brenda flared. 'And he'll be here any minute now, if you must know. I think it would be best if you left before then, don't you? He mightn't like it if he caught you spying on him.'

Without waiting for a reply, Brenda turned on her heel and flounced back into the pub, grabbing up a couple of glasses from the window-sills as she went.

Concerned, knowing that if Brenda was telling

the truth then Frank might appear at any moment, Lucy hurried to the nearest bus stop in Victoria Road and caught the next one that came along.

She was still thinking about Frank and Brenda when she reached Belgrave Road. She couldn't believe that someone as worldly as Brenda would be so gullible as to be taken in by his brash charms, not after she'd told her what he was really like.

She didn't bother to knock, but let herself in and was halfway up the stairs when Stanley Jones came out of the sitting-room.

'You've come back then, Lucy.'

Lucy froze. She should have known he might be there, but she hadn't given it a thought. Now, seeing him standing there, and hearing the warmth in his voice, all her mother's admonishments that it wasn't right or proper for a young unmarried girl ever to be alone in the house with a man came rushing back.

'I . . . I've come to collect the rest of my clothes,' she said almost apologetically.

'Oh!' He looked crestfallen. 'I was hoping you had decided to come back for good. This is your home, you know, Lucy. It always will be,' he added mildly.

She bit her lip; she didn't know what to say. He was such a gentle man and so kind and thoughtful, the exact opposite to her boorish cousin Frank. She wanted to tell him that she'd love to come back. Yet she couldn't. Her mother's voice was ringing in her ears, reminding her of the promise she'd made, and which she knew she must keep.

'If I put the kettle on while you collect your things together will you have a cup of tea with me before you go?' Stanley asked hopefully.

'Yes, that would be nice,' she agreed.

Upstairs in her old bedroom she sat down on the bed and cried. She'd never before appreciated how lovely the room was. It was so spacious and airy, compared to where she was sleeping at Anfield Road, that once again she was tempted to stay there. If only she could do that, she thought wistfully, without breaking her promise to her mother.

The sun seemed to have gone out of her day as she packed all her remaining belongings into her brown suitcase. Then she went into her mother's room and collected up her clothes and packed them into another suitcase that she found on the top of the wardrobe there.

When she took the two suitcases downstairs Stanley came out of the kitchen carrying a tray with cups and saucers and a plate of biscuits.

'Leave those in the hall and come and sit down,' he told her. 'It's all ready. You're lucky, I found some of your favourite chocolate biscuits in the tin. I bought them a few days ago because I had a feeling you might drop in.' He sighed wistfully. 'It's so lonely here without you, Lucy. I think about you all the time. Are you comfortable where you are? Are they looking after you?'

Lucy hesitated. She wondered what Stanley would say if she told him the truth. He'd be so upset if she described the house in Anfield Road, and told him how many people were living there.

If he knew she not only had to share a bedroom, but also share a bed, he'd he horrified.

'Why did you have to go away, Lucy?' he asked as he passed her a cup of tea.

'You know why! My mother made me promise to go and live with my aunt in Liverpool.'

Stanley studied her for a long moment. 'You're not happy there, are you, Lucy?' he said gently.

Lucy hesitated. She didn't want to lie; yet to tell him how bitterly unhappy she was would only make him more miserable, and even more insistent that she ought to return to Belgrave Road.

'You're not, are you, Lucy?' he persisted.

'It . . . it's different from here,' she prevaricated.

'In what way?' His grey eyes studied her intently from behind his horn-rimmed glasses.

'It's more crowded. As well as my aunt and uncle there are my cousins, Frank, Selina, Karen and Shirley.'

'Four of them? Does that mean you haven't got your own room?'

She shrugged disparagingly. 'I have to share with the three girls.'

He looked pained. 'And there's your room upstairs empty. Why don't you come back? I'll leave you to run your own life. You can do as you like. Simply having you here under my roof, knowing you are safe and that I am taking care of you, will please me so much, Lucy.'

'I can't do that, Stanley.' She shook her head emphatically. 'You wouldn't want me to break my promise to my mother, now would you?'

He didn't answer. Instead he picked up her empty cup, and poured her another cup of tea.

'You will think about it?' he persisted as he offered her the plate of biscuits.

She nodded and took one, too choked to speak.

'That's all right then. Now,' he said in a tone that was falsely bright and cheerful, 'tell me something about your new life.'

'I'm working. I started last week.'

'That's wonderful news. I'm really pleased for you! What are you doing?'

'I'm working in a factory.'

'In a factory?' The concern was back in his voice.

'Yes. H & Y Foods. Have you heard of them?'

He gave a dry laugh. 'I would have thought everyone had. You know why they call it that!'

She shook her head, her brown eyes puzzled.

'H and Y. Get it?' He shook his head at the bewildered look on her face. 'If you spell it out, in full, not the way it's written on their sign, you get the word H AND Y. Handy Foods. Meat and fish in tins ready to be served up when you're in a hurry.'

She laughed. 'Oh dear, I hadn't worked it out! I must be dumb,' she admitted. 'The women I work with think I'm pretty slow,' she confessed. 'They tease the life out of me, all except Emma. She's about my age and she's blonde and very pretty. Rather sweet really.'

'Not as sweet or as pretty as you, Lucy,' he said softly.

Suddenly the barrier was back. Lucy replaced

her cup on the table and stood up. 'I must be getting back, Stanley. Thank you for the tea and the chat. I enjoyed both.'

He looked crestfallen. 'Promise me you'll come again.'

'Some time, when I'm more settled.'

'You never will be settled living under those conditions, and working in a factory, now will you?' he said sadly. 'You're used to a lot better than that.' His face brightened. 'I tell you what, Lucy, why don't I try and get you a job at the Cotton Exchange?'

'For a moment her hopes leaped, then her face clouded. 'I can't type, nor do shorthand, so what sort of job would I get there except as a cleaner?'

He pursed his lips. 'As a telephonist, perhaps? You have a lovely voice, Lucy, and I'm sure you'd pick up the work in no time.'

Chapter Seven

Lucy found her life settling into a monotonous round. She was working from eight in the morning until six at night, except on Saturdays when she finished at one o'clock. In the evenings, after helping Aunt Flo to clear away the remains of their meal and wash up, she would sometimes go for a walk with Karen around the nearby streets, or as far as St Cuthbert's church, before going to bed.

Most people knew Karen and would call out a greeting to her. Lucy felt them looking curiously at her and she sensed they were gossiping about her after she and Karen had walked on. Occasionally they met the two women she'd encountered on the day she'd arrived, but apart from 'Hello, chuck' or 'Are you OK then, luv?' they didn't chat.

Sometimes she felt too weary to sleep, but would lie there in the fetid darkness, listening to her uncle's loud, guttural snores, or to the sibilant sighs from Karen curled up at her side. Often she was still wide awake when Selina came tiptoeing up the stairs, or she heard the heavy pad of Frank's footsteps before drifting off into oblivion.

Each day started with her uncle hammering on the bedroom door to rouse them as, belching noisily, muttering and mumbling to himself, he thudded his way downstairs.

Lucy would lie stiff and straight in the bed she shared with Karen, waiting until she heard Frank follow his father down the stairs. Then, as the smell of the fried bacon Aunt Flo cooked for the two men each morning wafted up the stairs, she would slide from under the coarse grey blanket, and hurriedly slip into her clothes while she knew both men were fully occupied eating their breakfast.

Selina would pull the bedclothes over her head and try to snatch another few minutes' sleep. Shirley would wait until the very last minute and then, the moment Selina started dressing, decide to get dressed as well. Arguments between the two of them usually ended in a shouting match as they battled for space in the confines of the overcrowded room.

Once Lucy was out of bed, Karen rolled herself into a tight ball, like a curled-up kitten, pulling the blankets in around her body and over her head as well.

Lucy had no idea what time Karen eventually got up. She hoped her Aunt Flo let Karen stay where she was while she was quiet or sleeping. Her fits were so frightening that each night as she crept into bed beside the sleeping girl, Lucy silently prayed that Karen would sleep the night through.

Twice since they'd been sharing a bed, Karen had had one of her fits. Screaming, twisting, her body contorting, foam spewing from the corners of her mouth, she'd been a frightening sight. Lucy hadn't known what to do. Both Selina and Shirley had turned over in bed so that their backs were towards what was happening and pretended to be asleep. Lucy had called out to her Aunt Flo, but it had been Frank who'd come blundering into the room. He'd known what to do. He made sure Karen's tongue wasn't slipping back down her throat and then soothed and tended her until her breathing quietened, her twitching stopped, and she fell into a natural sleep.

Lucy had been amazed at his gentleness and the softness of his voice as he spoke to Karen. She had also been alarmed by the look in his eyes as he'd stared at her, crouched on the side of the bed anxious to do anything she could to help. It was almost as if he was staring right through her nightdress and studying her naked body.

Before he left the house after eating the fry-up his wife had cooked, Fred Flanagan would again start shouting up the stairs.

'The whole bloody lot of you'll be late if you don't shift your arses,' he'd bellow. 'Are you out of those flea-pits or not?'

Selina and Shirley would scream back at him, but his bawling voice frightened Lucy into a state of panic, so she never said a word.

As soon as Fred and Frank had gone off to work, Selina and Shirley grabbed their own breakfast. They rarely sat at the table, but gulped down a cup of tea, and ate the hunk of fried bread their mother cooked for them as they finished dressing.

There was always a heated argument between Shirley and her mother about what sort of sandwiches she wanted to take for her midday lunch break.

'Why d'you always pack me cheese-and-pickle sarnies?' Shirley bleated. 'You know I hate them.'

'Tell me what you do want then, chuck?'

'I don't know, do I? What else you got?'

'If you don't want cheese then what about sardines?'

'Yuk. They make your breath smell all afternoon,' Shirley whinged.

'Cheese, sardines or jam, which is it to be?'

'Isn't there any ham?'

'Ham! Where do you think I am going to get ham from for sandwiches for you?'

'Well, make me a bacon butty then.'

'There's only enough bacon for your dad and Frank's breakfasts for the rest of the week,' her mother pointed out patiently.

'Why do they have bacon and I can't?' Shirley grumbled.

'When you're working and bringing in some money then you can have bacon,' her mother promised.

'Our Selina doesn't get bacon.'

'That's because she doesn't want it. Says it's too greasy and will spoil her looks.'

Shirley's face brightened. 'Then can I have Selina's bacon?' she wheedled.

The same argument went on almost every

morning. In the end it simply became a back-ground noise, something Lucy found she could shut out and completely ignore.

During the first part of her second week at H & Y Foods Lucy found the only way to get to work was to travel at the same time, and on the same tram, as Selina, and then Selina would pay her fare. It would have been so much easier if Selina had simply given her the money, but she refused to do this. She seemed to enjoy embarrassing Lucy by making a scene on the tram so that everyone knew Lucy hadn't the money to pay her own fare. First thing in the morning it wasn't too difficult to co-ordinate their times, although Selina did tend to leave setting off until the very last minute and they had to run so fast to catch the tram that they were breathless.

Coming home was more complicated. Selina usually hung back after the others left in order to meet up with Jack Carter. Sometimes this meant waiting around at the bus stop for merely ten or fifteen minutes, at other times it could be as long as an hour.

When she mentioned it to Selina on the third evening, after she'd been waiting in the rain for almost half an hour, Selina shrugged indifferently. 'You don't have to wait. You can always walk. Anyway, once I sell some of your clobber you'll have money in your pocket so you can pay your own tram fare! Or ask Frank to pay them. He did offer and he'll do it like a shot just for the sheer hell of having some sort of hold over you. Reckon our Frank has taken a shine to you,' she added with a sour laugh.

'I don't think so,' Lucy told her sharply. 'He's taken up with my friend Brenda over in New Brighton.'

'Who?'

'Brenda. The girl whose father owns the pub where Frank is working in the evenings.'

Selina gave a shrug, but said nothing. 'So when do I get the money for my clothes?' Lucy demanded.

'When I've managed to sell them, of course,' Selina snapped.

When she'd collected the clothes from Belgrave Road, Lucy had felt disloyal because every item brought back so many memories. Dresses that belonged to her mother and herself, some bought for them as presents by Stanley Jones. Clothes bought for special occasions, skirts and blouses her mother had spent hours and hours making for her. She'd been filled with guilt, but she needed the money so badly.

The entire transaction went against the grain, especially having to sneak back into the Flanagans' house hoping that neither her Aunt Flo, Karen nor Shirley were back from church and would ask what was going on.

Selina had quickly gone through the clothes, picking out those items which she wanted for herself and hiding them amongst her own things. The rest she'd bundled up and stuffed under her mattress. For the next two mornings they'd smuggled them out of the house and taken them to the factory so that Selina could show them to her workmates.

At midday break on Thursday, when her special cronies were all sitting outside in the yard eating their packed lunches, drinking the bottles of cold tea they'd brought from home, and enjoying the sunshine, Selina conducted her impromptu sale.

Lucy had been embarrassed even though she'd known what would happen when she'd helped Selina to bring the clothes to work. She kept as far away from what was going on as possible, and tried to avoid looking or listening to what was happening. The ribald laughter and coarse quips as Selina had held up different items for inspection, and invited offers for them, sent shivers of embarrassment through her, and brought a lump to her throat as she struggled to hold back the tears.

Minutes before the hooter sounded to tell them the lunch break was over Selina called out to her. 'Here you are, Lucy,' she announced, 'come and get your loot, you're in the money now!' She jingled the coins. 'There won't be any need for me to pay your tram fares any more.'

Lucy, cheeks flaming as the laughter rang out, was inwardly seething as she walked across to where her cousin was sliding a pile of coins from one hand to the other in a tantalising way.

'Hold your hands out, then!' She tipped a pile of coins into Lucy's hands. 'Happy now?'

Lucy looked down at the assortment of coppers

and silver she was holding in her cupped hands. 'How much is here?' she asked.

'Count it. You can count, can't you?' Selina sniggered.

Lucy bit down on her lower lip, refusing to be goaded. Squatting with her back against the factory wall she dropped the assortment of money into her lap and began sorting it and, at the same time, counting it.

Frowning, she looked up at the women gathered round watching her. 'Is this all there is?' she asked.

'All there is? What d'you mean by that?' Selina snapped. 'You suggesting I'm diddling you or something?'

'No, no, not at all. It's just that there is only two pounds, three shillings and ninepence.'

'Well?' Selina said aggressively. She stood with her hands on her hips, winking broadly at the crowd of women who were watching.

Lucy looked puzzled. 'I thought there would be more . . . a lot more.'

'For that load of old tat?' Selina laughed derisively. 'Think yourself lucky you've got that much. Some of the stuff I've sold for you was only fit for cleaning rags.'

'That's a lie,' Lucy defended hotly. 'My mother only ever bought good-quality clothes.'

'Yeah, luv, but when did she buy them?' one of the women questioned. 'None of us would be seen dead in most of those dresses. Those styles date back to the ark!'

'She's right, chuck. We only bought them

dresses because we cover 'em up with overalls while we're here at work,' another woman told her.

'That's right. So's we can save our decent stuff for going out,' one of the younger ones agreed.

Lucy shook her head in bewilderment. She couldn't believe that her mother's clothes had been so valueless. Deep inside she wished she'd kept them, a last memory and tribute to her mother, but common sense told her that had been out of the question. Not only had she nowhere to store them, but she was also desperately short of money.

'So what about my dresses?' she asked Selina. 'There were ten of them and they were all quite new.' Tears filled her eyes as she remembered how her mother always insisted on her having the best. She would never let her wear anything cheap or shoddy. If you buy quality items they always look good on you and they wear twice as long, had been her mother's maxim.

'They're gone too. You've got all the money you're going to get,' Selina said sharply.

'They were only kids' sizes, and only worth coppers,' a buxom girl told her. 'Your dresses weren't big enough for most of us, and your mam's dresses were well out of fashion.'

'You're such a skinny runt,' a middle-aged woman commented. 'I bought one of your old frocks for my kiddie, but I'm not sure if she'll get into it. If she doesn't then I'll want my money back, so don't go blowing it all.'

'Are you sure we've brought everything, Selina?' Lucy persisted.

'What are you saying now? Are you still suggesting I've twisted you?' Selina asked in an annoyed voice.

'Well, no. Of course I'm not!' Lucy prevaricated. Her eyes were bright with unshed tears, her face flushed from the open combat, and from the grins and knowing stares of the women gathered round Selina. 'It's just that it doesn't seem much money for all my mother's clothes and most of mine as well.'

Selina regarded her contemptuously, her blue eyes flashing angrily. 'That's gratitude for you,' she announced loudly, looking round at the other women. 'I put myself out, I flog her rags, and then she's not satisfied. What do you want me to do, Lucy, collect them all back up again and hand the money back?'

Lucy was saved from answering by the deafening blast of the hooter. The women dispersed in a flash, knowing that if they were late back at work their pay would be docked.

Lucy followed them. She was sure she'd been short-changed by Selina, but she had no proof, and from the grinning faces of the women who'd bought the clothes she suspected they knew and that they were in cahoots with Selina.

Back at her workbench, she tried to enlist Emma's support, but her new friend refused to be drawn into the discussion.

'I didn't buy any of them so I don't know what went on,' she said flatly.

Lucy tried to put the matter out of her mind as she got on with her work, but it was impossible. Inside she was churning. Anger with herself for being duped, anger at Selina for twisting her – as she was sure she had done – and anger at the women who'd profited from her misfortune. She wished she'd given the clothes to her Aunt Flo for Karen and Shirley instead of trying to sell them.

That night she didn't wait for Selina, but made her way back to Anfield Road alone. Her only consolation about the entire episode was that she now had the money to pay her own tram fares.

Lucy felt her future was bleak. The only person at H & Y Foods who showed any signs of friendliness towards her was Emma, and she took care not to appear too friendly in case she antagonised any of the other women. So many of them seemed to be cronies of Selina's and when Lucy mentioned this to Emma she simply shrugged. 'What do you expect when she's so matey with Jack Carter? Upset your Selina, and one word in his ear from her and you might find yourself out of a job.'

The more Lucy thought about this the more she longed to turn the clock back to before her mother had been taken ill. To the days when she'd been fourteen, and still studying for her School Certificate.

'That's impossible, but you could move back into Belgrave Road and keep house for Stanley Jones,' a voice inside her head kept telling her over and over again.

It was a tempting idea. And never more so than

when they all sat round the table for their evening meal, and she found herself being subjected to her Uncle Fred's jibes and blaspheming, to Frank's lecherous stares, and to Selina's contempt. Or when she was forced to strip wash in the scullery, afraid that at any minute Frank might walk back into the house and catch her in a state of undress. Or when she was forced to use the primitive lavvy in the yard outside, and to try and keep a foot on the door so that it stayed shut while she was in there.

If only she hadn't made that fateful promise to her mother then possibly she could have stayed in Belgrave Road, and with Stanley's help passed her exams and gone to college. Or trained to become a secretary. Even working in a shop would be better than in a factory, and yet that seemed to be the only sort of work she'd ever be able to get if she stayed with the Flanagans.

Chapter Eight

Collecting her first pay packet seemed almost mundane to Lucy. She had been waiting so long for it that it had none of the glamour or excitement she had originally thought it would have. Opening the small brown packet on the way home on the tram, counting and recounting the money inside it, she could hardly believe that it could be so pitifully meagre.

She still didn't know how much her Aunt Flo was expecting her to pay for her keep and until she did she couldn't work out how much she'd have left. Whatever it was she'd have to put fourpence a day aside for tram fares to work. And it would take at least another shilling every time she wanted to go over to New Brighton to see Brenda.

She needed to save for some new shoes and to have the ones she was wearing repaired. She could use some of the money Selina had got for her clothes, but old habits died hard, and she wanted to keep at least one pound safely tucked away for emergencies as her mother had always taught her to do. The last few weeks had shown her how valuable such a precaution could be. If she'd had a pound in reserve she would never have been forced into selling all her mother's clothes and most of her own for such a pittance.

Thinking back to when Selina had handed over the money, and the smirking faces of the women who were gathered round watching what was going on, Lucy was convinced that Selina had cheated her. Whether she'd kept back some of the money, or whether she'd sold the clothes to the women at bargain prices, she wasn't sure, but something wasn't right.

It was no good worrying about it, she told herself firmly. It had happened, it was all in the past. If she'd been taken in there wasn't very much she could do about it. She'd learned her lesson though, and she'd be more careful next time she had any dealings with Selina or anyone else, because she would never trust anybody again.

The Flanagans' ritual of handing over their pay packets began as soon as they'd finished eating their evening meal. Lucy felt uneasy when first her Uncle Fred, and then Frank and Selina, passed their unopened pay packets across the table to her Aunt Flo.

'Where's yourn then, Lucy?' her Uncle Fred bawled. 'Come on, girl. Hand it over like the rest of us.'

Lucy sat bolt upright on her hard wooden chair, colour staining her cheeks. 'I'll hand over what-ever you require for my keep if you tell me how much it is,' she said defiantly.

'Oh, you will, will you, missy,' he glowered. 'I

said hand over your pay packet and that's that. Understand?

'I can't hand it over because I haven't got it.'

'Haven't got it?' His face grew purple with anger. 'What the bloody hell do you mean by that? Jack Carter's not missed you out again this week, has he?'

'Of course he hasn't,' Selina said derisively. 'She's playing up. She's hoping you'll be a soft touch and let her off for another week.'

'That's not true!'

'Then hand over your damn packet and let's have no more monkeyin' about,' growled Fred Flanagan. 'And God help you if you've already opened it.'

'Of course I've opened it, it was mine,' Lucy told him, her brown eyes flashing. 'And I'm not trying to cheat on you. Tell me how much I have to pay you and I will.'

'How the hell do we know how much it will be if you don't hand over your packet, you silly bitch? Your Aunt Flo will give you back some pocket money. Can't you get that into your thick skull, girl?'

'I know perfectly well what you are saying, Uncle Fred, but it's not the way I want to do things. I'll pay whatever you ask for my keep, but my pay packet is mine and I don't want to hand it over unopened. Can't you understand that?'

Fred Flanagan's face mottled with anger. He raised his fist, and remembering what the two women she'd met in the street had told her about his temper, Lucy quaked inwardly. She was sure he was going to hit her. Even when his fist came crashing down on to the table, making the dishes rattle, she resolutely refused to let him dictate what she must do.

Aunt Flo tried to mollify him. 'Leave it, Fred, I'll deal with it after our meal is over,' she said quietly.

'You shut your mouth, you silly cow,' he raved. 'Taken in by her and her sodding fancy ways, aren't you! Never paid you a penny, has she, the mingy-arsed bitch!'

'Only because she's been skint ever since she spent the last of the few pounds her mother left her.'

'And how much of that has she been squirrelling away for herself? Tell me that, you daft moll? She hasn't been bloody walking to work, has she?'

'Lucy's been borrowing off me for her tram fares,' Selina said quickly.

'Yer what?' He looked taken aback. 'Another Lady Muck with more coppers than sense,' he snarled. 'Leave me to find the wherewithal to keep this bloody family going. I turn over every penny of me bit of bunce to keep you lot, and Father O'Reilly and his cronies, in the sodding lap of luxury.'

'I've told you, I'll pay my way once you tell me how much,' Lucy said stubbornly.

'Right! Ten shillings a week, how does that suit you?'

Lucy blanched. She was only earning fifteen shillings. She'd only have five shillings left.

She'd already calculated three shillings a week

106

for tram fares and to go over to see Brenda, which left her with only two shillings for everything else. It would cost her at least a shilling to have her shoes repaired, more if she had both the soles and heels done at the same time.

Pride stopped her from arguing, but she suspected from Aunt Flo's expression that she would be handing over far more than Selina did.

Fred Flanagan pushed back his chair. 'I'm off to the boozer, you coming with me, Frank?'

'Not tonight.'

'Off to see that new judy over the water, are you?'

Frank looked uneasy. 'Might be!' he said evasively.

His father laughed raucously. 'Don't wet your bloody self, I'm not thinking of coming with you. Just watch your step and don't put her in the club. One sodding stranger living here is more than enough.'

As Fred made to leave there was a sharp knock on the front door.

'Who the sodding hell is that? If it's Father Bunloaf mind you don't let him in, I'm not in the mood for that sanctimonious bastard,' he warned as Flo went to answer it.

Lucy gasped and a hot flush of embarrassment suffused her face as Flo Flanagan came back into the room followed by a slim, slightly built man with thinning light brown hair, wearing horn-rimmed glasses.

'Stanley! What are you doing here?' she asked in surprise.

She felt acutely uncomfortable as she saw how they were all staring at him. In his navy blue three-piece suit, white shirt with its stiff white collar and a plain dark blue tie, and holding his black trilby hat in his hand, he looked out of place in the Flanagans' house.

'Hello, Lucy. I hope you don't mind me calling like this. I tried to catch you when you left work tonight, because I have some good news for you,' he said, smiling.

'Good news?' Her face lit up. 'Do you mean about a job at the Cotton Exchange?' she asked eagerly.

'Yes, that's right.' He was beaming at her as if he was as pleased about it as she was.

'Who the bloody hell are you, and what are you yammering on about?' Fred interrupted. 'She's got a bloody job in a factory so what does she want another job for when half of Merseyside is unemployed?'

Lucy felt indignant. Did her uncle have to be so rude? She found herself seeing her surroundings as they must appear to Stanley and wondered if he was comparing them with his own home.

Aunt Flo, in her cotton wraparound apron, Uncle Fred, his tie loosened and his collar unbuttoned, Frank looking even scruffier with his shirt open halfway down the front exposing his hairy chest.

Selina hadn't changed since coming home. Her low-cut blouse showed inches of cleavage and with her tight-fitting skirt and heavy make-up she looked more like a floozie than a hard-working factory girl.

Not that I look a lot better myself, Lucy thought uneasily. She knew her hair was straggly, because she hadn't trimmed it for weeks, her blouse was stained and her fingernails grubby. One of her stockings had a ladder in it and her shoes were down at heel.

The smell of stewed lamb from their meal of scouse still hung on the air, the lumps of grey fat and half-chewed gristle still on their plates. Shirley had arranged hers around the edge like plum stones and had been counting 'This year, next year' when Stanley had arrived.

Stanley took off his glasses and polished them with the silk handkerchief from his top pocket. 'This is a different sort of job,' he said nervously. 'It's one I think Lucy will find more conducive.'

'Conducive? What the hell is conducive when it's at home?' Fred sneered. 'What's she going to be doing there, serving the bloody tea?'

'No, no, nothing like that.' Stanley replaced his glasses and stared owlishly at Fred Flanagan. 'Lucy will be training to be a telephonist,' he said solemnly.

'Gerraway! Answering the sodding blower all day, what sort of a bloody job is that?'

'A much better one than she is doing now,' Stanley said confidently. 'She'll be given full training and if she works hard and passes the exams it could prove to be a very worthwhile career. Anyway, I'm sure Lucy will be much happier working under such conditions than on an assembly line in a factory.'

'Are you the bloke she was living with before she got chucked out and had to come over here and move in with us?'

'Lucy and her mother were living in my house,' Stanley said primly. 'Lucy wasn't "chucked out", as you put it. She left of her own accord. As I'm sure you already know it was all to do with a promise she made to her mother.'

'That's my sister-in-law you're talking about. Uppity bitch, always thought herself too good to mix with the likes of us when she was alive so what did she need to send her kid to live with us for? What sort of feller are you, whacker, that she couldn't trust you?'

Stanley stared at Fred in horror. 'What on earth are you getting at?' he spluttered.

Fred scratched his chest thoughtfully. 'Must have been some reason for Maude making the girl promise to come here. It wasn't because she liked us!'

'You are her family,' Stanley said lamely.

'More to it than that,' Fred sniffed, scratching underneath his armpit. 'So when's she starting this new job?'

'Lucy can start on Monday if she wishes to do so.'

'No, she can't,' Selina chipped in. 'She's got to give a week's notice.'

'Really?' Stanley looked across at Selina in surprise. 'Do you have to comply with such formalities in a factory?' he asked blandly.

'Yes, she does, and no skipping off sick instead of working her week out. I went to a lot of trouble to get Lucy taken on there.'

'I know that and I don't want to let you down, Selina,' Lucy said quickly. 'Will it be all right if I start a week on Monday then, Stanley?' she asked. Her heart was thudding in case he said no. She could hardly believe her good luck. Getting away from the factory and working in an office was something she'd dreamed of doing.

'A week on Monday. Right!' He took off his glasses and polished them again. 'Be there at half past eight. I'll wait for you at the entrance to show you where you have to go, and introduce you to Miss Ford, the supervisor.'

'Thank you.' Eyes shining with relief, she reached out and touched his arm. 'I'm very grateful.'

He smiled back at her. Replacing his trilby on his head he turned towards the door. 'I'll see you a week on Monday then, Lucy.'

The Flanagans waited until they heard Flo closing the door behind him before voicing their varied opinions. Then they came thick and fast.

'So that's Stanley Jones, yer fancy man,' Selina said, raising her carefully shaped eyebrows in an expression of surprise. 'Old for you, isn't he?'

'One of them sort, if you ask me, with his cut-glass voice. Did you see the way he was polishing his glasses with a silk hanky,' Frank guffawed.

Lucy resented their comments, but she was too relieved at the prospect of a job at the Cotton Exchange to even rise to Stanley's defence.

'Bloody Wallasey boy,' Fred sneered. 'Great nancy! What the bloody hell does he want coming all the way out here to tell you about a job in the Cotton Exchange?'

'He's being very kind and helping me find a better job,' Lucy retorted.

'Better job, is it? Sitting on your fanny all day talking posh into one of them damn things instead of doing an honest day's work. What are they going to pay you, then? I didn't hear him mention money.'

Lucy bit her lip. Uncle Fred was right. She should have asked what the pay was going to be. Supposing it was less than what she was earning at the factory, what would she do then, especially now that she was committed to handing over ten shillings a week for her keep?

'I thought he was very nice,' Karen said dreamily. 'He had a kind face and such a lovely gentle voice. I like him.'

Lucy gave her a warm smile. 'You're right, Karen. Stanley is very kind and gentle.'

'I go to all the trouble of putting in a word for you with Jack Carter and you hand your notice in after two weeks! Where does that leave me?' Selina demanded sourly.

'I'm sorry, Selina. I really am grateful for your help, but this is more the sort of work I want to do.'

'Oh my, oh my,' Selina mocked. 'The factory was too hard for you, was it? Or didn't you like the company you had to keep while you worked there?' she jeered.

112

'When did you ask Stanley Jones to help you, Lucy?' Her aunt frowned.

'On Saturday, when I went over to Wallasey to collect the rest of my things,' Lucy mumbled. 'I didn't exactly ask him to help me, I told him about where I was working and he said he thought he could get me something more suitable.'

Her aunt nodded, but she still looked doubtful. 'Well, I suppose you know what you are doing, luv, but watch your step, that's all.'

'What do you mean?'

'It may be his way of trying to persuade you to go back and live in his house again, Lucy.'

'He'd make a lovely sugar-daddy,' Selina mocked. 'Not much good for anything else, I shouldn't think, but you probably wouldn't mind that as long as he bought you pretty clothes, and you didn't have to slave in a factory.'

'For Christ's sake, cut it out, mouthy,' Frank snapped. 'You're a fine one to talk, anyway.'

'And what's that supposed to mean?' Selina flared, her blue eyes blazing.

'Leave the kid alone. Good luck to her if she manages to get a better job. It's about time you did the same. Or are you content to be Jack Carter's bit on the side, and stay as factory fodder for the rest of your life?'

'Mind your own damn business!'

'Then you mind yours!'

'Stop this squabbling,' Aunt Flo interrupted wearily. 'Anyone would think you were still children!' She turned and smiled at Lucy. 'You do what you think is best, my dear.'

'Except going back to live in that fellow's house,' Frank warned.

'Jealous?' Selina jibed. 'I saw you in our bedroom the other night when you thought the rest of us were asleep.'

'You dirty-minded bitch,' Frank snarled. 'Karen had a fit and it upset Lucy. After I'd settled Karen I was trying to reassure Lucy that there was nothing to worry about. She does have to sleep in the same bed as Karen, remember.'

Lucy cringed. She knew Frank was only defending her to save his own skin.

'Karen had a fit? The other night? You should have called me, Frank,' his mother said worriedly.

'Sorry, Mam. I meant to tell you, but I forgot. It wasn't a bad one. She was out of it in no time.'

'She had one the other day, but that was only slight, too,' his mother agreed. 'Father O'Reilly has been saying special prayers for her so perhaps that's helping.'

'You'd better get him to say some for Lucy to help her make the right decision,' Selina quipped, flouncing out of the room.

Chapter Nine

Lucy found that working at the Cotton Exchange was like a holiday after her factory job at H & Y Foods.

Stanley was waiting for her on her first morning and introduced her to the supervisor. Miss Ford was a severe-looking woman in her late thirties. She was smartly dressed in a tailored navy suit teamed with a high-necked plain white blouse, sensible flat shoes and dark stockings. Her mid-brown hair was brushed back from her face into a neat roll.

In her short white skirt and frilly green blouse, Lucy felt frivolous, self-conscious and unsuitably dressed.

Miss Ford took down details of her age and working experience. Her frown as she wrote down the address in Anfield Road set alarm bells ringing in Lucy's head, but as the interview continued she became more relaxed.

Then she was taken to where the telephonists were working, and for a moment she had a feeling of panic as she viewed the immense switchboard that seemed to completely fill one wall of the room. It contained hundreds of holes, each one labelled with a different letter or number. The board itself seemed to be in two parts: at the base were the incoming lines and from these came plugs, which were inserted into the holes at the top to connect them to the internal numbers and extensions.

There were about ten girls sitting at the switchboard, and each of them had a headset clamped over her ears, and a horn-shaped mouthpiece hanging around her neck. Each of the girls seemed to be in control of a set portion of the board.

As Lucy watched them dealing with incoming calls, and deftly inserting plugs into the right extension or removing them when a call was finished, she felt sure she would never master the complex maze of numbers and plugs that was involved.

For the first morning, Lucy found that all she was expected to do was sit beside an older woman, and watch how she handled each incoming call, and dealt with the requests from different offices for a line or for an outside number.

In the afternoon Lucy found herself sitting alongside a red-headed girl called Wanda, who was to instruct her on how to deal with internal calls.

'If you make a mistake don't worry,' Wanda told her as she adjusted Lucy's headset. 'I'll be right here beside you, and I will put your plugs right if you get them wrong. I can hear exactly the same as you are hearing, remember.'

The first two calls were easy. The callers knew which extension number they needed, and it was simply a matter of inserting the plug into the correct hole. The third call was more complicated because the caller wanted another member of staff, but didn't know the extension. 'Ring me back when you get them,' said a man's disembodied voice. He replaced his receiver before Lucy had time to note which extension number he was calling from, or to check who it was he wanted.

Wanda made light of it. She suggested it might be a good idea if Lucy kept a notepad handy whilst she was still learning.

'Write down the extension that's calling, and then cross it through when you've dealt with it,' she advised. 'It's also a good idea to ask for their name as several people may be using the same extension.'

By the end of the second day Lucy was dealing with internal calls fairly competently. Her confidence faded a little, however, when she was transferred to the main switchboard and expected to handle incoming calls.

Since she was a newcomer, the supervisor, Miss Ford, kept a close watch over Lucy. She was never very far away, so that if Wanda, or one of the other girls, was too busy to help her out of a predicament then Miss Ford would come to her aid.

Lucy was quick to learn, and one of the things she liked most about her new job was that the girls she was now working with were all so welcoming. Although she had become friendly with Emma at the factory, no one else there had made any effort to be civil. But here there was no teasing, no abuse. Most of them came from

Wallasey or the better parts of Liverpool, like Blundellsands.

They not only spoke differently from the girls she'd worked alongside in H & Y Foods but they were well groomed, and much more smartly turned out. She realised as she listened to them chatting in the staff rest room that trying to keep up with them was not going to be easy, and she bitterly regretted parting with so many of her clothes, especially since Selina had cheated her over selling them.

Her new wages she was pleased to discover would be seventy-five pounds per year, nearly twice what she had been earning in the factory! She felt quite well off, especially since she had been promised a rise of another five pounds a year at the end of her three months' training.

Provided Aunt Flo didn't ask for more than the ten shillings a week she was already paying for her keep, then even after she had paid her insurance stamp, her tram fares, and bought a drink at lunch time each day, she would still have almost ten shillings left.

It would soon mount up, she told herself gleefully. Restocking her depleted wardrobe would be her first goal, she decided. She'd seen skirts in C & A Modes in Church Street for only twelve shillings, and a complete costume for only a little over two pounds. Of course they were not nearly such good quality as the clothes she'd handed over to Selina to sell for her, but she'd learned her lesson. She wouldn't be taken in like that ever again.

After that she'd try and put a regular sum away each week so that perhaps in a year's time, or even sooner, she'd be able to afford a bedsitting room of her own well away from Anfield Road.

She still had her mother's wedding ring and a pearl-encrusted gold brooch that her mother had treasured because it was the first present she'd ever had from her husband. Lucy knew she could sell or pawn these, but their sentimental value meant more to her than hard cash, and she would only part with them if she was really desperate.

Her Uncle Fred spoiled her feeling of euphoria by raising the question of how much she would be paying for her keep.

'Now you've got this bleeding highfalutin new job I hope you're going to turn up a bit more,' he told her in between shovelling a forkful of faggots and peas into his mouth.

Lucy didn't know what to say. She wished she knew how much Frank and Selina handed over for their keep each week, but this was a closely guarded secret both by them and by her Aunt Flo. When she'd said, 'I'll give you the same as the others,' her Aunt Flo's mouth had tightened, and her Uncle Fred had reminded her that they handed over their pay packets unopened the same as he did, and that they were handed back pocket money.

She still felt this was demeaning. She was quite willing to pay her fair share, but she refused to comply with the family tradition. She was pretty sure that the amount her Aunt Flo handed back was meagre. That was why Frank had been so

119

keen to go and help out at the pub Brenda's family ran in New Brighton. How Selina earned her extra spending money she didn't know, but she suspected that she had some sort of scam going, and that was the reason why she went round to her friend's house each evening.

She and Selina had hardly exchanged a civil word since Selina had duped her and sold off her clothes for such a measly pittance. Now, as Fred Flanagan harangued her over how much she was going to pay, she saw Selina was watching her reaction, a sly grin on her face, and that she kept exchanging knowing looks with Frank.

To Lucy's surprise it was Frank who spoke up in her defence.

'Why does Lucy have to hand over more money just because she's changed her job?' he asked in a puzzled voice.

'Because she's earning more money, you silly bugger!' his father roared back at him.

'You mean if I get a rise you'll take more out of my pay packet and then I'll be handing over more?' he asked blandly.

'Course you bloody well will. And why not? All for one and one for all in this family, or hadn't you noticed?'

'All I notice is that I'm skint by mid-week while you still manage to cadge the odd bob or two off me mam to go boozing.'

'Buys you a bloody pint whenever you come with me, don't I?'

'You never buy me one,' Selina commented.

'Never come to the bloody pub, do you. And if

you think I'm going to call round at Anytime Annie's, my girl, to see if you want one, then you can think again. Anywise, you've probably got plenty of fellers there ready to pay for more than beer.'

Bristling with anger, Selina pushed back her chair and flounced out of the room.

'You shouldn't have spoken to her like that, Fred,' Flo remonstrated, her full face looking pale and drawn.

'I'll speak to her and everyone else as I damn well please,' he muttered. 'My house, isn't it? If she don't like it then she can bugger off somewhere else.'

Lucy swallowed down the last of the food on her plate, and wished she was anywhere but in Anfield Road. She felt it was her fault that the row had started, but she still intended to stick to her principles about not handing over her pay packet. She hadn't even told them how much she would be earning, and she was sure that this was a further source of annoyance to her uncle.

The next morning, when they were handing out pay packets at the Cotton Exchange, she found that she was caught in the same trap as she had been on her first pay day at H & Y Foods. Instead of receiving the amount she'd calculated, she found only half as much.

'Three days are kept in hand,' Miss Ford told her. 'It's company rules, there's nothing I can do about it.'

The problem of how she was going to manage until the following Friday haunted Lucy all day.

As she walked down the steps that night to catch the tram back to Anfield Road she found Stanley Jones waiting for her.

'You look rather exhausted,' he said worriedly. 'Have you found the work hard?'

'No, not at all. I've loved every minute,' she told him quickly. 'I'm really grateful to you for arranging it.'

'I didn't do anything very much,' he said dismissively.

'You must have done or I would never have got the job with so many out of work!'

'Well, I knew you'd score top marks on how you spoke and how you dressed. The only thing I was worried might be against you was your address.'

Lucy grinned. 'I noticed the way Miss Ford frowned when I told her where I was living.'

Stanley nodded. 'Never mind. Later on, if you think it might be stopping you from getting promotion you can always move back to Wallasey. Anyway, that's not what I wanted to see you about. I know they hold back three days' pay so take this to make it up,' he said, holding out a one-pound note.

Colour stained Lucy's cheeks. 'I don't know, Stanley. It's kind of you, but I hate to be under an obligation.'

'Obligation?' He looked hurt. 'How can you feel under an obligation to me, Lucy? Look,' he added quickly as she still hesitated, 'you can pay me back later if you want to, you know.'

Sorely tempted, Lucy thought quickly. She'd

already spent the money Selina had given her for the clothes on new stockings, having her shoes repaired and paying back the money Selina had let her have for tram fares. There had only been fourteen shillings in her pay packet and she had to pay Aunt Flo ten shillings of that for her keep and pay her fares to work every day. If she refused Stanley's help then it would mean she wouldn't have anything to spend, not even enough to go and visit Brenda.

'Well, if you are quite sure it won't leave you short, Stanley.'

'Leave me short! Don't talk rubbish. It won't leave me short even if you don't pay me back. In fact, I wish you would take it as a present, Lucy. You can even have more if you need it,' he told her, beaming with pleasure at being able to do something for her.

'It's very nice of you to help me like this,' Lucy repeated as she took the pound note he held out to her. 'I only wish there was something I could do for you in return.'

'The one thing you could do that would please me more than anything else would be to come back to Belgrave Road to live. Will you think about it, Lucy?'

She sighed. In her heart of hearts there was nothing she would have liked more. She hated living at Anfield Road. Never a day passed without her remembering the comforts she'd enjoyed when she'd been living in his house, but her conscience wouldn't let her break the promise she'd made to her mother.

'I do understand, Lucy.' He laid a hand on her arm. 'I won't pester you. Perhaps one day you'll change your mind. Just remember, there's always a home for you at Belgrave Road.'

'Thank you, Stanley, it's comforting to know that,' she said quietly. Leaning forward, she kissed him on the cheek before quickly walking away.

Chapter Ten

'Well, that's the bottling-up finished in record time so does that mean you have the rest of the night off then, kiddo?' Frank Flanagan asked as he helped Brenda Green restack the shelves with bottled beer.

Brenda patted her short red hair provocatively and shot him a saucy look. 'What's it to you?'

Frank shrugged laconically. 'Seeing you're not working tonight I thought it might be nice to take you out somewhere, get to know you, like.'

'You can do that working with me, can't you?' she quipped.

'Yeah, but it's not quite the same, is it? I thought perhaps we could go to the Tower Ballroom, that's if you like dancing, or to see a show at the Tivoli or the Winter Gardens, or for a fish supper and a walk along the prom. Or we could go to the Trocadero if you prefer the pictures. Whatever you fancied, really.'

Brenda raised her eyebrows. 'Know how to turn a girl's head, don't you, Frank Flanagan?'

'You say where you'd like to go and I'll take you there. How's that?'

'Dinner at the Adelphi?'

He let out a low whistle. 'Bit out of your league,

isn't it? I don't even know if you have the right clothes for places like that.'

Brenda looked annoyed. 'Cheeky sod! You saying I'm scruffy or something?'

'Course I'm not. I think you've got a smashing figure, almost as curvy as Mae West's, and you've got a great pair of pins. What's more, you know how to dress to show off all your assets, and get the men going.'

'Well then? What's wrong with the Adelphi Hotel?'

'Sooner take you to the new Lyons Corner House and treat you to egg mayonnaise topped with smoked salmon and mustard and cress.'

Brenda pulled a face.

'Orr right then,' Frank smiled. 'Let's make it the Tower Ballroom. Pick a night when there's a good band, though.'

'Victor Sylvester's on there tonight.'

'Like him, do you? I prefer Glenn Miller's band.'

Brenda shrugged. 'Suit yourself. You can take me to the Trocadero to see *King Kong*, if you'd prefer.'

'No,' Frank conceded. 'The Tower it is. Get your glad rags on and we'll be off.'

'I'll have to ask my dad first, I can't just walk out at the drop of a hat!'

'Go on then, he's bound to say yes because it's pretty quiet, and I've seen the way you can twist him round your little finger.'

Half an hour later, they were walking arm in arm along the promenade towards the Tower

Ballroom. Brenda was wearing a full-skirted, low-cut, pale blue dress cinched in at the waist with a black belt, and was teetering along on black suede, high-heeled shoes.

As they began circling the floor to the rhythmic dreamy music, Brenda relaxed and melted into his arms. Frank waited until her head was resting against his chest before he began to ply her with questions about Lucy.

He already knew that they'd known each other at school, but he wanted to know more about Lucy's relationship with Stanley Jones. Although Lucy was unaware of the fact, he'd seen them together outside the Cotton Exchange; he'd been intrigued when Stanley handed her a pound note and he'd wondered what was going on. He'd felt a small stab of jealousy as he watched Lucy kiss Stanley Jones on the cheek.

Brenda, resenting Frank's interest in Lucy, didn't want to talk about her. When she realised that the only way to get her name dropped from their conversation was to tell Frank what he wanted to know, she began to embroider spiteful stories about Lucy's relationship with Stanley Jones.

'She was always boasting at school about the marvellous prezzies he bought for her. Real expensive things like new dresses, and bangles, and everything. She told me he said he was going to marry her one day.'

'Marry her?' Frank's voice was harsh. 'He's years older than Lucy!'

"Aven't you ever heard of a sugar-daddy?'

Brenda smirked. 'Better to be an old man's darlin' than a young man's slave!' She looked up at Frank with a teasing smile. 'I know which I'd prefer to be!'

'You do? What about Lucy?'

Brenda shrugged, rubbing her breasts provocatively against Frank's chest. 'Probably an old man's darling if the way she goes on about Stanley Jones is anything to go by.'

'She's too pretty to waste herself on a creep like him!' Frank said savagely.

'Do we have to talk about her?' Brenda snapped. 'I thought we were coming here to enjoy ourselves?'

'And we are, aren't we?' Turning on his charm, Frank held her closer, crushing the full skirt of her dress as he held her tightly against his body and they swirled round in time to the band. Then he slipped a hand under her chin, tilting her head back, and kissed her. It was a long, hard kiss that brought a whimper of ecstasy from Brenda.

'That's better,' she murmured, snuggling even closer to him. She felt sublimely happy. She'd fancied Frank Flanagan from the moment she'd first met him despite the picture Lucy had painted of him and his family.

He might be a rough diamond, but he was a very handsome one with his thick dark hair and hypnotic blue eyes. So he was rugged, and swaggering, and loud-mouthed, but then most of the dockers who came into the pub were like that.

She liked a man who enjoyed a smoke and a bevvy, especially when they were young and tall with powerful shoulders and solid biceps. Compared to Stanley Jones, Frank was a giant among men, and she didn't intend to lose him to Lucy Patterson.

Brenda had had enough experience of men to know that showing any jealousy or spite towards Lucy would only damage her own chances with Frank. She realised that there were other, more subtle ways. For the rest of the evening whenever Frank mentioned Lucy's name, or asked questions about her, she went out of her way to feed him the information she wanted him to have.

She felt no disloyalty in doing so. Lucy was only a friend from schooldays, after all, not a close buddy. She didn't really care if she never saw her again, because now she'd met Frank she didn't need her. If she played her cards right she was sure he'd soon be as keen about her as she was about him.

As they slowly circled the floor to the strains of the final waltz, Brenda's thoughts raced ahead. She knew her mam and dad liked him because they thought he was good behind the bar, and had a winning way with customers. In her mind's eye she saw the diamond ring flashing on her engagement finger.

She wanted him desperately, every fibre of her being cried out for him, and from the way he had been kissing her, and holding her as they danced, she was sure the need was mutual.

She wondered whether, if she let him make love to her when he took her home, he would declare his feelings for her. Or perhaps it would be better to play hard to get. She didn't want him to think she was a cheap floozie with no holds barred, but neither did she want him thinking she was a prude like Lucy.

Probably he didn't think Lucy was any nun, not now, she thought smugly, not after the picture she'd built up about her and Stanley Jones. Brenda smiled contentedly. She'd done a good job there. She'd made Frank think that Lucy really was soft on Stanley so, hopefully, that would turn Frank right off her.

As the dance ended, and they strolled the short distance from the Tower Ballroom back to the pub where she lived, Brenda tried desperately to think of a way to keep Frank with her. She chatted animatedly, squeezing his arm, clinging to him like a limpet.

Gazing up at the stars she sighed pensively. 'It's been a wonderful night, Frank, thank you for taking me.'

He grinned down at her wickedly. 'I haven't yet, though, have I?'

She felt the colour flooding her face; it was almost as though he could read her mind, and that he was teasing her deliberately. Not sure what to say, Brenda pouted prettily, and tried to look demure as if she didn't know what he meant.

To her annoyance, Frank didn't pursue the matter. Instead, he once again began questioning her about Lucy. It seemed as though he couldn't get enough information about her. Although he soaked up every tiny detail about their school-days, what they'd said to each other, and how they'd spent their time, it was facts about Lucy and Stanley Jones that seemed to really intrigue him.

Finding it was the only way to keep his attention, Brenda stretched her imagination to dish up every nugget of gossip about Stanley Jones that she could.

'So when did he start to show a real interest in Lucy?' Frank questioned.

Brenda shrugged. 'I don't know. I didn't know her until she moved to Wallasey High. When he had his annual holidays he used to come and meet her. At first I thought he was her father. When I asked her she told me that her dad was dead, and that she and her mum lived with Stanley Jones, so I thought he must be some sort of relation.'

'How did you find out he wasn't?'

'I told my mum and she asked around. In the winter we get a lot of customers in the pub from Liscard village and it didn't take her long to find out that Lucy's mum was Stanley Jones's house-keeper.'

'Housekeeper? That's all?'

'Yeah!' Brenda's lip curled. 'Yer only gorra look at him to know that. Not much lead in his pencil. Though people who lived near them in Belgrave Road, and knew him to talk to, always reckoned he had his eye on Lucy. They said all he ever went on about was what a smashing little number she was, and how clever she was. Seems he once told someone he meant to marry her when she was old enough.'

'And do you think Lucy liked him?'

Brenda shrugged. 'I don't know. He always gave her a tanner for sweets when he got his pay and when you're a kid you'll like anyone who does that, now won't you?'

Frank nodded thoughtfully. 'You're probably right, kiddo.'

Brenda shivered. 'I'm cold, so I'm off home if all we're going to do is talk about Lucy Patterson, and whether she likes Stanley Jones or not.'

'Come on, kiddo, no need to get in a huff,' Frank told her. He pulled her into his arms, leaning her back against the promenade railings, and his mouth covered hers, preventing her from saying anything more.

Brenda shivered; her body arched into his as his hands began roaming inquisitively up and down her spine. As she felt his fingers move inside her low-cut neckline, fondling her breasts, she let out a low moan of pleasure.

His head moved down and he began to caress her nipple with the tip of his tongue as he freed her right breast from the confines of her dress. She whimpered in ecstasy, her fingers grasping his thick dark hair as she pulled his head more firmly against her.

Freeing her, he put his arm around her waist, guiding her along the prom to the privacy of a shelter. Here, protected from the wind blowing in from the Mersey, his lovemaking became more tactile.

Ignoring her half-hearted protests he ran one of his hands up under her skirt. Rapidly unfastening his trousers, and pushing aside her flimsy under-wear, he rammed into her so savagely that she let out a gasp that ended in a scream as she surrendered to his passion.

Quickly he dropped his head, and covered her mouth with his own to smother the noise. He tasted blood as their teeth grated and he bit down sharply on her lip.

Her mouth was stinging, but she felt elated at having stirred him to such an intense display of his needs. He certainly isn't thinking about Lucy Patterson now, she thought triumphantly.

Although she felt exultant, Brenda wished she hadn't capitulated quite so readily. Struggling to free herself from his embrace, she let her body go limp as he held her even tighter. His breath was rasping and he leaned heavily on her as if exhausted.

Murmuring words of endearment, she trailed her lips over his neck and face, and then nibbled at his ear lobes. He kissed her again, but this time it was merely a meeting of their lips as he let go of her.

Straightening her clothes, and tidying her hair, Brenda slipped her arm through his, nestling into his side as they began walking back along the prom towards the pub. The evening had been full of surprises. It was thrilling to know she had such an effect on an experienced man like Frank Flanagan.

Lovemaking was no novelty to her, but she had never been possessed so savagely, and she was eager for their next encounter.

When they reached the pub, Frank made no attempt to take her in his arms again. It was left to her to kiss him good-night, standing on her toes, and pulling his head down so that she could reach his mouth. The passion was gone; his lips were cold and unresponsive.

Chapter Eleven

As he hurried to catch the ferry, Frank Flanagan's mind was in turmoil. Too agitated to sit in the saloon, he paced around the top deck of the boat all the way back to Liverpool. Staring out at the moon-washed river, and gulping down the keen night air, he mulled over the information he'd managed to glean from Brenda about Lucy.

The more he thought about seeing Stanley Jones outside the Cotton Exchange passing Lucy a pound note, the more convinced he became that she had feelings for the man. Her whole manner had been so relaxed, her attitude so friendly, and she'd been so animated. Yet with him, Frank reflected, she was either cool and distant, or bristling with anger.

She rejected even the smallest advance he made towards her, refusing so much as to talk to him, unless it was something involving Karen.

By the time he reached Liverpool he was in a towering rage. His temples were pounding and his throat was tight with jealous frustration. His mind was seething. How in God's name could she prefer a nancy like that to him, he asked himself over and over again?

Stanley Jones was the sort of man Frank despised. Cultured, bookish and intellectual. A right Mary with his soft hands and timid ways, he thought cynically. He found his gentle voice, with its slight Welsh singsong undertone, effeminate. His grey eyes behind horn-rimmed glasses made him look owlish.

Frank found he'd missed the last tram so he walked home from the pier head to Anfield Road, viciously kicking at any rubbish on the pavement, and thumping lampposts with his fist whenever he passed one. He strode along filled with vengeful yearnings, telling himself that a girl like Lucy was wasted on a cretin like Stanley Jones.

When he reached Anfield Road he found the house was in darkness. He sat downstairs, smoking one Woodbine after another until the packet was empty.

The vision of Stanley Jones handing Lucy a pound note, her smile of acceptance, and the way she had kissed his cheek before they parted, haunted Frank.

He wanted Lucy. He found everything about her tantalising. He was used to brash girls like Brenda and his sister, Selina, who flaunted their charms. Their favours could be bought for a few shillings or even, like Brenda tonight, they used them as a token payment for a night out.

Lucy wasn't like that. Her wary glare if he even touched her arm, or the way she turned on her heel and walked away when he tried to be friendly towards her, signalled that she was no easy-to-lay judy.

He ran his hands through his thick dark hair in despair. All his life, ever since his schooldays, he'd been able to charm the girls. He constantly boasted to his workmates that he could have any woman he fancied, married or single. And if any of them doubted Frank's word he quickly proved to him that even the man's own wife, or girlfriend, found him irresistible.

It often ended in a fight, but even there he was always the winner. Even if the man could boast of a physique comparable with his he ended up with a black eye or broken nose and bruised knuckles. The punier ones turned a blind eye to both Frank's taunts and his conquests. Some even bought him a pint to show there were no ill feelings.

Then the man would go home and vent his anger, shame and frustration on his unfaithful partner. If she was lucky, it was nothing more serious than a black eye. The more disgraced the man felt the more severe the retribution. Some even deliberately disfigured their women's faces to make sure that Frank Flanagan would never be interested in them again.

Making his way upstairs to bed, Frank paused outside the room where Lucy and his sisters were sleeping. Cautiously, he pushed open the door, and stood there surveying the four sleeping girls in the pale shafts of moonlight that filtered into the overcrowded room.

Shirley was lying on her back, arms spread above her head in a childlike pose. Selina lay spread-eagled, face down, her bare shoulders exposed. Karen, so fragile that her thin bony frame looked almost as if it was wrapped in a shroud, was lying in her usual position, curled into a ball, in the bed she shared with Lucy.

Lucy, lying on her side with one hand underneath her cheek, looked innocent and virginal, her lips parted in a faint smile as if she was dreaming of something that made her happy.

Frank's feelings were in mutiny. He wanted her so much that desire, hate, bitterness and hopelessness all churned inside him simultaneously.

Stealthily he moved closer to the bed, and saw her dark lashes flicker slightly against the delicate cream of her cheeks. It was as though she was aware that someone was there, standing looking down at her. Her lips moved and she murmured a name. Leaning closer, he tried to catch what it was, then pulled back angrily, convinced she had murmured 'Stanley'.

He stood there seething, his pulse hammering, his body suffused in sweat. He felt as if he was choking with pent-up passion. Gasping for breath, he loosened his tie and undid the collar of his shirt.

Consumed by anger and jealousy, and no longer able to control his lust, Frank whipped away the bedclothes. He stood there for several seconds, staring down at Lucy. Her cotton nightdress was ruckled up, exposing the creamy ripeness of her thighs.

Bending over, with one savage movement he ripped her nightdress from the neckline right down the front to its hem. Panting, his eyes glazed with animal pleasure at the sight of her slim white body glistening in the moonlight.

Startled, Lucy's eyes opened wide, dark with fear. Before she could move or cry out he was on top of her, pushing her legs apart, forcing her into submission before she had fully awakened.

The noise as Lucy tried to fight him off roused the other three girls. Selina rolled over in bed, propping herself up on one elbow. The moment her eyes focused on what was happening she started urging Frank on, laughing out loud with glee.

The disturbance brought Karen out of a deep sleep. She was so frightened by what was taking place alongside her that she became hysterical. Cowering away from the two thrashing bodies she covered her ears with her hands, and screwed up her eyes to try and blot out what was happening. Then she suffered a deeper reaction, and her whole body stiffened, and went into uncontrolled spasms.

Within seconds she was in the throes of one of her epileptic fits, frothing at the mouth, and throwing herself violently off the bed on to the floor, twitching and shaking.

Shirley woke, screaming in terror. Sobbing and shouting she yelled out, 'Mam! Dad! Come quick, our Frank's attacking Lucy, and our Karen's having a fit.'

Cursing loudly because his sleep was being disturbed, Fred Flanagan came blundering into the bedroom. Yawning, and scratching his enormous beer gut, he stood in the doorway trying to fathom out what was going on.

'Christ Almighty, Frank, what the bloody hell d'you think you're playing at?' he roared when he saw Frank, half undressed, sprawled on top of Lucy who was naked on the bed. 'What's this, a bloody whore-house?' Without waiting for an answer he grabbed him by the hair and yanked him to his feet. Raising one of his powerful arms, Fred fisted his son hard in the jaw, then threw him bodily towards the door. Lifting one foot, he booted him hard in the backside. Frank was out on the landing before he had a chance to speak.

'Mother of Jesus, whatever is going on here?' Flo Flanagan exclaimed in a shocked voice. 'Selina, why didn't you put a stop to this? And couldn't you have done something to help Karen?' she said in a concerned voice as she knelt on the floor beside the writhing girl, and began tending to her.

Selina didn't answer. Scowling, she slid out of bed, grabbing a black kimono lying across the foot of it and slipping it on. Tying it tightly round her waist she asked in a sulky voice, 'What do you want me to do then?'

Karen had stopped writhing and was lying supine, her breathing laboured as if she had been running too fast. Her eyes were still rolling under her closed lids, and she was bathed in sweat.

'For the love of God, give me a hand with her, Fred,' Flo begged. Together they pulled Karen up into a sitting position, and while Fred supported her Flo gently mopped her face.

'Bugger off downstairs and make us all a

cuppa,' Fred roared at Selina, 'or else do something to shut that squalling bitch up,' he said in an exasperated voice, nodding in Lucy's direction.

'I'll make some tea. Do you want me to bring it up here?'

'Use your bloody head, girl,' Fred rumbled. 'Once we can quieten Karen down we'll put her back in bed, and then we'll come downstairs. And for God's sake take that whining little cow with you,' he added, pointing towards Lucy who was still sobbing her heart out.

Selina scowled at him.

'Don't bloody well argue,' her father snarled before she could speak. 'You can tell our Frank that I want some answers about what's going on. Randy bugger forcing himself on her like that. What the hell does he think he's playing at? He's always boasting he can have any woman he wants so what's the bugger doing trying to rape that little cow?'

'Don't go blaming our Frank, she's been leading him on ever since she came into the house,' Selina told him. 'She's behaved the same with him as she has with my Jack. Pretends to be little Miss Innocent when all the time she's nothing but a cock-tease.'

'Selina!' Looking shocked, Flo Flanagan crossed herself. 'Dear God! What a terrible thing to say.'

'It's the truth. You don't see half of what goes on, our Mam. All you think is what a sweet little innocent thing Lucy is and that she can do no wrong. Look at her now, standing there listening to all we say and not saying a word. She looks as

141

if butter wouldn't melt in her mouth, and it's not like that at all. Just because she takes our Karen for a walk round the block some nights, doesn't mean she's not a man chaser, because she is. You want to hear what the girls at the factory say about her. They all noticed the way she made eyes at Jack Carter.'

'Shut your great gob and get down them stairs and make that cuppa,' Fred Flanagan growled. 'I'll talk to her, and our Frank, and to you as well, if it comes to that, when I've helped your mam to get our Karen back into bed. Some bloody night this is. Be time for me to go to work before I get any shut-eye the way things are going on.'

'You go back to bed, Fred, and I'll go down and sort this lot out,' Flo told him.

'Not sodding likely! I know you, you silly old biddy. You'll believe every bloody word our Frank tells you, and then you'll be comforting that little bint and saying bloody prayers for her. Before we know what's happening you'll be tucking her up in her bloody bed, and telling her not to worry, she's not to blame!'

'I don't for one minute think it's her fault,' Flo answered spiritedly.

'Will you bugger off and make that cuppa!' Fred raised a hand threateningly in Selina's direction. 'I'll have mine strong, and mind you put plenty of bloody sugar in it.'

Chapter Twelve

Next morning the atmosphere at Anfield Road was so bad that everyone avoided each other's eyes. Unspoken accusations hung in the air, and Lucy was afraid that even her Aunt Flo thought that she was in some way to blame for what had taken place.

'You must have done something to lead Frank on, Lucy,' she probed, her plump face drawn and worried.

'How can you say that! I was asleep when it happened,' Lucy defended herself tearfully. Her face and lips were drained of colour; her eyes had a haunted look as if she was reliving the ordeal she'd endured the night before.

'Earlier in the day then,' Aunt Flo persisted. 'Something you said to him that he may have taken the wrong way?' she questioned worriedly. 'Think back, Lucy.'

Lucy's lips tightened. 'I hardly ever speak to him!' she answered coldly.

'It might have been the way you looked at him then,' Aunt Flo insisted 'I do understand that you're not used to living in such a crowded house. Perhaps when you walked in on him, when he was stripped off having a wash ...' Her voice trailed away and she sighed deeply as if she knew she was wasting her time cross-questioning Lucy.

She hadn't slept at all for the rest of the night, and lying awake, listening to Fred snoring, she'd gone over and over what had happened, trying to puzzle out what could have possessed Frank to do what he did.

She couldn't believe he would have gone into the girls' bedroom unless Karen had cried out in her sleep and he'd thought she was having a fit and needed help.

He was so good like that. Right from when Karen had been a little tot, and the fits had first started, Frank had always been there for her. He's always been closer to Karen then he's ever been to Selina, she mused.

He'd only been three when Selina was born, but he'd resented her from the moment she'd given her first cry, Flo remembered. There had always been jealousy between them, the pair of them always squabbling for attention right from those very early days.

At first it had been over their toys, not that they'd had very many. Fred had been called up, and was in the army for three years while they were growing up. She'd had to struggle hard, pinching and scraping, to bring them up on soldier's pay.

Her family had refused to have anything more to do with her after she'd told them she was expecting Frank.

'It's not so much the fact that you are pregnant and unmarried, Florence, but the type of man who

144

is the father,' her mother had said disdainfully. 'Liverpool Irish and a Catholic! He may be very handsome, and swept you off your feet with his blarney, so that you think you're madly in love with him, but what sort of life do you think you will really have with him? One child after another, mark my words, and most of the time he will be drunk!'

Karen had been born while Fred was in the army. She'd been a puny little thing, more like a skinned rabbit than a human baby.

Frank had been almost ten and with his father away he'd considered himself the man of the house. Right from the first moment he'd seen Karen he couldn't do enough for her. Selina, who'd been six at the time, should have been a little mother to her, but she'd practically ignored her.

Karen had been a fractious baby, and it was Frank who gave her a bottle, found her dummy for her when she lost it, and nursed her to sleep. He never tired of pushing Karen up and down the pavement in the big battered pram that hadn't even been new when he'd been a baby.

As Karen grew older, and toddled out to play in the street, he always watched over her. He made sure the bigger kids didn't bully her, or knock her over when they played kick-the-can, or chased each other up and down the jigger, or swung from ropes looped round the lampposts.

When the fits started, when she was about three years old, he'd been terribly upset because he'd thought Karen was going to die. He'd watched over her even more closely. He seemed to sense when it was going to happen, and would skulk around the house, refusing to go out and play with his mates, in case she needed his help.

Selina had never attempted to help Karen when she had a fit, but Frank had insisted on knowing what to do for her.

So how could someone as caring and considerate as Frank try to rape his cousin? Lucy must have given him some encouragement, Flo was certain of it.

It didn't take much to stir up a virile young chap like Frank, and by the sound of it Lucy hadn't had anything to do with lads of her own age so she mightn't have known what she was doing.

Stanley Jones was supposed to be keen on her, but he was far too much the gentleman to make any rash moves and overstep the mark. Anyway, from what she recalled of her brother's wife, Maude had been strait-laced, and she'd bet she'd kept a close eye on what was going on. There'd be no hanky-panky with her around!

The minute Fred and Frank went off to work, Aunt Flo insisted that Karen and Shirley got ready to go with her to church.

Pulling her black shawl around her shoulders, and shepherding the two girls out of the door, she told Lucy, 'We'll light a candle to the Blessed Virgin, and we'll all pray for your forgiveness, chuck.'

Lucy felt incensed. Frank was the one who needed forgiveness, not her, she thought huffily.

146

He'd tried to rape her, and she'd been sound asleep at the time, so how could she be in any way to blame for what had happened?

She looked round the drab room, and knew she couldn't face coming home and sitting down to an evening meal with the Flanagans. Grey ash was spilling out of the range on to the floor, the table was covered in dirty dishes, and Uncle Fred's greasy cap was lying on his armchair. She was almost tempted to set her principles aside, forget the promise made to her mother, and go back to Belgrave Road.

Was rape the sort of thing that her mother had been afraid might happen if she had stayed on her own with Stanley Jones? Surely not! Stanley was so gentle, so kind and thoughtful, he would have had more respect for her than to commit such an outrage.

It was all so confusing that she felt the need to talk to someone about what had happened. Aunt Flo would defend Frank, and it was much too embarrassing a subject to discuss with Stanley Jones, so who was there she could talk to?

Brenda was the only other person she knew who'd met Frank, but since she liked him so much was it fair to tell her what had happened? Anyway, would she believe that he could behave in such a despicable way?

She struggled to fight off her feeling of despair. What had happened wasn't her fault, and she shouldn't be feeling dirty and degraded, she told herself over and over again.

Lucy finally made up her mind that she would

147

go and see Brenda when she finished work that evening. She left a note to let her Aunt Flo know where she was going and that she wouldn't be in for the evening meal.

At work, although the switchboard was extremely busy all day, she found she couldn't stop brooding about what had happened. The image of Frank's massive bulk pinning her to the bed, after he had ripped off her nightdress and exposed the most intimate parts of her body, filled her mind.

Miss Ford noticed her distraction and twice spoke to her quite sharply, telling her to concentrate on what she was supposed to be doing, and not sit there day-dreaming.

When the afternoon eventually came to an end, Lucy couldn't wait to get away. As she left the Cotton Exchange she spotted Stanley's dapper figure ahead of her and made sure she kept out of sight. She knew if he saw her he would want to know why she wasn't going home to Anfield Road.

When they reached the pier head both the *Royal Iris* and the *Royal Daffodil* were berthed alongside so she waited to see which one he boarded. The crowd was so dense that at the last minute she lost sight of him so she scurried on to the *Royal Iris*, which was going to New Brighton, fairly confident that he would take the other one, bound for Seacombe. As both boats pulled out into the river she spotted Stanley walking around the top deck of the *Royal Daffodil*, and breathed a sigh of relief.

Twenty minutes later she was in New Brighton, hurrying along the prom to the pub at the corner of Victoria Road where Brenda lived, hoping she'd be able to talk to Brenda before they got busy, and before Frank arrived for his night's stint.

'Hey, what's brought you over here then, kiddo?' Brenda asked in surprise when Lucy walked up to the bar where she was polishing glasses. 'Come straight from work, have you?'

'That's right. I wanted a word with you. Can you get a few minutes off?'

'No, not really. Mam and Dad are having their meal. Talk to me here, if you like. Want some crisps?' She passed a half-eaten bag over the counter, and filled two glasses with shandy, one of which she pushed towards Lucy.

'So what's up now?'

Brenda studied the bright pink varnish on her long nails as Lucy related the events of the night before.

'Well, you do wind him up, don't you!' she grinned. She spread her hand and held it against the deep cleavage of her emerald green dress. 'Do you think this colour looks right, or would dark red be better?'

'Wind him up? I do everything I can to keep out of Frank Flanagan's way!' Lucy exclaimed indignantly.

'Yeah kid, but it's the way you do it. He takes all that meek and mild simpering stuff as a come-on! Look at the way you blush and lower your eyes whenever he speaks to you! As if you didn't

149

know that pretending to be so shy only makes him want you all the more.'

Lucy looked puzzled. 'I don't know what you mean. Selina, his sister, said something the same. But I don't mean to encourage him, Brenda, I really don't,' she persisted. 'I wouldn't do anything like that, I'm too scared of him.'

Brenda laughed sourly. 'You've no cause to be. All he can talk about is you, and he's as jealous as hell of Stanley Jones.'

'How on earth can you know that?'

'He took me dancing at the Tower last night, and he talked about you all evening trying to find out what sort of relationship you had with Stanley.'

'Well, I hope you told him that my mother was Stanley's housekeeper, and there was nothing at all going on between me and Stanley,' Lucy said heatedly.

Brenda shrugged. 'I tried to, but he didn't seem to believe me. Anyway,' she went on in a disbelieving tone, 'I think you're exaggerating about what happened, or making it all up.'

Lucy's dark brows shot up and she looked puzzled. 'Making what up? What do you mean, Brenda?'

'This story about Frank attacking you in bed last night, and trying to rape you. He was with me until midnight, and after the session we had in the promenade shelter I wouldn't think he'd want to do it again for a week!'

'Brenda! Do you mean what I think you mean?' Lucy asked in a shocked voice.

'Of course!'

Lucy's brown eyes widened in astonishment. 'And you let him?' Amazement and disbelief mingled on her face.

'Why not? He's not the first, and he'd taken me out dancing for the evening so he deserved some sort of reward,' Brenda grinned.

'You really are unbelievable, Brenda,' Lucy told her heatedly, unable to keep the revulsion she felt out of her voice.

Brenda looked affronted; her green eyes glittered dangerously. 'You know your trouble, Lucy Patterson, you're too pure for your own good. Frank says that since you've been working at the Cotton Exchange you've become ever so uppity. He probably thought you needed taking down a peg or two.'

'And trying to rape me was his way of doing that?' Lucy asked bitterly.

Brenda shrugged. 'Don't ask me, I don't know how men think. I don't understand why he's so besotted by you when you're so rude to him, but there you are, that's men. I'm crazy about him, and more than willing to do whatever he asks, and give him what he needs, and yet he still wants you. How do you think I feel?'

'Oh, Brenda, I'm sorry,' Lucy said contritely. 'I shouldn't have said the things I did. I came to ask your advice, not to criticise you.'

'Advice? What sort of advice can I give you?'

Lucy shrugged despairingly. 'I don't know what to do, Brenda. And I'm so scared that he will try it on again. Do you think he will?'

Brenda looked amused. 'You really don't know the first thing about men, do you, Lucy? If you gave in, let Frank make love to you, then he'd probably leave you alone after that. It's because you try and keep out of reach that he's so madly keen. Give in, let him do it! What harm is there in it?'

'Brenda!' Lucy bristled and began to blush furiously. 'I wouldn't dream of going that far with any man until after I'm married.'

'More fool you,' Brenda snapped, her green eyes full of contempt. 'Would you buy a new dress without trying it on first?'

'That's completely different.'

'Not really. Except you can chuck the dress away when you're fed up with it, but you're stuck with a man for the rest of your life if you marry him.'

Lucy shook her head in despair. 'We're not talking about marrying. What I want to know is what I must do to stop Frank pestering me.'

'And I've told you. Stop fighting him! Give in.'

Lucy's mouth tightened. 'I can't do that, it's completely out of the question,' she declared emphatically.

Brenda gave a breathy little laugh. 'More fool you! You don't know what you're missing! Frank's a great lay . . .'

'Brenda! Stop talking like that,' Lucy said heatedly.

Brenda shrugged. 'I bet if Stanley Jones tried to make love to you then you'd let him because you think he's respectable. It's only because Frank

Flanagan is a docker, and a bit rough and ready, that you think he's beneath you. Well, let me tell you this, Lucy Patterson, I'd marry him tomorrow if he asked me, so there!'

Lucy slid off the bar stool and picked up her handbag. 'I may as well go, Brenda, if that's what you think.'

'Off to weep on Stanley Jones's shoulder, are you?' Brenda smirked.

'No, I'm off back to Anfield Road, and I hope Frank isn't at home when I get there,' Lucy told her wearily.

'He won't be. He's coming over here tonight. You'll probably pass him on your way back. You should be safe though,' she taunted, 'he's unlikely to grab you in broad daylight.'

'You think it's funny, don't you, Brenda, but it isn't. He's family! My own cousin! I should feel safe and protected when he's around and yet I'm so frightened of him that I'm not only scared of meeting him, but I'm afraid to go to bed in case he tries it on again.' She shuddered, her eyes becoming glazed. 'I don't think I will ever be able to forget that terrifying moment when I woke up and found him ripping my nightdress off.'

'Then why didn't you fight him off?'

'I tried to, believe me, but I was completely powerless. He was lying on top of me. I could hardly breathe because of his weight as he pinned me to the bed.' She buried her face in her hands and her shoulders shook uncontrollably as she relived the nightmare. 'I can feel his hands invading my body even now.' She shuddered.

153

'And you didn't enjoy it? Not one tiny bit?' Brenda asked.

'Enjoy it? I was petrified! And I still am. Can't you understand that, Brenda? How would you have felt in a situation like that?'

Brenda shrugged, then grinned. 'If it happened with Frank I'd lie back and enjoy it! If you weren't so stuck up, and so prim and proper, you'd have done so as well. It's time you grew up, Lucy. You can't go on being a virgin all your life.'

'We've been through all this. I happen to think differently from you.'

'The more you run away from him the more he'll chase you, that's men for you,' Brenda told her sagely.

'Couldn't you talk to Frank, and ask him to leave me alone?' Lucy pleaded. 'He might listen to you.'

'I'll think about it,' Brenda promised. She looked pointedly at her watch. 'Hadn't you better skedaddle before he turns up here?'

Chapter Thirteen

Frank Flanagan nursed his pint of beer and brooded over the things that Brenda Green had told him the night before when he'd visited New Brighton.

Never in his whole life had any girl resisted his charms, and to be told by Brenda that Lucy hated him, and wanted him to leave her alone, was like a red rag to a bull.

He was young, good-looking, possessed a fine physique, and he was free with his money when he was working and had any to spend. And at the moment he was pretty flush since he was working steady at the docks as well as helping out at the pub.

He admitted that he'd been a fool to let lust dominate his actions a couple of nights ago, and he had the bruises to prove it. Even though his dad resented Lucy living with them he still didn't hold with rape, especially when it happened in his house.

Grabbing hold of him, taking him out into the back yard, and giving him a first-class bashing, had proved that.

'It's not that I bloody well think you were to blame,' his father admitted after he'd thumped him, 'but I don't want that sort of sodding thing going on under my bloody roof. Do you under-stand?'

Frank had contained his anger with difficulty. He'd never apologised in his life, and he didn't intend to start, so he merely grunted.

'There's your bloody sisters to think about, and your mam to consider,' his father told him. 'She'll probably have Father Bunloaf round to bless the sodding house after what went on here tonight. Come to that, you'd better get yourself down to bleeding confession first thing in the morning now that I'm through with you!'

He hadn't gone to confession, though. He'd left the house early, before his father came down-stairs. His mam had understood. As well as his sarnies, she'd slapped his rashers of bacon between two thick slices of bread and pushed it into his hand as he went out of the door.

He'd spent a pig of a day. They'd been unloading oil cake, and other cattle feed, and it had smelled so abominable that it had made his stomach churn.

Added to that his thoughts had been in turmoil. He was sorry for frightening Lucy. He blamed the drink, and the way Brenda had got him worked up with all her talk about Lucy and Stanley Jones.

He wondered if Brenda had said the things she did because she was jealous of Lucy. They might have been at school together, but as far as he could see that was about the only thing they had in common.

Brenda was flashy; a busty barmaid from the tip of her red head to her painted toenails. She

156

was a looker, he'd give her that, if you liked red hair, green eyes, peaches-and-cream skin and a slightly turned-up nose.

She was a good armful, too. Plump breasts, a small waist and shapely hips. And she was generous with her charms; they'd been his for the taking.

Yet it was Lucy, quiet little Lucy with her neat dark hair, heart-shaped face, dark brown eyes with their long lashes, and her cupid's bow mouth, who tugged at his heartstrings.

Lucy was so different from the girls he'd known all his life. She was the exact opposite of his eldest sister. Selina was a lush! By the time she was fourteen her brash ripe beauty had all his mates drooling. He'd hated the way they bragged that she was an easy lay, and free with her favours. Then he found that most of the girls he knocked around with were the same.

Lucy was different. She had the same look of innocence and purity that Karen had; untouched, an almost spiritual aura.

He was ashamed of the way he'd attacked her, and he would give anything to turn the clock back. The things Brenda had said about her had inflamed him. All evening she had been hinting that there was some sort of understanding between Lucy and Stanley Jones.

He wished he could be certain it wasn't true. He was quite sure Stanley had strong feelings for Lucy. It was in Stanley's eyes when he looked at her, in his voice when he spoke to her.

Frank tried to convince himself that this didn't

mean she felt the same, but it was so difficult to know what she did feel. She was so polite, so restrained, so sweet and gentle whether she was talking to Stanley Jones, or to Karen, or to his mother. Even when his father cursed and swore at her she never lost her temper or answered him back.

Selina, and even Brenda, both gave as good as they got, and their language was as ripe as that of any docker, but he'd never once heard Lucy swear.

Yet she could stand up for herself. He grinned to himself remembering how defiant she'd been about refusing to hand over her pay packet.

When he finished work at the end of the day, Frank was in two minds about going home, but his conscience was bothering him, and he felt he had to make sure Lucy was OK. When he got there, and his mother told him that Lucy had gone over to Wallasey straight from work, he felt incensed because he was sure she'd gone running to Stanley Jones to cry on his shoulder about what had happened.

To take his mind off it, he went over to see Brenda. He couldn't believe his ears when Brenda said Lucy had been there, bleating for sympathy. He was even more riled when Brenda said, 'Lucy asked me to tell you to leave her alone.'

'What the hell does she mean by that?' he raged. Couldn't she see that it was only because he wanted her that he'd acted as he had? He'd never intended to hurt her!

Frank brooded about it all evening; in between

pulling pints for the customers, he became more and more angry, and by the end of the evening it was as if his feelings for Lucy had undergone a metamorphosis.

He began to believe the things Brenda had been saying, and accept that perhaps, after all, she was right and that Lucy was a tease.

He was so upset that his temples pounded, and there was a sour taste in his throat that even repeated nips of whisky couldn't take away. Hatred churned inside him; rage turned his feelings for Lucy into something cruel and sinister.

He was determined to sort the little bitch out one way or the other. Gradually a plan formed in his mind, and he couldn't wait to put it into operation. He told Brenda's father that he wasn't feeling too good and left early so that he could get back to his own local before closing time.

Now, as he sat nursing his beer, and chain-smoking one Woodbine after another, as he waited for his workmate Doug Baldwin to come in, he was going over and over in his mind the plan he'd dreamed up earlier.

As a general rule he didn't believe in revenge. Life was too short to bear grudges. Even when his old man thumped him one, like he had last night, he shrugged it off. He didn't retaliate although he knew he was quite capable of giving as good as he got. Better, in fact. If he landed one on his father it would put him out cold. He had as much strength, was a good foot taller and twenty-five years younger. He sometimes thought his old man forgot that when he was in a temper and lashed out at him. It was as if he thought of him as a kid, someone he could still dominate.

This was different. It wasn't really a family row, even though Lucy was his cousin. It went deeper than that. It cut him like a knife that she could prefer a nancy like Stanley Jones to someone like himself.

Not for much longer, though. He was determined to change all that. If he couldn't have her he'd make sure no other bloke would want her, not even Stanley Jones.

Doug Baldwin would see to that for him and enjoy doing it. He smiled grimly to himself. Doug had been in Walton Jail three times for GBH and rape so there wasn't much he didn't know when it came to accosting women. And this time he wouldn't be taking potluck. He'd have a full description of what she looked like, and details of her movements, and every possible scrap of information he needed to know.

As Frank drained his glass, stubbed out his Woodbine and mooched over to the bar, Doug Baldwin came in. He was a short, broad-shouldered man, heavily built with brawny arms and stocky legs. He'd been in so many fights that his face was badly disfigured. His nose was squat, he had a cauliflower ear, and there was an ugly scar running from his left eye to his chin. His lank fair hair hung over one eye, and he was constantly running his thick nicotine-stained fingers through it, and pushing it back from his face.

They'd been working together at the docks for years. Frank was by far the more astute of the two men, but Doug was far more cunning. He was also ruthless, and without any kind of conscience. Other people's suffering had no effect on him, not even when it was his brutality that had caused it.

Frank waited until they had both been served, then, with a movement of his head, indicated an empty table in a quiet corner at the far end of the room.

'Feel like a bit of fun, Douggy?' he asked as they settled themselves and he held out his packet of Woodbines.

Doug's eyes narrowed. 'What sort of fun?' he asked suspiciously. 'Unless it involves a judy you can count me out.'

'Oh, it involves one of them all right!' Keeping his voice low Frank outlined his plan of waylaying Lucy when she left the Cotton Exchange.

'After that, it's up to you, Douggy, what you do with her,' Frank grinned.

Doug Baldwin inhaled a lungful of smoke, held it, then let it out very slowly so that they were both shrouded in a blue haze.

'What the bloody hell are you getting out of this?' he asked in a baffled voice.

'Revenge!'

Doug ground out his cigarette. 'Turned her nose up at you, has she?' he leered.

'Something like that.'

'And you say she lives in your house?'

'Yeah.' Frank's face hardened, he took a deep gulp of his beer.

Doug grinned, showing a mouthful of chipped,

yellowing teeth. 'Christ! You never tried it on, did you?'

Frank nodded. 'The silly bint screamed her lungs out, and woke the whole house up. All hell was let loose. One of me sisters had a fit, and me old man half murdered me.'

'Bloody hell! And your mam went rushing off to St Cuthbert's to pray for forgiveness.'

'Something like that,' Frank admitted morosely.

Doug took a deep swig of his beer, then wiped the back of his hand across his mouth. 'Bloody women, they're all the same,' he muttered. 'Lay a finger on 'em and they scream for help, even though they're panting for it, or leading you on something chronic. It gets my bloody goat, I can tell you!'

'Yeah, we know all about your bleeding love life,' Frank said impatiently, 'but are you on? You going to do it or not?'

'Yeah, course I bloody well am.' He licked his lips. 'Of course I'll bloody well do it! I'm always up for a bit of Bayonet Practice, you know that.'

'Well, let me know when it will be so that I can be there.'

'What for?' Doug looked taken aback. 'Don't you bloody well trust me or something?'

Frank held out his packet of Woodbines. 'Have another fag! Of course I do, you dozy-arsed bastard, but I want to see the little bitch get her comeuppance!'

'There's no point in hanging about.' Doug took one of the cigarettes and lit it from the glowing tip of Frank's. 'The sooner the better, I reckon.'

162

Frank laughed cruelly. 'It'll teach her a lesson. She'll be shit scared for one thing.'

Doug was as good as his word. The next evening he was skulking in an alleyway off Old Hall Street waiting for Lucy to leave the Cotton Exchange. As she walked across the road to catch the tram home he grabbed at her.

With a hand over her mouth to stop her screaming he half dragged, half carried her towards a back jigger. Ignoring her flaying arms, and the way she kicked hard at his shins, he pushed her up against the wall, jammed his knee between her legs, and pushed a hand up under her skirt.

The next minute he felt a hand on his collar, and someone wheeling him round to face them. In the same instance, a fist caught a glancing blow at his chin which so surprised him that he staggered backwards, still holding on to Lucy.

'Stanley, help me,' she screamed, struggling to pull herself free from Doug Baldwin who still held her in an iron grip.

Frank, watching from a doorway, and seeing that things were not going according to plan, was afraid that Lucy's screams might alert a patrolling scuffer, and so he joined in the mêlée. Grabbing at Stanley's jacket he tried to pull him away, and give Doug a chance to make a run for it.

Stanley was not so easily deterred. Lucy had been threatened, and it made him see red. Boiling with anger, he ignored Frank's intervention and lashed out again, even though her assailant was almost twice his size. This time Stanley's fist caught Doug Baldwin underneath the chin, sending him reeling backwards. As he fell, his head slammed hard against a concrete lamppost, and he crashed to the ground unconscious.

As Frank had feared, the noise of the fight had brought two policemen to the scene as well as a crowd of interested bystanders. One of the policemen unfastened Doug's collar, and checked for his pulse. He looked grave when he stood up. An ambulance was called, and Doug Baldwin was loaded into it and taken away to Liverpool General Hospital.

While the police were concentrating on Doug Baldwin and Stanley Jones, Frank grabbed hold of Lucy who was still cowering against the wall sobbing, with the idea of getting her away before she could say anything to the police that might be incriminating.

Lucy was so overwrought that instead of responding quietly, she protested vehemently. Her ear-piercing scream when Frank touched her arm alerted the policemen, and one of them walked over, and demanded a full explanation of what was going on.

Frank tried to bluff things out by saying he knew who Lucy was, and that he wanted to see she got home safely. The police were having none of it.

They took down all her details, and listened carefully to Lucy's account of how she had been attacked as she left the Cotton Exchange, and how Stanley Jones had come to her assistance.

'Did you know your attacker, Miss Patterson?' one of them asked her.

She shook her head. 'I've never seen him in my life before.'

'And what about these two men who came to help you?'

'Yes, I know both of them.'

She was about to explain who they were, but the police decided that it would be better if Lucy, Frank and Stanley all went along to the police station and made a detailed report.

Lucy found the gruelling cross-questioning almost as terrifying as the assault had been. At the end of it all she felt completely drained. She also suspected that her story, far from clearing either Stanley Jones or Frank Flanagan, had only landed both of them in even deeper trouble.

She was taken into a side room, given a cup of tea, and told to wait there until both men had been interrogated.

An hour later, she was told she was free to go, but would be needed some time in the future to give evidence. Both Frank Flanagan and Stanley Jones were under arrest for causing a breach of the peace, and they would remain in custody.

Chapter Fourteen

Lucy felt so traumatised by what had happened that she had no idea how she found her way back to Anfield Road. In a complete daze she managed to board the right tram, and automatically got off at her destination.

As she walked the few hundred yards from the tram stop to the Flanagans' house, she tried desperately to sort out in her mind how she was going to break the news to them that Frank was in custody.

The moment she went in the door she realised they already knew. They were still sitting round the table having their evening meal, but most of the food was congealing on their plates as if none of them had any appetite.

There had obviously been a heated argument going on, but they stopped speaking the moment Lucy walked in. She could feel the hostility in the air as they all turned to stare at her.

Her Uncle Fred's face was thunderous, Aunt Flo was weeping, Shirley looked like a frightened rabbit not knowing what to say or do, and even Selina looked worried. Only Karen was untouched by the drama going on around her. She was rocking backwards and forwards, singing softly to herself, completely oblivious to what was happening.

'Bloody hell! I wonder you dare show your bleeding face in this house after the disgrace you've brought down on our heads,' Fred bawled.

'Shurrup, Fred, give the girl a chance to tell us her side of the story,' Flo Flanagan protested, dabbing at her eyes.

'Listen to her side of the bloody story! We've heard all we want to know from that sodding scuffer who came banging on the door. Our Frank's been carted off to Walton Jail and locked up, isn't that bloody well enough for you, woman?'

'For God's sake, Fred, Lucy was there when it happened, that policeman wasn't, so shut up and let's hear what she's got to say, and see if we can get to the bottom of it,' Flo Flanagan insisted stubbornly.

The expression on her round face was grim. Frank was her eldest, her first-born, and especially dear to her heart. As a young boy he'd been so obedient, and so attentive at church, that she'd hoped that one day he would enter the priesthood. She'd been so proud of him when he sang in the choir, or seeing him in his little white cassock, standing in front of the altar by the side of Father O'Reilly at Mass on Sundays.

Fred looked taken aback by her tone of voice. The whole evening had been a series of shocks. He knew Frank had a reputation on the dockside as a bruiser, and that there were very few who would ever take him on, especially when he was

167

in a temper. Frank seldom got into a fight deliberately, though, and when he did he knew his own strength, and he always held back when he saw his opponent had had enough.

He was mystified about what had happened outside the Cotton Exchange, and how Stanley Jones came to be mixed up in the fracas, but he wanted to know the details from Frank and not from anyone else. Even so, he couldn't summon up the courage to go to the prison, not even to find out from Frank exactly what had happened.

He certainly didn't want to hear a garbled story from Lucy since it was bound to be one-sided, but it looked as if he had no choice. The very fact that she was involved in what had happened spelled trouble as far as he was concerned.

For his wife to tell him to shurrup, something she'd never done before, was a further blow to his pride.

Whoever else might argue or contradict him, Flo never did when other people were around. She respected him, knew he was master in their home, and if she didn't see eye to eye with him over something then she waited until they were on their own and had it out with him then. But for her to stick up for Lucy, and shut him up in front of Selina, Karen and Shirley, left him feeling decidedly uneasy.

There was no doubt about it, he told himself, things hadn't been the same since that girl moved in under his roof. He hadn't liked her from the start. She was like a bloody, timid mouse, too quiet, too wrapped up in herself. He couldn't understand why the hell she'd needed to come to live with them when she'd a perfectly good roof over her head in Wallasey. And why Flo had agreed to it without even asking him was another thorn in his side.

Flo'd had nothing to do with her family since the day they'd married. Her brother, Lucy's old man, had said outright that she was marrying beneath her.

If I wasn't bloody good enough to marry his sister then why the hell do I have to provide a home for his sodding daughter, Fred thought bitterly. She's caused nothing but mayhem in this house from the moment she came through the door.

Who the hell did she think she was refusing to hand over her pay packet like the rest of them did? It was a family ritual. None of the others ever objected. He handed his over, and so did Frank, and so did Selina, but not that little bint.

She'd started something, too. Selina had begun questioning why she had to hand the lot over, and only get a few bob back. He'd soon put her straight. A backhander across the face for her bloody nerve had soon shut her up. And Flo hadn't said a word about that! Crossed herself, and muttered a few 'Ail Murrys, but then she did that so often he didn't take any notice.

Now for Flo to stand up to him, tell him to shurrup and let that little slut Lucy tell them what happened, and why the scuffers had stuck Frank in the nick, was beyond belief. It turned his blood to piss.

'Well, bloody well get on with it then.' He scowled at Lucy. 'Let's hear what you have to tell us.'

'Someone attacked me as I was leaving work,' she said nervously.

'Who the bloody hell would bother to do that?'

'I've no idea who he was. He was massive, dirty looking, badly in need of a shave and he smelled vilely,' Lucy told him. 'He grabbed hold of me, and then he put his hand over my mouth to stop me screaming. Then . . . then he dragged me down an alleyway,' her voice faltered.

'That's a fine bloody tale,' Fred scoffed. 'Who'd bloody well want to do that with you when there's plenty of willing bints on the game?'

Lucy took a deep breath. 'I've told you, I've no idea who he was, but he was horrible and terribly strong. I don't know what he'd have done next if Stanley hadn't seen what was happening and come rushing over to help me.'

'Stanley? Who the bloody hell is this Stanley?' Fred asked in a baffled voice. 'I thought it was our Frank who put up a bloody fight and got nabbed by the scuffers and stuck in the dog's 'ome for his trouble?'

'Stanley Jones is the man my mother kept house for in Wallasey. You met him when he came over here to tell me he'd found a job for me at the Cotton Exchange.'

'That nancy! What the hell was he doing there?'

'I don't know, but it was lucky for me that he was nearby. He punched this man, and then grabbed hold of him to try to pull him off me . . .'

'So where does our sodding Frank come into it all, then?' Fred interrupted, completely bemused by the story she was telling them.

'Why don't you let her finish, then perhaps we would know,' Flo said wearily. 'Go on, Lucy. You were saying that Stanley Jones tried to pull your attacker away, is that right?'

'Yes! Then Frank appeared, and he got involved, and they were all fighting each other,' she added lamely.

'And between the pair of them they knocked this bugger down, is that what you're saying?' Fred asked.

'Well,' Lucy frowned. 'Sort of. One of them hit him, and as he fell he crashed against a lamppost. He was lying on the ground, and he didn't seem to be moving. That's when the police arrived, and they said he was dead.'

'And you're not sure which of them hit this fellow? Not sure whether it was our Frank or Stanley Jones?' Aunt Flo asked quietly.

Lucy shook her head. 'No, not really. All three of them were fighting and struggling and shouting. I was so frightened I couldn't take it in.'

'Did you hear either our Frank or Stanley Jones call this man by name?' Selina asked.

Lucy frowned, trying to recollect exactly what had happened. 'I think someone said "Doug" or "Douggy" but it didn't mean anything to me.'

'Douggy?' Selina came to life. 'You say he was a thickset chap, about the same age as Frank?'

'Mother of God! It could be that reprobate Doug

171

Baldwin. They work together sometimes,' Flo murmured agitatedly as she crossed herself.

Selina's lips curled. 'You been leading him on as well, you little slut?' she demanded.

Lucy's face blanched. 'Leading him on? I've never heard of him or seen him before.'

'And you expect us to believe that, do you?' Selina sneered. 'You wouldn't have been trying to play him off against our Frank, just to make Frank jealous, by any chance?'

Lucy looked shocked. 'Of course not! Why ever would I do a thing like that?' she asked indignantly.

'Why? Because you know our Frank's sweet on you and you like leading him on and then walking away, you little cock-tease. You even tried playing the same hard-to-get game with Jack Carter when he offered to lend you a couple of bob.'

'I did no such thing!'

Selina wasn't prepared to let it go at that, even though she knew that what Lucy was saying was true, and that Jack Carter would have done the same for any new girl to help her out the first week when there was no pay packet forthcoming. What had niggled Selina was Jack Carter's comments about Lucy afterwards. 'Are you sure she's your cousin?' he'd joked. 'She seems to be too well brought up to be a Flanagan.'

His remark had sparked off a row between them. They'd said things to each other that they both knew they'd regret when they'd cooled down. The rift had been widened further when

172

she'd told him to get back to his wife and he'd retorted that he would, because she was a damn sight better than a slag like her.

'Oh yes, you did, little Miss Innocence! You toadied up to Jack Carter and caused a flaming row between the two of us, and now he's gone back to his wife and kids.'

Lucy shook her head, bewildered. 'You breaking up with Jack Carter had nothing at all to do with me, Selina,' she insisted. 'He was my boss, so of course I was polite to him, that was all though.'

Selina was still not mollified so she changed her tactics.

'You make me sick! After me putting myself out to get you a job at H & Y Foods what did you do? Chucked it in my face when your precious Stanley gets you a job working with him. Why the hell don't you sod off and marry him? If you'd done that in the first place, instead of coming over here and mooching off us, none of this would have happened, and our Frank wouldn't be in jail.'

Flo crossed herself again. 'That will do, Selina. Slagging off Lucy, and blaming her for what's happened won't get us anywhere. It's too late now to do anything about what has happened. All we can do is pray.'

'Pray! What bloody good is prurs going to do, you bloody knee-bender?' Fred roared. 'Half the rat-arse scuffers are Prots and they wouldn't know a prur if they heard one.'

'I'll ask Father O'Reilly to go along to Walton Jail in the morning and put in a good word for our Frank,' Flo went on as if she hadn't heard him.

'And give them all a bloody laugh by telling them that he was once a choirboy? A lot of sodding good that will do.'

'There's not very much else we can do!'

'That little bint is the one that should go along there and tell the scuffers exactly what happened. Tell them it was her fault they were fighting in the first place. Tell them it was all an accident, and that they've made a mistake arresting our Frank.'

'A man's died, Dad, so someone's got to take the can back,' Selina pointed out maliciously.

'Then let it be that Jones fellow. Bloody ponce! If he hadn't poked his nose in then none of this would have happened.'

'You mean if Madam there hadn't been up to her usual tricks, flirting with every feller in sight,' Selina sniffed. 'She probably knew that Doug Baldwin was one of our Frank's mates, and she was trying to make our Frank jealous.'

'That's not true!' Lucy was almost hysterical with anger. 'I've already told you that I'd never seen this man in my life before. He was dirty and smelly and horrible. He grabbed hold of me. Frank saw what happened and he was trying to save me . . .'

'He certainly wasn't trying to save Stanley Jones, and you still haven't told us what he was doing hanging around there. Had a date with him, did you?' Selina jibed.

'No, I didn't have a date with Stanley,' Lucy snapped. 'He does work at the Cotton Exchange, you know, so he was probably leaving for home the same as I was doing.'

'Watching over you like a guardian angel, more likely,' Selina sneered.

'That will do, Selina,' her mother interjected. 'Lucy is only telling us her side of the story as I asked her to do.'

'It still doesn't sort out which of the buggers killed Doug Baldwin, does it?' Fred grumbled. He took a crumpled packet of Woodbines from his pocket and lit one, drawing on it heavily as he pondered the dilemma they were in.

'As I see it,' Flo reasoned, 'it was just unlucky that this man fell badly and hit his head. That was what killed him, not the fact that he was punched.'

'You silly cow! Try telling that to the scuffers!' Fred scoffed. 'A man's dead. He was in a fight with two other men so one of them must have bloody killed him. That's the way they'll see it.'

'Yes, but it wasn't the fight that killed him, just the way he fell,' Flo Flanagan persisted doggedly.

'They've arrested both the other men who were in the bleeding fight, haven't they?' Fred bawled at her. 'And our Frank is one of them.'

'I know that, Fred, but if Lucy tells her story to the police, and they see how it happened, they'll realise it was an accident and let both our Frank and Stanley Jones go.'

'I've already made a statement,' Lucy reminded them.

'Then bloody well get down the nick and make another one. And this time make it clear that it wasn't our Frank's fault that Doug Baldwin died!' Fred roared. His face was mottled with anger and the sinews stood out on his neck like window cords.

'She won't do that because that would be putting all the blame on Stanley Jones,' Selina pointed out smugly.

'One look at that limp bugger and they'd know he couldn't knock a man the size of Doug Baldwin over,' Fred muttered gloomily.

Flo picked up her black shawl from the back of her chair and fastened it round her shoulders. 'I'm going to ask Father O'Reilly what we ought to do. I'll see if I can persuade him to speak up for our Frank. A good word from a priest can work wonders,' she said confidently.

'Only if the scuffer is a Cat'lick himself and then you have to say a dozen 'Ail Murrys and make sure the beak's one as well,' Fred said scornfully.

'It might do some good, Fred Flanagan, if you got down to the church and bent your knee, and lighted a candle to Our Lady,' Flo told him sharply.

'Me! Christ, what the hell do I need to go for when there's youse lot to do the praying for me? You and our Karen live in the bloody church. And the way you go to confession every week you must be the biggest sodding sinner on Merseyside.'

Tears welled up in Flo's eyes and began to trickle down her cheeks. 'Don't start, Fred,' she begged. 'I converted to your religion when we married and I've tried my best to live up to all the promises I made. I've brought the children up to believe in God, pay their respects to the Holy

176

Mother, and to go to confession, Holy Communion and Mass regularly.'

'I know, I know.' He got up from his chair and put his arm roughly around her shoulder. 'You've been a good wife and mother, but I don't like to see you put too much faith in what Father O'Reilly can do in a case like this because I know you're going to be bloody disappointed. A bleedin' lawyer is more likely to get him off than a sodding priest.'

'Perhaps if Lucy tells them that Frank was defending her honour because they're engaged to be married he might get away with it on compassionate grounds,' Selina suggested craftily.

'You want me to tell them I was going to marry Frank?' Lucy eyes widened in dismay. 'I couldn't tell a lie like that!'

'If it will save our Frank's sodding neck then I'll bloody well make you,' Fred roared.

'But it's not true,' Lucy protested. 'We don't even like each other.'

'What the hell has that got to do with it, you stupid bint?'

'She's playing the little innocent again,' Selina said scathingly. 'She does it all the time and the men fall for it.'

'Well, this one bloody well doesn't,' Fred snarled. 'I don't give a damn if she lies her head off so long as it saves our Frank.' He glared at Lucy. 'You do know that a charge of manslaughter can mean hanging or imprisonment for life? D'you want that on your bloody conscience?'

'Please, Fred, don't talk like that,' Flo begged.

177

'Of course Lucy doesn't want that to happen, and I'm sure she'd be only too willing to say she's going to marry Frank if she thought it might help him.'

Lucy looked bewildered. 'But if I do that then it puts all the blame on Stanley,' she protested.

'And we don't want dear Stanley to be hanged or imprisoned for life, do we,' Selina said bitterly.

'I don't want anyone hanged or given a life sentence,' Lucy said quickly. She looked at each of the Flanagans in turn, and as she saw the hate and hostility on the faces of her Uncle Fred and Selina she knew they blamed her for what had happened, and that nothing she said or did would make any difference. Her eyes filled with tears as she turned and ran out of the room.

Chapter Fifteen

Lucy couldn't sleep. She tossed and turned all night and woke so bleary-eyed the next morning that she decided it was pointless going into work because she knew she wouldn't be able to concentrate on dealing with a busy switchboard.

By now, she reflected, everyone at the Cotton Exchange would know what had happened, and after the grilling she'd had from the Flanagans the night before she couldn't bear the thought of fending off all the questions she was bound to get from the other girls.

All through the night she'd been trying to recall the details of exactly what had happened. It had all taken place so quickly that she couldn't really be sure who had struck the blow that had toppled her attacker.

She went over and over it in her mind. She remembered coming out of the Cotton Exchange and starting to cross the road to catch her tram. Then, out of the blue, someone had grabbed her, clamped a hand over her mouth, and dragged her up an alleyway near the Cotton Exchange.

The man had smelled vilely of sweat, and his hand had been so greasy and sour that she'd retched. He'd not been very tall, but he was powerfully built and terribly strong. She'd kicked out at him, but struggling had been useless. He'd lifted her under one arm, her feet trailing the ground, as if she'd been a sack of potatoes.

The minute they were in the alleyway he'd changed his grip, pinioning her up against the wall. She would never forget those terrible moments when she'd felt his hands under her clothes. She'd tried to push him away, but she'd been completely powerless. Then, as she feared the worst, Stanley had appeared, fists waving, trying to force her assailant to let her go.

At almost the same moment, Frank had materialised from nowhere. He seemed to be fighting both Stanley and her attacker, but she'd been so frightened she'd cowered back from them, and couldn't tell one from the other, or who was hitting whom.

Lucy heard her Uncle Fred slam the front door as he went out of the house. He hadn't called out to either her or Selina to get up. The noise of his leaving woke Selina, however, and Lucy heard her getting out of bed and starting to dress.

When Selina spoke to her, telling her she'd be late for work if she didn't get a move on, Lucy burrowed down under the clothes and pretended to be asleep.

She stayed there until Selina and Shirley had both left the house before getting out of bed. Karen was still sleeping so she dressed as quietly as she could, and then waited until the house was completely silent before going downstairs.

The used breakfast dishes were still on the table, and there was no sign of her Aunt Flo. Lucy made her mind up quickly. News of what had happened must have reached Brenda by now, but she felt she owed it to her friend to go and see how she was.

All the way to New Brighton she wondered if she was wasting her time since they weren't on the best of terms, but she felt she owed it to Brenda to tell her exactly what had happened.

The pub was still closed, but when she banged on the door, the woman who cleaned there each morning eventually unlocked it.

'Oh, it's you, chuck! Early bird, aren't you? I suppose you want young Brenda?'

Lucy nodded.

'You'd best step inside, luv. If I leave the door open some hopeful will think we're ready for business, and come demanding to be served.'

Brenda looked surprised to see her when she came down in response to the woman's shouts. She was still in her dressing-gown, and although she'd run a comb through her red hair she had no make-up on. 'You're early,' she yawned.

Lucy nodded. 'Have you heard what happened to Frank last night?'

Brenda frowned. 'What do you mean, what happened to him? He left here early, said he wasn't feeling too good, so what's wrong?'

Lucy looked pointedly at the cleaning woman who was busily wiping down the bar counter, but who was obviously within earshot and listening to their conversation.

'Come on through,' Brenda invited. 'You can

tell me while I make a cuppa. I suppose you want one?'

Brenda listened in stunned silence as Lucy told her all about what had happened the night before.

'And the police have arrested Frank?' she exclaimed in horrified tones.

'Yes, and Stanley Jones. They arrested both of them.'

Brenda clamped a hand over her mouth, her green eyes saucer wide. 'Oh, my God!'

'They took them both into custody and now they're both in Walton Jail.'

Brenda looked stunned. 'And they let you go?'

'Why shouldn't they? I hadn't done anything wrong!'

'Didn't they question you at all about what had happened?'

'Of course they did! I had to make a statement.'

'Well, surely you could have said something to get Frank off. He was trying to help you, you know.'

'I told them the truth about what had happened.'

Brenda shook her head in disbelief. 'What do Frank's family have to say about all this?'

'They're pretty cut up.'

'I bet they are!'

'They want me to say that I was engaged to Frank so that the police will say it was a crime of passion, and give him a lighter sentence.'

'You, engaged to Frank!' Brenda bristled. 'You couldn't stand the sight of him!'

'I know. That's why I don't want to do it.'

'And what about Stanley Jones? Don't forget, if

Frank's let off lightly then he'll take most of the blame.'

'I know that, too,' Lucy admitted miserably. 'That's why I don't know what to do for the best. That's why I've come over here to see you. I need someone to talk to, Brenda, and to tell me what I ought to do.'

'I told you what you ought to do a long time ago,' Brenda said smugly. 'You should have married Stanley Jones, and moved back in with him. Instead, you flirted with Frank, led him on so that he lusted after you, and now look at the mess you've got us all into.'

'I never encouraged Frank for one minute. I barely spoke to him,' Lucy said heatedly.

'That was the way you played it, wasn't it. Flutter your eyelashes, let him think you were a sweet little innocent, and drive him mad with desire. It's a game as old as the hills, Lucy Patterson.'

'And not one word of it is true!'

Brenda shrugged. 'Whatever you say. So what about this man who grabbed you? Are you saying you hadn't been leading him on, either?'

'I'd never seen him in my life before!' She shuddered. 'He was really horrible, Brenda. His name's Doug Baldwin and Selina said that he worked with Frank on the docks, and sometimes they went drinking together. Did he ever come in here?'

Brenda shrugged. 'How would I know? There's new faces in here every night.'

'I thought you might have noticed him if Frank talked to him a lot.'

Brenda pulled a face. 'What difference does it make, anyway? He's dead now, and Frank is in the jug, and looks like being charged with killing him. And it's all your fault, Lucy Patterson. If you'd used your brains and married Stanley Jones then none of this would have happened. And if you'd been settled with Stanley Jones then Frank would have asked me to marry him, and we'd both have been set up in homes of our own and perfectly happy.'

'Frank marry you, Brenda! What are you talking about?'

'Of course he would have done. If he'd known you were marrying Stanley Jones then there would have been no problem. You leading him on like you did got him all fired up. You know what men are like. They always want what they can't have,' she snapped gloomily, her face creased with anger.

Lucy realised she'd been stupid to come. There was nothing to be gained by talking to Brenda any more. 'Thank you for the tea,' she murmured as she stood up. 'I won't hold you up any more.'

'Have another cup before you go. And a piece of toast if you like. I'm sorry if I snapped,' Brenda added contritely. 'It's just that I'm so worried about Frank. I really do love him, you know, Lucy.'

'Yes, and I'm sorry things have turned out like this,' Lucy said wearily. 'I'd better get to work.'

'I thought you were having the day off?'

'There doesn't seem to be much point.'

'You'll be awfully late.'

'If I manage to get a boat right away I'll only be about an hour late. I expect Miss Ford, the supervisor, will understand – under the circumstances,' she added wryly.

'Hang on, let me get dressed, and I'll walk to the ferry with you,' Brenda offered.

'No, don't bother, I'm sure you've plenty to do here that you should be getting on with.'

As she waited for the ferry, and the sun became obscured by thin cloud, the brightness of the early morning faded. Fine rain was falling by the time Lucy reached Liverpool, adding to her already despondent mood.

Miss Ford looked at her watch rather pointedly, but accepted Lucy's excuse that she'd overslept without any comment.

News of what had happened, and Stanley Jones's part in rescuing Lucy from her attacker the previous night, had already filtered through to the Cotton Exchange. All eyes were on Lucy as she took her place at the switchboard, but because of Miss Ford's presence no one dared ask any questions.

Later in the morning, two uniformed police officers, a sergeant and an inspector, arrived. Lucy was asked to go to the manager's office. Speculation about Lucy's involvement in the fracas was rife amongst the girls, but none of them had an opportunity to talk to her about it until the midday break.

'Which of those two blokes who did the killing

was the one you're supposed to be marrying, then?' one of the girls asked as they all sat around in the rest room unwrapping their sandwiches and drinking tea.

'I'm not marrying either of them,' Lucy said primly.

There were exclamations of surprise and amazement.

'You mean the man who was killed was the one you were going to marry?'

'No!' Lucy shuddered. 'That was the man who attacked me! I didn't even know him.'

They waited breathlessly, avid for more details, but they were disappointed. The police had already cautioned her that she must not discuss the matter before the case came to court.

'If you remember any further points you must contact us immediately,' the inspector told her. 'Even the smallest detail might be of use to us. Whatever you do, don't talk about it to anyone else. Come straight to us, you understand?'

'Can you tell me what is going to happen to Stanley Jones and my cousin Frank Flanagan, the two men you have in custody?'

The faces of both the sergeant and the inspector became inscrutable. 'We haven't completed our inquiries yet,' the sergeant told her. 'They will both remain in prison until we do. Which is why it is extremely important that you tell us as much as you can about what happened.'

'I've already done that. I told you everything in the statement I made last night.'

'Yes, yes, but as Inspector Jarvis has already

186

said, if you remember anything else you must let us know right away.' His face relaxed. 'Very often people recall something long after the incident took place, and which they've forgotten in the heat of the moment.'

The other girls' curiosity was not easily stemmed, and there was such a general air of unrest on the switchboard that finally Miss Ford called Lucy to one side.

'I think it would be better if you went home for the rest of the day, Miss Patterson,' she said sharply.

Lucy looked stunned. 'But why? I've not done anything wrong. I'm trying to do my job. It's not my fault the other girls keep asking me questions.'

Miss Ford's face tightened. 'Be that as it may, Miss Patterson, you're causing a disruption, and that is something I cannot tolerate on such a busy switchboard.'

'I'm not discussing the case with them, really I'm not,' Lucy told her earnestly. 'The police said I wasn't to talk about it to anyone. Perhaps if you told them that they would stop asking me questions,' she pleaded.

'That will do, Miss Patterson!' Miss Ford snapped. 'I said take the rest of the day off, but under the circumstances I think it might be better if you took the rest of the week off. In fact, I don't think you should come back until both Mr Jones and the other man have appeared in court, and we know exactly what the outcome of this débâcle is going to be.'

'But . . .'

'That will do, Miss Patterson. Call in on Friday, and you can collect whatever money is due to you. It will be waiting for you at the porter's office.'

Lucy stared at her in dismay. There wouldn't be very much in her pay packet at the end of the week if she stopped work now. How on earth was she going to manage? Uncle Fred would have something to say if she couldn't pay for her keep. With Frank in prison there would be a shortage in Aunt Flo's housekeeping so they'd be counting on her contribution more than ever.

'Does this mean I'm being suspended?'

Miss Ford avoided Lucy's question. 'It will be best if you stay away until we have more detailed information about what is happening,' she said stiffly.

Chapter Sixteen

The trial of Frank Flanagan and Stanley Jones lasted three days and made banner headlines in both the *Liverpool Daily Post* and the *Liverpool Echo*. It even merited quarter columns in most of the national dailies.

In his summing-up the judge portrayed Doug Baldwin as the villain of the incident because he had attacked a young girl as she left work at the Cotton Exchange.

'In any other circumstances,' he told the court, 'the two accused men who rushed to help this young girl would be regarded as heroes. But for their quick thinking, and protective action, she might well have been murdered, or at the very least raped.'

He went on to state that Doug Baldwin was the real criminal. He then added, 'Since he has died, as a result of being knocked against a lamppost, by blows or punches inflicted on him by Flanagan and Jones, then they are guilty of taking a man's life and they must be punished accordingly.'

When the jury brought in a verdict of manslaughter there was a sigh of relief throughout the court, and this was repeated when the judge announced the sentences. 'Frank Flanagan,' he said, 'receives three months' imprisonment. Stanley Jones, because he delivered the actual blow, six months.'

The judge had obviously taken the accidental nature of Doug's death into account when passing sentence, and Lucy's heart felt lighter than it had since she'd been attacked. She'd been so afraid that their sentences would be much longer that she openly wept with relief.

The days leading up to the trial had been so fraught that she'd felt drained. As she anticipated, her Uncle Fred had been incensed when he heard she'd been suspended from the Cotton Exchange, because that meant she wouldn't be earning any money, and wouldn't be able to pay for her keep.

When he saw all the reports of the case in the papers, and realised that the entire family's name had been besmirched, his language became so abusive that Lucy was frightened for her safety.

Lucy found the general atmosphere in Anfield Road equally unpleasant. Her Aunt Flo said very little, but she'd aged visibly with all the worry. She seemed to spend every spare minute she could either down on her knees praying, or saying her rosary. Or else she was scurrying off to St Cuthbert's to seek solace from Father O'Reilly, and to light a candle to the Virgin Mary in the hope that the Holy Mother would intercede on Frank's behalf.

Most nights Shirley came home from school crying because the other children had been taunting her about her brother Frank being a killer and ending up in prison. When Lucy tried to comfort her she pushed her away saying that it was all Lucy's fault, and she wished she'd never come to live with them.

Selina totally ignored Lucy. It was not only that she didn't speak, it was as if she couldn't even see her. Since she no longer had to be out of the house early to catch a tram to work, Lucy took to staying in bed in the morning out of Selina's way.

Each evening, the moment their meal was over, Selina left the house, and it was usually long after midnight before she returned home, creeping up to bed in her bare feet so as not to wake her father.

Only Karen seemed unaware of what was going on. During the day she helped her mother around the house, doing whatever chores she was told to do the same as always. Or she sat singing to herself, or staring into space, happy enough in her dream world. Lucy spent more and more time with her, gaining strength from Karen's placid attitude.

Lucy felt relieved and optimistic as she returned to Anfield Road after the trial. Her Uncle Fred had refused to attend court, and Aunt Flo had said she couldn't bear to sit there on the final day since she was sure Frank would be found guilty and get a terrible sentence.

Even so, Lucy expected that they would have already heard the news. It had been blazoned all across Merseyside by the bold black headlines in special editions of the *Liverpool Echo*, which had been rushed out the moment the trial ended.

She went into the house expecting to find them elated. Instead she found her Aunt Flo in tears, and her Uncle Fred waiting for her return with a face like thunder.

'Have you seen this, you dozy little slut?' he bellowed, shaking a copy of the *Liverpool Echo* in her face.

'Yes!' Lucy smiled. 'It's wonderful news, isn't it? We can start planning now for when they both come home.'

'Come home? What the bloody hell are you blathering on about? Our Frank's staying in bleeding jail! He's been sentenced to three months in the bloody nick!'

'Yes, I know that, but it's a much lighter sentence than any of us expected.'

'You stupid little cow!' Fred Flanagan thundered. 'He's in jug! Don't you know what that means? He'll have a prison record that'll be round his neck for the rest of his life. No one will employ the bugger after this. He'll lose his job at the docks and his bloody reputation. The rest of us Flanagans will all be blackballed from now on as well. What sodding chance will young Shirley have of ever getting a decent bloody job now? Tell me that? All because of you, you stupid bitch!'

'Uncle Fred, the judge praised Frank's action . . .'

'That didn't stop him from bloody well sending our kid to prison though, did it?' Fred barked. 'And all because of you!'

Lucy felt angry. It hadn't been her fault that she'd been attacked. If it came to it, if Frank hadn't been hanging round the Cotton Exchange then he wouldn't have been there to rescue her when Doug Baldwin attacked her.

How did it happen that it was someone Frank knew, and often worked alongside, who had attacked her? It had puzzled her so much that she'd even asked Aunt Flo how it was that if Doug Baldwin worked on the docks then what was he doing outside the Cotton Exchange when she left for home. She'd asked why Frank had been there as well, but Aunt Flo said she had no idea at all, and refused to discuss it.

Lucy tried desperately to think how she could explain all this to her Uncle Fred without making him even angrier. Before she had a chance to do so, he was thrusting a sack into her arms, and pushing her towards the door.

'What are you doing?' she gasped, the colour draining from her face.

'That's your clothes and stuff in there, now bugger off,' Fred grunted.

Startled, Lucy gaped at him completely dumbfounded. She'd thought he'd be relieved, pleased even, that Frank had been let off so lightly. What had happened wasn't her fault. Suspicion that in some mysterious way Frank was responsible for the whole incident pushed itself to the forefront of her mind. She'd been the victim, and so too had Stanley Jones if it came to that, and he'd been given a longer sentence than Frank.

'Beat it! Don't just stand there. Don't ever come back here again, you understand?' Fred bellowed.

'You can't turn me out into the street, I have nowhere to go,' Lucy protested, swallowing back her tears. She turned, appealing, to her aunt, but Flo Flanagan knew when Fred was the master.

'I'm sorry, Lucy, but there's nothing I can do,' she said uneasily. 'You'd best go quietly before your Uncle Fred makes a worse scene, and *throws* you out of the house.'

Lucy looked round at the rest of them in dismay. Shirley looked bemused, Karen was snuffling noisily, and protesting that she loved Lucy and wanted her to stay. Only Selina remained impassive, a smug sardonic look on her face.

With a deep sigh, Lucy looked at the sack with her belongings in it, and her mind went blank. She had no idea at all about what to do next or where she could go. Her only hope was that Brenda would let her stay with her.

'Could I leave my things here ... just for tonight?' she asked her Aunt Flo. 'I'll go across to New Brighton, and see if I can stay with my friend Brenda. I'll come back tomorrow and collect them, but I can't walk around the streets carrying that sack, it's too heavy.'

Fred opened his mouth to refuse, but her aunt agreed to the arrangement before he could speak.

'Leave the sodding thing out in the bloody lavvy then,' he growled, 'and make sure you bloody well pick it up before I get home from work. And now bugger off, I never want to see your sodding face again!'

As he slammed the door shut behind her, Lucy walked dejectedly towards the tram stop. Her legs felt like jelly, and she was shaking so badly that her teeth were chattering. Her life had started to disintegrate the day she left Belgrave Road and moved in with the Flanagans, and become even worse when she'd started work at H & Y Foods.

She'd thought things were on the mend when Stanley had fixed up for her to work at the Cotton Exchange. She'd even thought that her foot was on the first rung of a worthwhile career. Now she was back in the gutter again. Miss Ford had made it plain that she thought the fracas reflected on the good name of the Cotton Exchange so it was very unlikely that she'd take her back again.

Her only hope now was that Brenda would let her stay with her. She wasn't sorry that she'd been turned out of Anfield Road. She'd hated it from the moment she'd first arrived. The things the two women she'd met on her very first day had told her should have been a warning of what she might expect, but she'd thought it was idle gossip.

She gulped back her tears. So much had happened to her since then that it seemed like a lifetime away. If only she'd never promised her mother that she'd go and live with her Aunt Flo then none of this would have ever happened. If she'd stayed on in Belgrave Road her life might have been uneventful, but she would have been living the kind of life she was used to.

If Stanley Jones had got someone in to do the cleaning and run the house, then she could have earned her living any way she chose. He'd said as much when she had first gone to see him, even reminding her that there was still a chance to finish her education and become a teacher.

She smiled to herself; she would probably have

ended up working at the Cotton Exchange anyway. The only difference would have been that today she'd still have her job, and Stanley would still have his, and they'd both be living in Belgrave Road.

As it was, because she'd insisted on keeping her promise to her mother, they'd both lost their jobs, Stanley was in prison, she was homeless, and a man neither of them had known was dead. It was like living in a nightmare.

If she could only stay at Brenda's, and get fixed up in a job, either as a telephonist or receptionist, and then find somewhere to live, perhaps she could start all over again. The trouble was she had no references, and it would be no good asking Miss Ford for one.

Unable to sit still, Lucy walked round and round on the top deck of the boat all the way from Liverpool to New Brighton. She tried desperately not to feel sorry for herself, but instead to think of other ways she could earn a living. She still fancied being a Nippy in one of the Lyons Corner Houses, then realised that would mean working in Liverpool. The moment she mentioned her name they were sure to recognise it, and to have read all about the murder case in the *Liverpool Echo*.

So too would most people in Wallasey and New Brighton, she thought gloomily. Yet she had to find work locally, she had no friends or relations in any other part of the country. In fact, Brenda was her only hope.

As the boat bumped up against the pier, and

she waited for the landing platform to be lowered, she mulled over the possibilities of working at Brenda's place as well as staying there. It was mid-season so New Brighton would be packed with trippers and holidaymakers, and with Frank in prison they were bound to be short-handed.

Feeling suddenly light-hearted and optimistic she almost ran the few hundred yards from the pier to the pub.

Brenda looked disconcerted by her arrival, but Lucy barely noticed. She was so keyed up that she didn't know which to ask first, whether she could work there, or whether she could stay there.

When she did ask her hopes were quickly shattered.

'You work here? Don't be daft. You haven't a clue about working in a pub! And as for staying here, that's right out of the question.'

'Surely, you could ask your mum if I could stay for a few days,' Lucy begged.

'No, I couldn't,' Brenda told her sharply. 'They said I was to have nothing more to do with you. You've cost us a barman for a start, so we'll be rushed off our feet for the rest of the season now.'

'I know! That's why I thought you'd like me to come and work for you. I could be here full-time, not just evening shifts like Frank did. You suggested it yourself, Brenda, when I first told you I was living over in Liverpool after my mother died.'

'My dad can't afford full-time staff,' Brenda said evasively.

'It wouldn't cost him as much as employing

Frank, not if I lived here as well,' Lucy pointed out.

'No, it's out of the question after what's happened. I wouldn't even dare to ask them,' Brenda told her.

Lucy ran a hand through her hair in a despairing gesture. 'Then where am I to go?' she asked.

'Back to Belgrave Road, of course. I would have thought that was obvious. Stanley's in prison, and the house is empty, so why not live there?'

'I couldn't do that, I haven't a key,' Lucy said lamely. 'I handed it back to Stanley the night I came over to collect all my things.'

'Then you'd better nip along to Walton Jail and ask for it back,' Brenda told her brusquely. 'He'll give it to you. He'll be only too glad to know you're there waiting for him when they let him out,' she added snidely.

Lucy shook her head adamantly. 'I can't do that, Brenda. I promised my mother I wouldn't, didn't I?'

'Promises are made to be broken,' Brenda told her complacently. 'Anyway, Stanley's not there at the moment so you wouldn't be under the same roof as him, now would you?'

'It's still his house.'

'Well, it's up to you.' Brenda shrugged and turned away hurriedly as her mother came into the bar.

Mrs Green totally ignored Lucy. 'Come along, Brenda, you can't stand here talking, we're much too busy,' she said officiously.

'Please, Mrs Green, will you let me stay here, just for tonight? I've nowhere else to go.'

Mrs Green shook her head. 'No, Lucy! In case Brenda hasn't already made it clear, I've told her that after what's happened I don't want you on the premises, and I don't want her seeing you. Now please leave at once, and don't ever come back here again. Do you understand?'

Chapter Seventeen

Fred Flanagan's temper came to boiling point as he faced the ganger who was doling out the quayside jobs. To be told there was no work was one thing, but to be stood off because his son was in trouble with the law was something else again.

He belched noisily. 'What the bloody hell has it got to do with me? I can't keep me sodding son under lock and key, not at his age!'

'How you control your family is your own affair, Fred,' the foreman told him. 'All I know is the bosses don't want anyone working here whose family has a prison record, so bugger off quietly or I'll have to call in the scuffers.'

Fred's heavy dark brows were drawn together in anger. He looked menacingly at the crowd of workmates within earshot. 'Tell him, you lot,' he shouted, 'tell him you won't stand for it, singling me out like this.'

The men shrugged, or shook their heads. A couple of them even voiced aloud their refusal to comply.

'Can't risk taking sides, Fred, we can't afford to lose our jobs.'

'The wife would scalp me if I got stood down, we've got three kids to feed.'

'Bugger off, Fred, before you get us all stood off!'

'Your son's a bleeding murderer, what do you expect, you old sod, a welcoming committee?'

Fred took off his greasy cap and ran a calloused grimy hand through his thick black hair.

'You're a right load of bleeding ponces!' he exclaimed in disgust. He dragged off his donkey jacket, balled his hands into fists, and took up a sparring stance. 'Fight the bloody lot of you if I have to,' he snarled.

'Put your fists away before you kill someone the same as your son did!' a voice shouted.

'That's all you Flanagans ever do when there's a problem to be solved, bloody well use your fists!'

The ganger looked at him contemptuously. 'Clear off, Fred. Don't start trouble here or you'll find yourself in Walton Waldorf Astoria, in a cell alongside your Frank.'

Fred picked up his jacket and slung it over one shoulder. 'I'll swing for the lot of youse if I have to,' he bawled back at them as he strode away.

He felt so enraged he didn't know what to do with himself. They were supposed to be his mates, men he worked and sweated alongside, risked his neck with when they were handling a dangerous cargo. They were men he went boozing with; men he knew as well as he did his own family. He'd helped them to fight when high spirits caused a drunken brawl; he'd got a cauliflower ear and a broken nose to prove it. And now they were turning against him. Not one man had spoken up in his defence.

The leaden skies reflected his mood as he trudged along the dock road. Life was still shit, he thought gloomily. He'd thought he'd left the struggling behind him, but it looked as though with no job, and Frank in prison, he was back at square one.

Nothing could be quite so grim as his early days in Liverpool. The eldest of seven children living in southern Ireland, he'd been half starved because there was never enough work. His father had kicked him out when he was twelve, telling him they couldn't afford to feed him so he'd better find himself some work.

He'd walked all the way to Dublin, and lived rough on the streets for a couple of months, sleeping in shop doorways or alleyways. Then the weather had become so bad that he knew he had to move on or freeze to death.

He'd stowed away on board a cargo boat, and by the time one of the deck hands found him they were putting in to port at Liverpool so he scarpered before they could hand him over to the authorities.

Liverpool was no better and no worse than Dublin. For a while he'd managed to exist on scraps from the rubbish bins behind the big stores and hotels like the Adelphi. One day he was caught thieving from a market stall and handed over to the scuffers.

He admitted to being Irish, and a Catholic, so they called in a local priest who promised to look after him. The priest took him along to an institution for boys who were homeless. It was run by lay brothers whose idea of caring for the boys in their charge was to treat them as slaves by day and then abuse them by night.

As soon as he got the chance he ran away. This time he stowed away on a boat going to Panama, only to find that he was changing one form of slavery for another; the abuse was identical.

He stuck it out, swapped boats when they reached Buenos Aires, and worked his passage back to Liverpool via South Africa and the Mediterranean. By the time he came ashore again on Merseyside he was eighteen, twice as big physically as he'd been when he left, and twenty times more aggressive. He'd learned to take care of himself, mainly by using his fists.

He'd also discovered girls. At least one in every port had fallen for his handsome Irish looks and his glib tongue. He could charm the birds off the trees; they sighed and giggled as they succumbed to his needs.

The fact that he had a reputation as a bruiser, and was known to take on any man, no matter what his size, and usually to be the winner, earned him a good deal of notoriety. Shipmates were always eager to have a wager when Fred Flanagan was using his fists.

Meeting up with Flo Patterson may have been purely accidental, but it was a meeting that changed his entire outlook on life. He was suddenly tired of his nomadic existence, being at sea for months on end and never sure where he was going to end up next.

He was also fed up with being turned away

when he tried to sign on for a voyage. There were a number of captains who refused to have him on board because he was known to be aggressive. They knew that once they put to sea, if there was the slightest upset he became vile tempered and belligerent. A fight inevitably followed, and usually one of the crew ended up seriously injured.

Now and again Fred would come off worse, and it was one of these rare occasions that changed the entire course of his life.

The fight was no great deal. Bare-knuckle fisticuffs rather than a fight according to Lonsdale rules. An uppercut blacked his eye, and sent him sprawling so hard that he fell awkwardly and broke his left arm, and had to be taken to hospital.

The first thing he knew when he came round from the anaesthetic was that a plump young nurse with an incredibly gentle touch, and the voice of an angel, was looking after him.

Flo Patterson was charmed by his blarney, his dark curly hair, and intense blue eyes. His Irish brogue was music to her ears. His roistering ways, and outspoken manner, were so different from the respectable middle-class society she was used to that she fell head over heels in love with him.

After being forced to stay three months ashore while his injuries healed, he decided to remain in Liverpool permanently when he was fortunate enough to be offered a job at the docks.

For a while, living in a seaman's hostel, he was content with his lot. He had money in his pocket, a woman he was crazy about – even though she was from a totally different class from him – and he really began to enjoy shore life.

He was besotted by her. She was plump, and in those days placid, with dark eyes and a warm heart. She wasn't a Catholic, but she loved him so much that she was willing to convert. That was a terrible shock to her parents because they were staunch Methodists.

When they met Fred for the first time it was an uneasy confrontation. It was obvious from the very start, although they were far too polite to say so, that they didn't think he was good enough for their daughter.

When he met her brother, John, the difference between their lifestyles became even more apparent. John was well spoken, his voice modulated, his words clipped. He wore a conventional three-piece suit, and a white-and-grey striped shirt with a starched white collar. His manners were impeccable, but there had been no mistaking the sneer on his face or the contemptuous look in his eyes.

Fred was secretly elated at the way Flo defended him. But even so, he was afraid that their relationship was doomed. He hadn't counted on Flo's devotion to him, or her rebellious streak. Far from turning her off him, the opposition had made her even more keen.

The moment he asked her to marry him she accepted, and she was even willing to let him make love to her with no holds barred. The sandhills at New Brighton, and the ones out towards Southport, became their stamping ground. Life for Fred had never been so good, or the future more promising.

Then Florence became pregnant. At first she was elated. Then as she realised the more sombre facts of what this meant she started to worry. When she told her parents about the coming baby they were horrified. They tried to talk her into going away until after the baby was born, and then having it adopted. When she refused to even contemplate such a step her family turned her out, and barred their door to her.

One of his mates at the docks, an Irishman like himself, offered them a room in his two-bedroom terraced house. It was small and none too clean, but Flo scrubbed it out, washed the curtains and cleaned the windows, and he gave it a lick of paint. It had been somewhere of their own, the home they returned to after their unplanned wedding.

He'd told the parish priest, Father Murphy, of his predicament, and explained that they wanted to be married right away, before the baby arrived, so that it wouldn't be labelled a bastard.

The fact that Flo had not yet been fully accepted into the faith had been a bit of a problem, but with Father Murphy's help they managed to overcome that hurdle.

Flo even managed to keep their wedding secret from the hospital, and carry on working. Then nature took over and it became obvious to the sister in charge that the reason Florence Patterson's uniform no longer fitted her was nothing to do with her diet, but the fact that she was pregnant.

When she was summoned to Matron's office, and threatened with dismissal, Flo merely smiled and said she was leaving anyway because her husband didn't like her working.

Fred had been lucky enough to stay in full employment even though times became increasingly hard on Merseyside. Flo was a brilliant manager and they saved every halfpenny they could.

Her training as a nurse stood her in good stead. Right up until the last minute of her pregnancy she was able to earn the odd shilling or two by helping out at neighbours' confinements, laying out the dead, dressing the odd cut or boil, and dealing with other minor ailments.

Before their baby was born, Flo had saved up enough for them to rent their own place a few streets away. It was identical to where they were living, only this time it belonged to them.

Fred would never forget the wonder of that first day under their own roof. Being able to shut the front door knowing that no one else could walk in on them, or tell them to keep the noise down, or complain about the smell of what they were cooking, was like heaven itself.

Frank had been born a few days later. A strong, healthy seven-pounder with lungs that could make themselves heard the length of the street.

For the first few months it had been paradise. Then he'd been laid off. With no money coming in they'd been forced into letting out two of their rooms. Flo hated having anyone else living with them. She resented them using her kitchen, sharing her cupboards, even touching her pots and pans.

'It's like having burglars in the place,' she moaned.

'We'll have them out like a shot as soon as we can afford to do so,' Fred promised.

He was down at the docks at daybreak every morning, trying to catch the ganger's eye when he picked his team of men for the day. Occasionally he was in luck, but more often than not he returned home mid-morning in a sour, depressed mood.

Flo became the breadwinner. Her nursing skills were always in demand. Left to look after baby Frank, Fred felt emasculated. He took his temper out on Flo and they fought like alley cats. She changed from being a well-mannered, nicely spoken, middle-class girl into a harridan who because she couldn't always give as good as she got became irritable and withdrawn.

They always made up after their numerous fights, and vowed it would never happen again. Yet it always did.

They still loved each other despite all their squabbling, but when Flo told him that she was pregnant again, he felt the sky had fallen in.

Frank was barely three when Selina was born. She was a small, pretty, dark-haired gem of a child who was precocious from the moment she first opened her huge vivid blue eyes. Fred found her enchanting, but he was also very aware that it was another mouth to feed.

Flo had wanted to go across the water and ask her parents for help, but he wouldn't hear of it.

'They wanted you to have your baby adopted when you said you were expecting Frank,' he reminded her. 'They didn't think I was good enough for you then so why should they think any differently now, tell me that? And they didn't offer us any help after our Frank was born so to hell with them. I'll beg in the streets before I'll let you go crawling back to your family for help. We'll rub through somehow.'

And they had. At times, all they'd had to feed the four of them had been the rent they got for the two rooms plus the odd shilling or two Flo earned by helping out at somebody's bedside.

Surely to God, he thought as he tramped mindlessly through the drizzle that had begun to fall, they weren't going to return to those terrible times again.

Being turned away at the docks wasn't the end of the world. These days things were beginning to pick up, and there must be other sorts of work, carting or lumping, that he could turn his hand to, he told himself.

Selina was still working, thank God. Karen and Shirley were the main problem. Karen, with her fits and her airy-fairy ways, wasn't able to work in a factory or anywhere else.

She could help out in the house, Fred reasoned, and give her mother a hand so that Flo could do a bit more nursing. Shirley was still only a kid, but perhaps she could get herself a paper round. He'd never pressed any of the others into doing that, but times were going to be really hard and every penny mattered.

Chapter Eighteen

Lucy couldn't believe that Brenda's mother could be so unkind as to not only turn her away, and say she was never to come back, but also to refuse even to let her stay there for one night. Brenda had been her friend since schooldays, and though they'd often argued, and they sometimes disagreed about things, they'd never stopped seeing each other.

If she hadn't given her keys back to Stanley she would have been tempted to stay at Belgrave Road. There was no way that she could bring herself to go to Walton Jail because she was sure he'd hate her to see him in his prison garb. He'd always been so particular about the way he looked.

She walked for miles along the prom, almost as far as Wallasey village. Then turning round she retraced her steps again as far as Perch Rock. Feeling hungry, she went up the side streets looking for a fish-and-chip shop. She bought a fourpenny piece of fish and two pennyworth of chips, and walking back down on to the prom sat in one of the covered shelters to eat them.

By this time it was growing dark. She looked out across the Mersey towards Liverpool, where the streetlights twinkled, and the clock face on the

Liver Building was lit up so that she could read the time on it from where she was sitting.

A crowd of trippers, intent on catching the last boat back to Liverpool, came staggering along the promenade, arms linked, singing a rowdy song at the top of their voices. Lucy slunk back into the shadows of the shelter, praying that they wouldn't notice her, or that if they did they would leave her alone.

She'd never been out this late on her own before, and she felt scared to death. She even wished she was back in Anfield Road, going upstairs to the cramped little room she'd shared with Selina, Karen and Shirley.

The darker it grew the more nervous Lucy felt. She was too frightened to stay in the shelter so she began walking back along the promenade towards the pier.

She wondered if she went back to Brenda's place, and waited until the last of their customers left, whether Brenda's mother would change her mind, and let her stay there until the morning.

She'd sleep on the floor, or doze in an armchair even, as long as she was somewhere safe. She couldn't bear the thought of having to spend the rest of the night out in the open, or in one of the shelters on the prom. There were so many strange noises. Worst of all were the pounding footsteps of solitary men walking home. Supposing one of them came up and spoke to her, or attacked her like Doug Baldwin had done outside the Cotton Exchange. It would be no good screaming; there was no chance of either Frank or Stanley Jones being on hand to save her this time.

Thinking of them shut up in Walton Jail filled her with despair. She had no idea what it was like to be in prison, but the mere thought of being locked up in a cell, knowing you couldn't get out, must be terrible. And they were bound to think about the man they'd killed, especially Frank because he had known Doug Baldwin.

She stopped, and leaning on the promenade railings, stared out across the darkening water, shivering as the night air became colder. Suddenly she found herself crying. She'd been the cause of so much tragedy and now there was nobody left in the world who cared about her. Not even Brenda, and they had been friends for almost as long as she could remember.

Putting her head down on her arms she let her feeling of misery take over, and great noisy gulping sobs racked her body. She wished she could die. Perhaps if she climbed over the railings, and slipped down into the dark swirling waters, it would all be over. She'd have no more fears, no more worries, and as the waters closed over her she'd gently slide into a long dark sleep.

'You're out very late on your own, miss, is everything all right?'

Lucy froze as the sound of a man's voice cut through her reverie. She opened her mouth to scream, but no sound came, only a sickening retching, and the repugnant taste of regurgitated fried fish and chips filled her mouth.

Then she saw the uniform, recognised it was a

policeman, and for a moment she thought she was going to faint, her sense of relief was so great.

'Do you want to tell me what the problem is?'

'There's not really anything to tell,' Lucy snuffled, dabbing at her eyes, and blowing her nose.

'Come on, there must be some reason you're out here in the dark all on your own. Trouble with the boyfriend?'

Lucy stiffened. She turned her head away quickly, afraid he might recognise who she was. 'No, nothing like that,' she told him. 'I was expecting to stay overnight with a girlfriend, but I find it's not possible so I have nowhere to go.'

'You don't live locally?'

Lucy shook her head. 'No, I live in Liverpool, but I've missed the last boat.'

'Well, we can't have you wandering the streets. You'd better come back to the station with me.'

'No, no, I'll be all right,' she assured him quickly.

The policeman wasn't prepared to accept that. 'I tell you what,' he said, 'I know of a nice little boarding house where you can get a bed for the night. You do have some money?'

'Yes, but not very much.'

'This place is cheap and clean and you'll be safe there, if you know what I mean. I can vouch for Mrs Benson.'

Lucy nodded as she fell into step alongside him. They walked a little further along the prom, then he turned up one of the side streets. Stopping in front of a green-and-white front door, he rapped on it authoritatively.

The woman who opened the door was small and grey haired and wore a blue-and-white overall over a dark green dress.

'Customer for you, Mrs Benson. Just for tonight. Missed the boat back to Liverpool.'

'You're lucky, I've got one single left,' Mrs Benson smiled. 'Come along in, luv. I'll make you a nice cuppa and then you can turn in. Have you got time for a cuppa as well, constable?'

'I'm afraid not. I'll have Sergeant Scot on my back if I don't keep to my schedule.' He saluted and withdrew, but not before he'd given Lucy an encouraging smile.

When Lucy woke next morning she wondered where she was. The narrow room, with its striped blue-and-white wallpaper, the single bed with its blue bedspread, and the dressing-table with its frilly blue skirt were all so strange.

Then Mrs Benson knocked on the door and came in with a cup of tea and suddenly it all fell into place.

'Here you are, luv, did you sleep well?' she said as she put it down on the bedside table. Not waiting for a reply she added, 'It's eight o'clock, the bathroom is next door, and your breakfast will be on the table in half an hour.'

Lucy would have liked to lie there, but she sensed Mrs Benson expected her to be dressed and out of the house as quickly as possible. She still had no idea what she was going to do, or where she was going to live. She wondered about staying another night at Mrs Benson's, but she wasn't sure if she could afford it. She still had to find a job.

She ate every morsel of the bacon-and-egg breakfast that had been cooked for her, and both slices of toast, wondering when and where she'd get her next meal.

Church bells were ringing out all across the city when she arrived back in Liverpool, making sure that everyone knew it was Sunday. If it had been any other day of the week, she might have managed to talk to Aunt Flo on her own and persuade her to let her stay on until she could find a job and somewhere else to live.

Worse still, because it was Sunday her Aunt Flo, Karen and Shirley would probably all be at Mass so it meant facing her Uncle Fred and Selina. Unless she could creep round to the back of the house, and find her sack of clothes in the outside lavvy without disturbing them.

Lucy found her luck was out. Not only was the sack not where it was supposed to be, but the back door was wide open. Selina was in the scullery washing her hair, and spotted her immediately, so Lucy had no alternative but to face her.

'Come for your stuff, have you?'

'Yes, but it's not where I left it.'

'You didn't think it would be, did you? How did you think we were going to be able to use the lavvy with that great sack of rubbish stuck in there?'

'Sorry, but it was where I was told to put it. Do you know where it is now?'

'Dad took it back up to our bedroom. Come on in, I'll get it for you as soon as I've dried my hair.'

Lucy stood uneasily just inside the scullery door, straining her ears for any sound that her Uncle Fred might be in the house.

'Stop looking like a frightened rabbit,' Selina told her. 'There's no one else here.'

'Uncle Fred is out, is he?'

Selina stopped towelling her hair, and flipped it back from her face so that it spread out like a dark shawl around her shoulders. 'For the moment. Why?'

'I'd better be off before he gets back,' Lucy said uncomfortably. 'I think he'd be very angry if he found me here. Shall I nip upstairs and get my stuff?'

'Where are you going with it?'

Lucy shrugged. 'I don't know.'

'Where did you stay last night, with your friend Brenda over in New Brighton?'

'No, her mother wouldn't let me stay there.'

Selina began brushing her hair with long methodical strokes. 'Why was that? Was it because of what's happened to our Frank?'

Lucy shrugged. 'I suppose so. I couldn't believe it, I've been a friend of Brenda's for such a long time. I stayed the night in a boarding house in New Brighton.'

Selina looked surprised. 'And are you going back there?'

Lucy shook her head. 'I'd like to, but I can't afford it.' Tears pricked at her eyes and began to trickle down her face. 'I don't know what I'm

217

going to do, or where I'm going to stay. I've got to
find a job . . .'

'Oh, stop snivelling and feeling sorry for yourself,' Selina snapped. 'I can help you if you want
me to.'

'You can?' Lucy's mouth fell open with surprise. 'With finding a job, do you mean?'

'With finding a job, and somewhere to live. I
told a friend of mine about you. She said she'll
take you on.'

Lucy looked at her in amazement, wondering
what the catch was. 'Are you really saying you
know someone who will give me a job?'

Selina grinned widely. 'Yeah, kiddo, that's what
I said. I don't know how you will like the work, of
course. It's quite different from what you're used
to doing.'

'I'll do anything, absolutely anything,' Lucy
said fervently. 'If I can work in a factory I should
be able to do most jobs,' she added with a
shudder.

Selina looked thoughtful. 'You let me down
pretty badly over that one though, didn't you?'
she reminded her.

Lucy looked uncomfortable. 'I know, but it
won't happen again, I promise you!' she said
contritely.

'Let's hope not! My friend will be livid if you
do. She's doing me a favour, as well as you, by
agreeing to take you on.'

'And did you say that you also know somewhere where I can live?' Lucy asked in disbelief.

Selina looked smug. 'Yeah, that as well.' She

rubbed vigorously at her long hair again with the threadbare towel, then began brushing it into a different style.

'You'd better nip upstairs and get your stuff, it's on my bed,' she said, beginning to outline her generous mouth with a vivid red lipstick. 'It might be a good idea for us to go right away, before my dad gets back and catches you here. He hasn't much time for you at the moment,' she added with a smirk.

Chapter Nineteen

They left the house and walked down Anfield Road carrying the sack containing Lucy's belongings between them. Lucy wondered where they were going, but she thought it better not to ask. It was the first time she'd been on her own with Selina, apart from riding on the same tram. Even though she'd been living in the same house and sharing the same bedroom for almost three months, they'd had very little to say to each other.

It puzzled Lucy why Selina was being so helpful. Most of the time she treated her with contempt, or criticised her, or said spiteful things about her.

Remembering the incident over selling the clothes, Lucy wondered if she should trust her, because she was sure Selina had diddled her. Another thing, Selina had claimed that it was because of her that she'd split up with Jack Carter, so why should she want to help her now?

As they reached the end of Anfield Road, Selina stopped, dropping her end of the sack on to the pavement.

'This is too bloody heavy for us to carry, we'd better get a tram.'

'Have we far to go, then?'

'No, only a couple of streets away, but this bloody sack weighs a ton!'

They caught a tram, not into town, or down towards the pier head, but in a different direction altogether, to a part of Liverpool Lucy had never been to before.

They only went three stops and then they were off the tram and struggling to carry the sack along a road of large detached three-storey houses. Lucy noticed they all had imposing bay windows, smart front gardens with low walls in front of them, and paved pathways up to the glass-fronted vestibules.

Before she could ask where they were, or whom it was they were going to see, Selina turned in at one of the houses, went up the path and rang the bell. A maid wearing a brown dress and a frilly white apron opened the door.

The next minute they were inside the house, standing in a large square hall. There was dark red Wilton carpet on the floor and the walls were decorated with elaborately patterned red-and-gold flock wallpaper. A huge gilt-framed mirror filled one wall, and in front of it was a highly polished mahogany table holding a large silver tray.

As Selina put Lucy's sack down in one corner of the hall, a stylishly dressed woman in her early thirties came down the wide carpeted staircase to greet them.

She had marcel-waved, peroxide-blonde hair, and she wore a great deal of make-up that made her oval face look almost like a mask. She was dressed in a tight-fitting black dress, cut low in the neckline and with a skirt short enough to show quite a lot of her shapely legs.

She greeted Selina warmly, kissing her on the cheek and hugging her, as though they knew each other very well.

'This is my friend Maggie Mayer,' Selina told Lucy.

There was an enormous glittering diamond-and-emerald ring on the hand Maggie held out, and Lucy noticed she had earrings to match.

'So Selina has brought you along to see me at last!' She smiled in Selina's direction and raised her eyebrows enquiringly.

Selina bit down on her lower lip and looked amused. 'Lucy has lost her job, and my old man won't have her in our house any longer, so now she has nowhere to live.'

'What a terrible dilemma!' Maggie murmured in a throaty voice. 'Mind you,' her shrewd emerald-green eyes narrowed as she looked Lucy up and down, 'I can quite see why men would fight over you, dear.'

Lucy felt uncomfortable. 'What has Selina been saying about me?' she asked.

'Saying about you? Selina? Why nothing, dearie! I read all about the incident outside the Cotton Exchange in the *Echo*, and I recognised you the moment you walked through the door.' She patted Lucy's shoulder consolingly. 'Don't worry, it's all over now. Time for a fresh start, eh?'

Lucy nodded her head. She was trying hard not to cry but she could feel tears prickling behind her

222

eyelids. Was she never to live it down, never to be allowed to forget what had happened, she wondered.

'Come on then, and let me see if I can do something to help,' Maggie said, leading the way into a large room on their right.

Lucy gasped in amazement. She had never seen such opulence. The sitting-room at Belgrave Road had been spacious, and comfortably furnished with a carpet square on the floor, and pictures on the wall, but this room was quite magnificent.

It was carpeted wall to wall with dark red Wilton the same as in the hall. In front of the marble fireplace, with its gleaming brass fire irons, was an enormous cream sheepskin rug. Over the fireplace was an immense gilt-framed mirror, similar to the one in the hall.

The wallpaper was a shade of dusky rose, the woodwork dark but highly polished, and there were four armchairs and two huge Chesterfield settees all upholstered in a heavy cream velvet material. Numerous elegant brass lamps with pink shades stood on highly polished side tables around the room, and there was an elaborate crystal chandelier hanging from the centre of the ceiling.

'Come and sit by me, and let's have a little talk,' Maggie Mayer suggested, sinking down on to one of the Chesterfields, and patting the cushion beside her invitingly.

Lucy did as she was asked, but she sat nervously on the edge of the seat, fidgeting with her hands, and unsure what she was supposed to say or do.

The contrast between this house and Anfield Road was incredible, and yet Selina seemed to be quite at home here. She'd kicked off her shoes and curled up in one of the big armchairs, and Lucy wondered how she and Maggie Mayer ever came to know each other.

'So you have lost your job, and you have nowhere to live, is that right?' Maggie murmured softly. She reached out to a table at her side, and picked up an elaborate gold-plated cigarette box, opened it, and offered it to Lucy. 'Smoke?'

Lucy shook her head emphatically. 'I don't, thank you very much.'

Maggie took one and fitted it into an ivory holder, then held out the box to Selina. Selina uncurled herself and padded across the room to take it. Without being asked she picked up a cream marble table-lighter, and held it for Maggie before lighting her own cigarette.

'Has Selina mentioned my name or told you why she's brought you here?'

'No! I'd never heard of you before tonight.' Lucy's face went scarlet with embarrassment. 'When I went to collect my things from Anfield Road, Selina said she could find me somewhere to live and knew someone who would give me a job.'

'That's right!' Maggie tapped the ash from her cigarette into a gold-rimmed glass ashtray, and blew out a long stream of smoke. 'I can certainly do that,' she confirmed.

'That ... that sounds wonderful! I ... I'll do anything, anything at all. I'll work really hard, I promise you,' Lucy gabbled.

She stopped and held her breath, feeling suddenly uneasy as Maggie and Selina exchanged amused glances.

'Shall I show you your room first, and you can see if you like it before we talk about work?'

Again leading the way she took them up the red-carpeted staircase, and then by way of a narrower staircase on up to a second floor. Here they went along a passageway where there were six doors all painted white, and each one numbered.

Maggie stopped at one of them, and they followed her inside. It was a pleasant, medium-sized room furnished with a bed, a wardrobe, a dressing-table and a small chest of drawers. There was pink Wilton carpet on the floor, a pink flowered bedspread and matching curtains at the window that looked out on to a strip of grass at the back of the house.

'This would be your room. Do you like it?'

Lucy looked round her in delight. It wasn't as big as her bedroom in Belgrave Road had been, but after the cramped conditions she'd had to endure at Anfield Road it was sheer heaven. It reminded her of the room she'd slept in at the boarding house in New Brighton, except that it was a different colour scheme.

'It's lovely,' she breathed, 'only I'm not sure I can afford it. I haven't got a job yet, remember.'

'Selina told you I could offer you a job as well

225

as somewhere to live,' Maggie Mayer reminded her. 'If you like the room, then we'll go back downstairs and talk about the job, shall we?'

As soon as they were back in the luxurious sitting-room, the maid who'd opened the front door brought in a tray of tea and biscuits. As she sat drinking from a rose-patterned china cup, nibbling a shortcake biscuit, and talking about inconsequential matters to Maggie, Lucy found it hard to convince herself that it wasn't all a dream.

'So you've decided you like the room, then?' Maggie smiled.

'It's perfect! I'd love to have it if I can afford it. Can you tell me something about the job, please?'

'What sort of work have you done up to now?'

Colour stained Lucy's cheeks. 'I worked at H & Y Foods for a few weeks, Selina got me a job there,' she said, looking uncomfortable, 'but then a friend found me a job at the Cotton Exchange.'

'So what did you do there?'

'I worked as a telephonist on the switchboard.'

Maggie sipped her tea thoughtfully. 'Yes, I suppose you would be good at that. You do have a very nice voice, doesn't she, Selina?'

Selina grinned. 'Absolutely cut glass!'

Maggie nodded thoughtfully. 'And were you working before you came to live with Selina's family?'

Lucy shook her head. 'My mother was ill for several years before she died, and I was looking after her, and helping her to do her job.'

'What sort of work was that?'

'She was housekeeper to a bachelor. We lived in his house.'

'In Wallasey?'

'That's right. In Belgrave Road. It was a nice house. Not as big or as posh as this one, but it was . . .'

'Much better than living in our tip,' Selina cut in. 'Our house wasn't your sort of place at all, was it?'

'You were all very kind to me, but it was rather crowded,' Lucy admitted diplomatically.

'Kind to you! Our Karen was the only one who was even civil. Frank spent his time leering at you, my old man never stopped shouting and swearing at you, my mother used you as a drudge, and was always trying to press you into going to church, and our young Shirley cheeked you something rotten.'

'And what about you, Selina?' Maggie asked, her shrewd eyes with their heavy mascara narrowing.

'I was my usual bitchy self!'

The two women laughed in unison. Lucy felt bemused. She didn't understand the joke. As far she could see no one had said anything funny.

'Well, bitch,' Maggie sat forward in her chair and looked directly at Selina, 'if Lucy has decided to take the room I've shown her then you can take her belongings up there for her. Right, Lucy?'

'I love the room,' Lucy said quickly, 'but I don't know how I can afford it.'

Maggie's mouth tightened. 'I've already told

you not to worry about the rent. You can pay when you are earning.'

'I told you Maggie could offer you work as well as somewhere to live, remember,' Selina reminded her.

Lucy looked uncertain. 'What sort of work?'

'You could help out around the house.'

Lucy's heart fell. Working in the factory had been bad enough, but after her more prestigious job in the Cotton Exchange, to have to work as a maid or, worse still, as a cleaner would be quite a comedown.

She looked round the opulent room with its magnificent furnishings, and wondered if it was some kind of private hotel.

She thought of the comfortable room upstairs, and knew she couldn't afford to refuse Maggie's offer.

'Yes, all right,' she said a trifle reluctantly.

'You don't sound very sure. Isn't the room to your liking?'

'Oh no, that's lovely. It's just that I'm not very fond of housework, so I don't know if you will find me very satisfactory as a maid.'

Maggie and Selina both laughed.

'I'm sure she'll do fine,' Maggie chuckled, looking across at Selina.

'You're exactly the sort of maid Maggie is looking for,' Selina smirked.

'I think that's resolved then, Selina. Why don't you take Lucy and her belongings upstairs to her room, and leave her to get settled in, then you can help me find some clothes for her that are a bit more suitable than the ones she's wearing.'

Chapter Twenty

The moment Flo Flanagan walked into the corner shop at the junction of Anfield Road and Piper Streeet, there was a sudden uneasy silence, and she knew they were talking about her family's troubles. Peggy Sharp, who was serving behind the counter, as well as Fanny Nelson and Sal Hicks, all stopped speaking and looked uncomfortable.

Flo held her head high. Let them talk, she thought savagely. Her mother had abhorred gossip, and she'd been brought up never to talk about anyone behind their back because it showed a lack of respect, and was something only lower-class people did.

It was at times like this when you knew who your true friends were, Flo thought bitterly. After all she'd done for those three, and all the other people in Anfield Road, she'd have thought they'd treat her better.

She'd helped when most of their kids were born, and nursed them through childhood illnesses. She'd looked after most of their old folk when they became infirm and incontinent, and then, when the end came, she'd been the one who laid them out ready for the undertaker.

Cradle to grave they'd needed her, still did

if it came to that, and yet they gossiped about her.

She felt contemptuous, even though she knew it was the way they lived. They fed on every titbit of gossip like crows on carrion. It was their lifeblood, their only excitement. Gossip, the more sordid the better, got their adrenalin flowing, gave them a high that was more potent than any drugs.

She knew so much about the private lives of all her neighbours that she could have been the biggest gossip of the lot of them; only she wasn't. As well as the way she'd been brought up, her training as a nurse made her as tight-lipped as Father O'Reilly was over things he heard in his confessional.

They say a trouble shared is a trouble halved, she thought wryly, so perhaps if she had gossiped more, particularly about her own family, she might not be feeling so despondent.

The only relief she ever found for her own troubles was to pray to the Blessed Virgin, or go to confession, and spill out her troubles to Father O'Reilly.

He was a compassionate priest, and she valued his advice, yet what did he really know about everyday problems? He lived in a big warm house; six rooms just for him and his aged housekeeper. He ate four square meals a day, except in Lent when he piously abstained from his late supper snack.

He never had to scrimp and save, never had to go without food to pay for shoe repairs for one of the kids or for a coat from the bargain counter at the pawnbrokers to keep one of them warm in winter.

Flo longed to go to the end-of-season sales and buy herself a dress, or a blouse and skirt, clothes that no one else had ever worn. The nearest she ever got to replenishing her shabby wardrobe was at the church jumble sale. And there was always such a mad scramble for anything worth having that it was snatched out of your hand if you weren't sharp.

Over the years she'd gradually accepted it as all part of the life she'd chosen for herself. Then Lucy had arrived on her doorstep, and it had been like turning the clock back twenty-five years.

She'd been only about a year older than Lucy when she'd left home to train as a nurse. Although she'd lived in at the Liverpool hospital her home had only been on the other side of the Mersey, so she'd had the best of both worlds. Independence, because she was working away from home, yet able to enjoy home comforts on her days off.

She'd had money to spend, too. Her parents, though strict, were generous and they were always ready to help her out if she happened to overspend.

It was years since she'd thought about them. In fact, until the letter had arrived from her sister-in-law, Maude Patterson, written only a week or so before she died, Flo had put her parents and her brother right out of her mind.

She'd had nothing whatsoever to do with them from the day she refused to have the child she was expecting adopted, and told them that she was marrying the father. They considered Fred Flanagan totally unsuitable and warned her no good would come of it. They were even more shocked when she admitted that he was a Catholic, and that she intended becoming one as well.

In those days, though boisterous, Fred was so handsome with his dark curly hair, hypnotic blue eyes and his warm Irish charm, that she'd found him irresistible. If he'd asked her to jump off the top of the New Brighton Tower she would probably have done it to please him.

Hard luck and poverty had brought out a more strident side to his nature. Over the years he'd reverted to the raucous ways of his childhood.

She hadn't fared much better, she thought wryly. When they'd married she'd been pretty, and as refined as young Lucy. Deprivation, and the strain of scrimping and saving, had turned her into a frowsy, middle-aged woman whose once trim figure was sagging, and whose face had as many lines as Lime Street station.

She was sure the reason why Fred resented Lucy so much was because she stirred up memories from the past. Like her, he probably remembered the days when she'd looked as fresh and innocent as Lucy did now.

Listening to Lucy saying that after her father had died her mother had experienced hard times, made her smile. Living in a comfortable house in a respectable part of Wallasey, looking after a young bachelor, who by all accounts was the easiest person in the world to care for, sounded like her idea of heaven.

Holding her back straight, and conscious that although she had a black shawl around her shoulders she had, at least, removed her apron before coming out to the shops which the other two women hadn't bothered to do, Flo waited to place her order.

'Hello, Flo, what can I get you this morning?' Peggy Sharp asked. 'If you're in a hurry I'm sure Fanny and Sal won't mind waiting.'

'Terrible business about your Frank,' Sal Hicks said as Flo walked up to the counter. 'You been along to see him yet?'

Flo ignored the question and spoke directly to Peggy Sharp, asking for a loaf of bread and some margarine.

'That young girl who's staying with you had a rough deal getting attacked like that by a mate of your Frank's. Is she over it?'

'Bet she wishes she'd never come to live in Liverpool,' Fanny Nelson went on when Flo made no response. 'Sal and I met her the day she arrived, she'd no idea where your house was. We put her right, didn't we, Sal?'

'And told her what you thought she ought to know about us, no doubt,' Flo said sharply.

The two women exchanged glances.

'We were only trying to help. She said she was your niece, but she didn't seem to know anything at all about you or any of your family,' Sal said.

'She's my late brother's daughter,' Flo told them.

'She certainly has a family likeness about her,' nodded Fanny. 'Pretty little thing. Dressed really smart when she arrived, but she seems to have become as dowdy as the rest of us since she's been here. Only seems to have about two dresses to her name these days.'

Flo looked at them, startled. They were right. When Lucy had first arrived she'd worn a different frock, or blouse and skirt, every day. Lately, though, she'd seemed to have only one dress, a skirt, and a couple of blouses. So what had happened to the other stuff she'd brought with her? And a couple of times she'd gone back to Wallasey to collect the rest of her belongings so what had happened to all her pretty clothes? She'd not seen any sight of them in the bedroom, and there was nowhere else she could have stored them.

Flo felt uneasy. The only answer she could think of was that Lucy had sold them. But why? She racked her brains to think of what expenses Lucy'd had to make her do such a thing. Then she remembered her pay had been withheld the first week she'd been at the factory, but she'd thought Selina had let Lucy have money for her tram fares.

Selina! Yes, that was the answer, of course. Selina had a mercenary streak in her that worried Flo. She'd probably talked Lucy into selling her clothes, and done the deal for her, and probably benefited from it more than Lucy.

Selina had Fred's gift of blarney. She could charm the birds off the trees when she wanted to, the same as he could. She'd never been as close to her eldest daughter as Fred. Selina had been his favourite since the day she was born. She took after his side of the family in looks, too, with her thick black hair and vivid blue eyes.

She'd always regarded Selina getting involved with Jack Carter, a married man, as a terrible sin, and it broke her heart to think about it. She'd tried talking to her, but Selina wouldn't listen to a word she said.

'Leave me to run my own life or I'll bugger off,' was her standard response. And since Flo knew exactly where she would go, and considered that to be even worse than her affair with Jack Carter, she said no more.

Selina's friendship with Maggie Mayer was the greatest of all the burdens she had to bear, Flo thought bitterly. Selina and Maggie had been at school together, and being slightly older than Selina, Maggie had latched on to her, and dominated her. She hadn't bullied her; Flo could have handled that, but it had been far more insidious. She'd lured Selina into her way of life like a spider entrapping a fly. By the time Selina was twelve, she was already running after the boys, and long before she started work she was keeping late hours, and bringing down Fred's wrath on her head.

He'd taken his belt off to her more than once. The last time he'd brought up weals on her arms and legs that had burst the skin. She'd had to keep her away from school for a week to give them a chance to heal, and put the word out that she'd slipped down some steps and badly grazed herself.

People had accepted it, but they knew the truth all right. Many dropped hints about what went on when Selina and Maggie went off with a gang of boys. As they grew older it had been men, not boys, that the two of them began going with, and Flo dreaded the day when Selina would come home and say she was pregnant. She never did, of course. Maggie was too worldly to let anything like that happen to either of them.

Maggie left school ahead of Selina, and both she and Fred had hoped that it would be the end of their friendship. For a short time Selina had become quieter and easier to live with. She went out far less, and Flo thought they were over the worst.

She matured fast. She was restless at home. When she left school and went to work at H & Y Foods, and met Jack Carter, there'd been a new set of problems. She began to doll herself up, and go out every night, often not coming home until after midnight.

The rows between her and her father flared up all over again. He threatened her with a hiding, but she warned him that if he ever again raised a hand to her she'd walk out.

'And where the hell do you think you'd go?' he'd asked.

'To Maggie's place. She's set up in her own house, and she's in the money, and she says I can go and live with her any time I like.'

It was a threat she held over their heads,

knowing they'd find it hard to manage if they lost her weekly wage packet. She turned up every penny she earned, and accepted the pittance her mother gave her back without a quibble. Flo had often wondered how she managed to buy so many new clothes, and all the make-up she plastered on her face, but she'd never asked.

Father O'Reilly had been the one who put her wise.

'I never see that lovely daughter of yours at Mass these days, and I haven't heard her confession for many months. Now why is that?'

'I'm sorry, Father, I'll have a word with her about it.'

'You do that. She's in mortal danger these days, you know.'

She hadn't understood his meaning, and pressed him to explain. When he did she covered her ears with her hands, and refused to believe what he was saying.

When she'd told Fred, he confirmed every word of it.

'Maggie Mayer's is a bloody knocking shop. Thought you knew that!' he exploded. 'Why d'you think I threatened to tan her bloody arse when I knew she was seeing that Maggie again?'

Yes, Flo thought, as she paid for her few groceries, there had always been plenty of things going on in the Flanagan family for people to gossip about. This new scandal, Frank and Lucy

238

being involved in this murder, would stir up all the old stories.

Head held high, though her spirits were in her boots, Flo paid for her shopping.

'So where's that niece of yours gone to now?' Sal Hicks asked.

'We heard your Fred had kicked her out!' Fanny laughed. 'I saw your Selina helping to carry her belongings away yesterday morning while you were at Mass.'

Flo stared at them blankly. Selina helping Lucy? What on earth was she doing that for? She didn't like Lucy! For some reason she'd taken against her the moment she'd moved in. Flo had no idea why, unless it had been her own stupid remark, 'She's so like what I dreamed you'd be like,' that had started it.

When Selina had been a toddler she'd been so enchanting, and even during her early schooldays she'd been bewitching. Flo sighed. The rot had set in when she'd gone to senior school, met Maggie Mayer, and been influenced by her.

Selina had helped Lucy to get a job at H & Y Foods, of course. She'd wondered then what she was up to. To be helping her now, though, when she'd seemed to be so delighted that Fred had sent her packing, was beyond Flo's comprehension. Unless ...? Her blood chilled. That could mean only one thing! Dear God, no! Not that!

Her thoughts were in turmoil as she left the shop. Even before she'd closed the door behind her, she heard the buzz of voices as Fanny and

Sal jabbered away to Peggy Sharp, and she knew it wasn't sugar they were talking about.

Chapter Twenty-One

Lucy wasn't sure whether there'd been something in the cocoa Maggie sent up to her room, or if she was so utterly exhausted by all that had been happening over the past few days, but she didn't remember a thing until next morning.

She had no idea where she was, what time it was, or even how long she'd been asleep. The lined curtains screened out all the light, and even the noise from outside, and there seemed to be no sounds from anywhere inside the house.

She stretched, plumped up her feather pillows, then snuggled down again in the warm soft bed.

She dozed fitfully; in between times she tried to reason out how Selina came to know someone who lived in such a luxurious house.

What puzzled her most of all was that they seemed to be such close friends. So why did Selina stay in Anfield Road, in such dingy surroundings, when she could have moved in with Maggie and lived in luxury?

The question worried Lucy so much that she became restless and couldn't stay in bed. She slipped on the white dressing-gown that was hanging behind the bedroom door, padded over to the window, and peered out. It was a glorious day; the autumn sun was so high in the sky that she guessed it must be late morning at least, and she felt guilty about still being in bed.

She opened her bedroom door and stared down the long passage. Everywhere was quiet as if everyone had gone off to work. All the white doors were tightly closed. There seemed to be absolutely no one about or any household noises.

At the far end of the corridor was a pale green door and she dimly recalled Maggie telling her that it was the bathroom. She tiptoed along and nervously tried the door.

Inside, Lucy stopped and gaped in surprise. There was not only a huge bath, but also a big wash-basin and a flush toilet all in a matching pale green colour. She padded across the thick cream carpet and stared down into the bath, wondering if she dare use it. The thought was so tempting that the next minute she'd turned on the taps, and the bath was filling up.

Lucy had soaped every inch of her body, and was lying back enjoying the luxury of being immersed in hot water for the first time in months, when the door opened.

She gave a little scream and tried to cover herself with her hands, overcome with embarrassment.

'It's all right, it's only me,' Maggie called out.

Although her hair was elaborately styled, and she was wearing make-up, Maggie wasn't dressed. Her voluptuous figure was wrapped in an elegant black satin negligée, with rows of intricate bead embroidery down the edges.

'Did you sleep well?' she asked as she came

into the room, and stood staring down at Lucy in the bath.

Lucy slid down deeper in the water, wishing Maggie would go away. 'Yes, thank you. What time is it?'

'Almost midday.'

'I'm sorry, I seem to have slept the clock round!' Lucy exclaimed guiltily. 'I had no idea it was so late. Everywhere was so quiet.'

Maggie perched herself on the side of the bath, trailing her fingertips languidly in the water. 'Don't worry about it, Lucy. You were exhausted so it's probably done you good. Anyway, none of the girls here ever get up until early afternoon.'

'They don't?' Lucy looked startled. At Anfield Road everybody was up and eating breakfast long before eight o'clock, even on Sundays.

'They don't finish work until one or two in the morning,' Maggie yawned, covering her mouth with a manicured hand.

Lucy looked puzzled. 'Really? All of them? Whatever do they do to keep them up so late?'

Maggie took her cigarette case out of a concealed pocket in her robe and lit up. 'The same as you are going to do, of course,' she smiled.

'But you didn't tell me what I would be doing,' Lucy reminded her. 'You said you'd leave it until later.'

Maggie tipped her head back and exhaled a thin spiral of smoke. 'We'll talk about it when you're dressed.' She stood up and moved towards the door. 'You'd better get out of that bath now,

243

Lucy, the other girls will be needing it,' she said curtly and walked out.

Lucy shivered. The water had gone cold, and the sense of euphoria she'd felt earlier had completely vanished. Why couldn't Maggie tell her what her job was to be, why build up such a mystery?

She emptied the bath and was towelling herself dry when the door opened again and a girl of about her own age, plump with curly blonde hair and also wearing a white robe, walked in.

Covered with confusion, Lucy quickly wrapped the towel around herself. No one seemed to have any regard for other people's privacy, she thought indignantly.

She waited for the girl to leave so that she could discard the towel and slip into her dressing-gown, but the new arrival seemed to have no intention of doing so.

'God, I'm tired,' she yawned as she walked across to the bath, and turned on the taps to fill it. 'Half past two before I got to bed!'

The girl slipped off her robe. 'I'm Babs,' she smiled as she tested the bath water and tossed in a handful of pink bath salts from a jar standing on the edge of the bath. 'You're new?'

'That's right.'

'So what made you come here?' Babs asked.

'My cousin, Selina. Maggie said she would give me a job and a room.'

'Selina?' Babs bent over the bath, whisked the pink salts around, then stepped in and slid down in the water. 'You mean Selina Flanagan?'

244

'That's right. Maggie is a friend of hers,' Lucy told her. She reached for her dressing-gown and slipped her arms into it, pulling it round her so that she shielded her naked body from Babs's gaze before she discarded the towel.

'And you fell for it?' Babs regarded her curiously. 'Where are you from, Ireland or a convent?'

Lucy looked bewildered. 'Neither. I used to live in Wallasey, but I've been living over here in Liverpool . . .'

'Hold on,' Babs sat bolt upright in the water. 'I know who you are! You're the girl who was mixed up in that murder outside the Cotton Exchange. Am I right?'

'I'm Lucy Patterson, yes.'

Babs's green eyes widened. 'A man grabbed you and Selina's brother, Frank Flanagan, and another man – some of the papers said he was your boyfriend – tried to save you. Between them they ended up killing the bloke who'd attacked you. My God! Wait until the others hear about this!'

'Must you tell them?' Lucy protested, her face scarlet.

Babs shrugged her plump shoulders. 'Even if I say nothing some of the others will be bound to recognise you. Is that why Maggie took you on? I bet she thought it would bring in the punters, you being so notorious.'

Lucy looked puzzled. 'What do you mean, punters?'

For a moment Babs stared at her wide-eyed, then she started to giggle. 'You really don't know what this place is, or what goes on here, do you?'

Lucy shook her head. 'Why? What does go on here then?'

'What do you think?' Babs asked archly.

'I've no idea. Maggie said none of you finished work until very late at night and that you didn't usually get up until midday.'

'So what did you think we do for a living?'

Lucy looked thoughtful. 'Show girls? Dancers either here in Liverpool, or over in New Brighton? They have troupes of dancing girls at the Floral Gardens and ...' Her voice trailed away as she saw that Babs was doubled up with laughter.

'Oh, my God. You are a scream. Wait until I tell the others!'

'So what do you do for a living then?'

Babs regarded her strangely. 'Selina's your cousin and she didn't tell you what sort of place this is? It's a knocking shop, so what do you think we do? We entertain men.'

Lucy shook her head, bewildered. 'Entertain them? How exactly? I'm afraid I don't know what a knocking shop is,' she added apologetically.

'We're prossies, you silly bint! We give 'em a bit of what they want! That's why it's called a knocking shop! It's a very high-class one, mind,' she sniggered. 'And you didn't know that? I thought everyone in Liverpool knew that Maggie Mayer's place was a knocking shop!' she said in surprise. 'We only cater for the very best clientele, of course, or so Maggie tells everyone.'

'Oh no!' Lucy clapped a hand over her mouth.

246

She didn't want to believe what Babs was telling her, but suddenly it all made sense. The posh house, the lavish furnishings, the rows of bedrooms discreetly shut away behind the white numbered doors. The late nights, and Maggie allowing the girls to lie in bed until midday.

Was this what she had come to? Even the squalor of Anfield Road, and working in a factory, was nothing compared to the disgrace of a brothel. She shuddered, feeling sick with despair. Her mother would have been horrified to find she was involved in such depravity. What would Stanley Jones think? What had her life become since she left Wallasey? How could she have sunk so low?

Without another word, Lucy walked out of the bathroom and back to her room. She needed to be alone, to think what to do next. She'd thought Selina was trying to help her, but all she'd been doing was involving her in a life of shame.

She was sitting dejectedly on the side of her bed, still wrapped up in the dressing-gown, when Maggie came back.

'Aren't you dressed yet?' she said sharply. 'I want to talk to you about your work here.'

'One of the girls has been telling me what she does, but I don't believe her,' Lucy whispered.

Maggie's eyes narrowed as she drew heavily on her cigarette. 'I hope you're not going to be difficult about all this,' she said harshly. 'There are lots of advantages for you, you know. You've got a lovely room, a nice house to live in, and

247

you'll get very good meals. All you've got to do in return is smile, be pleasant, and pander to the whims of a couple of men each evening.'

Lucy shivered. 'I'm sorry, but I've never done anything like that in my life! I don't want to, either!' she added sharply.

'Then you'd better start packing your bags and leave,' Maggie said icily. 'Remember, though, I won't take you back if you do.'

'I wouldn't come back if that was what I had to do to get a room,' Lucy told her heatedly.

Maggie shrugged expressively. 'It's up to you, but I don't think you can afford to be so choosy. You have no job, your boyfriend is in Walton, and from what Selina has told me you're certainly not welcome at her place.'

Lucy stared hopelessly after Maggie as she walked away, realising that every word she said was true. What was she to do?

Somehow she must get away. But how? Where could she go? She had no money, no friends to help her. Stanley was in prison, and Brenda's mother had refused to let her stay with them. One question after another bombarded inside her head like pistol shots.

She'd felt so elated when Selina had told her she could get her a job. She'd thought that once she was working she'd be able to start life anew, and in time even fulfil some of her dreams.

She stared round the pretty bedroom in dismay. It had seemed so lovely when Maggie had brought her up here last night, but now she saw it as an evil prison.

It made her feel sick as she thought about what had gone on there in the past, and what Maggie expected her to do there in the future. She wanted no part of it. The sooner she left the better.

She went over to where Selina had dumped the sack containing her belongings. She'd get dressed, put on some clean clothes of her own, and then she'd face up to Maggie, and tell her she was definitely going to leave because she'd sooner earn a living some other way.

As she opened up the sack she gasped in dismay. Inside was a mass of old straw, a couple of bricks, and some old newspapers. Not a single item of clothing, not even her shoes or raincoat. She tipped everything out over the pink carpet. Nothing! Then she found a piece of cardboard with some writing scrawled on it in pencil: *'You owed us for your bleeding keep so I've taken youse bloody clothes to the pawnbroker.'*

Lucy had never seen her Uncle Fred's handwriting, but she knew instinctively that it was his.

She had no money, and now only the shabby clothes she stood up in. Soon it would be winter and the weather would be bitterly cold and damp. She'd let Selina sell the bulk of her best dresses, good shoes and her warm clothes. Now her Uncle Fred had sold the precious few that had remained. She didn't even have a raincoat.

She sat down on the unmade bed, held her head in her hands, and let the tears flow. She'd never felt so dispirited or forsaken in all her life. With no money, no job, no friends and no prospects, it seemed she'd have to do whatever Maggie asked of her.

Chapter Twenty-Two

Helped by Daisy, the little maid, Lucy carried the assortment of boxes and packages, all of them containing new clothes, up to her bedroom.

Maggie had taken her shopping. They'd spent the entire afternoon visiting all the big stores in Liverpool, and she'd never experienced a shopping trip like it.

Maggie had been emphatic that she must have everything new, from lingerie and silk stockings, to several gorgeous dresses.

Their shopping expedition had taken so long that Maggie had insisted on taking afternoon tea in Henderson's restaurant. That had been something Lucy had always dreamed of doing, but had never been able to afford.

Now, counting up all the boxes and packages, it made her feel quite dizzy trying to remember exactly what was inside each of them.

'We must have a dress parade, and make sure that everything fits you. If they don't, then they will have to go back, and be exchanged for something else,' Maggie said, coming into the room.

Lucy looked bewildered. 'I tried everything on before you bought it,' she reminded her.

'Of course you did, but they may look different

on you here. Our lighting is not the same, and even the surroundings can make a difference to the way an outfit looks.'

'Oh!' Lucy looked bemused. 'I didn't know that.'

Maggie smiled understandingly. 'Not everyone does, which is why so many people are disappointed by what they buy. I insist my girls only wear clothes that flatter them, and which emphasise their good points, so you must try everything on, and let me be the judge. We'll do it this evening, after the rest of the girls start work.'

Lucy looked away quickly, biting her lip, and feeling subdued and uneasy. That was the part she didn't like, knowing that all these wonderful clothes were for when she started work.

The other girls at Maggie's place seemed happy enough about what they were doing, but she found it impossible to accept that it was right. Her mother would have been terribly shocked.

Babs had laughed when she'd said that, and told her not to be a prude. 'We're supplying a service. You might as well say it's wrong to sell bread, or to answer the telephone. You are only supplying a service that someone needs.'

Lucy hadn't argued because she didn't want to antagonise Babs, or appear to be criticising Maggie, but it had haunted her conscience ever since she'd accepted Maggie's offer of a job and somewhere to live.

Now, after this shopping expedition, she felt even more deeply indebted to Maggie. It still didn't stop her feeling anxious about the fate that lay in store for her. Taking her place each evening with the rest of the girls in the salon, as the imposing sitting-room was called, filled her with dread.

The thought of being ogled by visiting men, picked out as their companion for the evening, and then having to take them upstairs to her bedroom, filled her with both disgust and panic. She wouldn't even contemplate what happened after that.

Babs had told her that she had nothing to worry about because Maggie would be instructing her in what she had to do. Even the thought of that was repugnant and sent her into a state of confusion.

Maggie was too wily to rush matters. She sensed Lucy's confusion and reluctance. She also knew from what Selina had told her that Lucy was inexperienced in sexual matters.

The two of them had laughed about it like a couple of schoolgirls as they sat in Maggie's private sitting-room enjoying a port and lemon. Selina told her about the way Frank had teased Lucy by walking round with only a towel wrapped round him, or following her to the outside lavvy, and pushing the door open when she was in there. When Selina went on to relate the incident when her brother had burst into their bedroom and tried to rape Lucy, they'd smiled knowingly at each other.

'She's such a pretty little thing, and speaks in such a refined way, that I think I will save her for someone special,' Maggie confided. 'I've one or two special customers who will pay well for a virgin.'

'You won't forget who brought her along, will you?' Selina said archly.

'Have I ever? You'll get your reward as soon as I'm paid, have no fears about that.'

'Have you anyone special in mind?'

Maggie smiled conspiratorially, and teasingly tapped the side of her nose with one finger.

'Don't rush her,' Selina advised. 'She loves clothes, so kit her out, and let her feel indebted to you first.'

It was sound advice and Maggie had taken it. Now, with dresses to soften her up, Maggie felt that Lucy was ready for her initiation.

Meals at Maggie's house were taken in the dining-room at times to suit individual requirements. Maggie employed a full-time housekeeper, Ada, as well as the little maid Daisy. Ada was in her late fifties, buxom and practical. It was her job to see that each of the girls had a well-cooked hot meal each day between two and three o'clock.

If they were sick, it was Ada who looked after them, cosseting and mothering them until they were well again. Her potions for headaches, sore throats and head colds were infallible. She could also cope with most other minor ailments or discomforts that the girls might incur, anything from bruises to corns.

As some of Maggie's clients arrived immediately after they'd finished work at their offices in the city, it was part of the daily routine for the girls to have afternoon tea in the salon. It was brought in by Daisy wearing her maroon uniform and white frilly apron so that she was ready to answer the door to any early arrivals.

All the girls would be dressed ready for the evening ahead so it gave Maggie an opportunity to check that they were all well turned out. Her standards were high. She paid particular attention to grooming as well as smartness.

For the first few days that she was at Maggie's, Lucy did not attend these gatherings. On the day of her shopping spree, however, Maggie suggested that she should put on one of her new dresses and come down.

Lucy quailed. Did this mean she was now going to have to start work? She knew it had to happen some time, but she dreaded the thought. Babs had said Maggie would instruct her about what she had to do, but that still didn't take away the feeling of revulsion she felt every time she thought about what that entailed.

She chose a pale blue dress, and as she slipped it on and smoothed it down over the new white satin slip, pulled on the skin-tone silk stockings, and slid her feet into new strappy black shoes, she felt a little more confident about the ordeal ahead.

Even so, it took every ounce of courage to walk into the salon and face all the other girls. A few she knew by sight because she'd passed them on the landing, or had been in the dining-room at the same time as them, but Babs was the only person who'd talked to her.

As she'd feared, everyone turned to stare at her. They all looked so glamorous, so self-assured, in their smart dresses, stylish hairdos and sophisticated make-up, that Lucy felt completely tongue-tied. She couldn't even say hello to any of them. Then Maggie appeared, introducing her, and as she listened avidly to the chatter going on around her, amazed and astounded by some of the things they were saying, she found herself wondering why she'd been so frightened.

None of them seem to regard what they did for a living as anything unusual. They talked freely and in some instances, actually exchanged information about the personal habits of the men who were their clients.

Lucy couldn't believe that several different girls had slept with the same man, or that one girl had slept with several different men. She was so astounded by this that she asked Babs in a whisper whether it was true or not.

'Of course it is,' Babs laughed. 'We're not married to them, you know. If a chap comes in and asks for a particular girl, and she is already with someone, then he'll pick somebody else.'

'But don't you mind when that happens?' Lucy frowned. 'Don't you feel jealous?'

'Of course not! Why should we? We don't have any deep feelings for these men. We're just providing a service. If they went into a barber's shop for a haircut, and the usual assistant wasn't available, then they'd have their hair cut by someone who was free, now wouldn't they?'

Lucy could see her point, but she still didn't feel it was right. It made her dread even more the ordeal that still lay ahead. She racked her brains to try and think of some way of putting it off, and yet, there were moments when she wanted it to happen so that she could get it over with.

Maggie knew she was becoming restless, but she didn't intend letting Lucy become part of the general salon. As she'd mentioned to Selina, she had other plans for her.

Among her many wealthy clients, one of the most fastidious and demanding was Richard Thomas. He was always eager for something special, and prepared to pay extra for a new experience.

Maggie had been watching Lucy carefully, and decided she was an ideal offering. She had been delighted by how pretty and fresh looking Lucy was from the moment Selina brought her to the house, and also pleasantly surprised by the way she spoke, and by her charming manners. It was obvious that she had been well brought up.

Maggie had known Selina for years, and the story of Lucy coming to live with the Flanagans had intrigued her right from the start. She knew Selina found Lucy an intrusion after she moved in with them, and she had hoped that it would make Selina realise at last how much better off she would be if she left Anfield Road and came to live with her.

As usual Selina had refused.

She came round to see Maggie most evenings, and she was always ready to help out when they'd booked in more clients than they could cope with, or when one of the girls was ill, but she refused to give up her independence completely by moving in permanently.

Bringing Lucy along at a time when she was seeking some new diversion for Richard Thomas had been a stroke of genius on Selina's part, and Maggie was truly grateful. Tonight when he came into the salon she might even introduce him to Lucy and gauge his reaction when he saw her for the first time.

She'd been dropping tempting hints over the past few days to intrigue him, and he had been responding exactly as she had expected. She was quite sure Lucy would entrance him, and that he would pay well for the privilege of being the first to be entertained by her.

She felt no qualms about the exorbitant sum she would be asking him for this privilege. He could afford it. He was young, about twenty-five, handsome, with an angular face, broad jaw, thin mouth and keen, dark eyes. He was the assistant manager at Bunney's, one of the largest department stores in Liverpool.

He was a regular customer at Maggie Mayer's, and she was determined not to lose him. She made all this very clear in the one-to-one chat she had with Lucy in her private office.

'I'll try to be nice to him,' Lucy promised, 'but I don't really know what I have to do.'

'You've never slept with a man?'

Lucy looked shocked. 'Of course not, I'm not married, am I?'

'You've not had any men friends?'

Lucy hesitated, wondering whether knowing

Stanley Jones over so many years counted, and decided it didn't. 'No, not really.'

Maggie felt herself becoming exasperated. 'Surely you've kissed a boy?'

Again Lucy hesitated. 'Only on the cheek, never on the lips.'

Maggie looked puzzled. She found it hard to believe that Lucy could be so completely innocent. Apart from the attack outside the Cotton Exchange, when the man had grabbed her, and Frank and Stanley Jones had rescued her, Selina had said that Frank had tried to rape her. She hesitated about asking Lucy what had happened because according to Selina she'd been so distraught that her screams had brought both her parents to the scene, and even caused Karen to have a fit.

Her dilemma was whether to enlighten Richard Thomas by telling him how inexperienced Lucy was, or whether to let him discover the fact for himself. She wondered which he would find most intriguing.

There was also Lucy to consider, of course. Should she forewarn her about the part she had to play, or let her remain innocent of what to expect? She didn't want her to take fright and spoil Richard's enjoyment.

She decided to see what Selina thought.

'Perhaps it might come better from one of the girls rather than from you,' Selina said. 'She seems to get on well with Babs, so why not ask her to explain things to Lucy. Tell Babs what to say, but don't tell her who Lucy's first client will be.'

259

Maggie looked puzzled. 'Why not?'

'She'd be jealous, of course! Think about it, he's smashing looking, plenty of money, and he's probably a great lover.'

'Fancy him yourself, do you?' Maggie teased.

'Yeah, but once I opened my mouth and he heard how I talk, he'd look at me as if I was a piece of shit,' Selina told her sourly.

Maggie sighed. Selina was probably right. She had the looks, with her lovely long dark hair, huge blue eyes and voluptuous figure – in fact none of the other girls could hold a candle to her – but she had no finesse. And Richard Thomas was top drawer.

'I'd soon put a polish on you if you came and lived with me,' she told Selina. 'Living under the same roof as your old man and Frank doesn't help you any with the way you speak.'

'Yeah, yeah, some day!' Selina laughed. 'I can hardly leave home at the moment with our Frank in nick, now can I? Me mam misses his wage packet, and she needs all the support she can get, poor cow.'

'Perhaps they should have let Lucy stay on,' Maggie mused. 'It would have been a bit more money coming in.'

Selina shook her head. 'She hadn't got a job, had she. And not likely to get one as long as people remembered her mug from the *Echo*. They'd be thinking she was trouble. Anyway,' she grinned, 'me dad said he'd bloody well swing for her if she ever crossed the doorstep again.'

'Right. Then I'll introduce her to Richard Thomas after I've asked Babs to have a chat with her, and we'll see how things go.'

Maggie topped up their port and lemon. 'Drink up!' She clinked her glass against Selina's. 'There will certainly be something in it for you as soon as Richard Thomas pays up.'

Chapter Twenty-Three

Lucy would never forget the first time Richard Thomas walked into Maggie Mayer's salon. She'd been sitting in one of the alcoves with Babs who was telling her exactly what working at Maggie's entailed. The more Babs explained things the more repelled she'd felt. Then she'd looked across the room and seen him walking in, and he seemed like the man of her dreams.

He was at least six foot tall, suave, well groomed and smartly dressed. He was so handsome that she couldn't take her eyes off him. His dark wavy hair was cut close to his well-shaped head. He was clean shaven, his skin tanned, and he had the decisive mouth, and firm jaw line, of a man who knew his own mind.

His sharp dark eyes swept round the room and she felt a tremor run through her as they met her gaze and his dark brows lifted the merest fraction.

'That man who has just come in, who is he?' she asked Babs.

'Richard Thomas. He's wealthy and he thinks a lot of himself,' Babs said disparagingly. 'When he wants something he can be quite ruthless.'

'Is he married?'

'No!' Babs shook her head. 'He's too selfish and

superior for that. He thinks women are merely for his pleasure,' she added scornfully.

'You don't seem to like him very much,' Lucy chuckled.

Babs shrugged. 'He's just another client as far as I'm concerned. I don't like or dislike any of them whether they're tall or short, fat or thin, black, white or any other colour under the sun.'

Lucy bit her lip. 'I don't think I could ever do what you do if I felt like that,' she confessed. 'I would need to like them.' She grinned. 'I don't suppose that would be too difficult if it was someone as handsome as Richard Thomas.'

'Well, here's your chance to find out,' Babs whispered. 'He's coming over this way, and I know it's not me he wants to talk to so I'll leave you to get on with it.'

Before Lucy could answer, or stop her, Babs had slipped away, and Lucy had found herself looking up into Richard's piercing dark eyes.

'Lucy, isn't it?' He held out a hand, and she felt a tremor go through her as their skin touched. 'Maggie has been telling me about you. I've been looking forward to meeting you.'

'I haven't been here very long,' she said shyly.

'So I understand.' His gaze swept the busy room. 'Perhaps we should go somewhere more private so that you can tell me all about yourself.'

'You mean . . .' Colour flooded her face. She felt hot and uncomfortable, and avoided his eyes.

'Your room?'

'I suppose so, if that is what you really want to do,' she agreed hesitantly.

263

His eyebrows lifted. 'That is why you are here, isn't it?' he asked in an amused tone.

She didn't answer. She felt panic-stricken and looked round for Maggie, but she couldn't see her. Reluctantly she got up and walked out of the room, conscious that Richard Thomas was at her side, and felt all eyes were on them.

When they reached her room he followed her in and closed the door firmly behind him. Then he walked over to the armchair and sat down, leaving her standing in the middle of the room and wondering what she was supposed to do next.

She tried desperately to remember all the tips Babs had given her, but her mind was in such turmoil that she couldn't remember a thing. From the way Richard Thomas was studying her she supposed he was waiting for her to undress, but she had no idea how to start.

She was so nervous that her fingers were incapable of unfastening buttons or doing anything at all. Frozen to the spot, she wished she were a thousand miles away. She felt as frightened as when she'd been attacked outside the Cotton Exchange, or on the night when Frank had climbed into her bed.

'Why don't you sit down and tell me something about yourself,' Richard Thomas suggested.

His voice was so quiet and reassuring that she wanted to cry with relief. Suddenly she felt completely safe, and slowly her confidence came back.

'Very well.' She perched on the side of her bed

264

and smiled tremulously. 'What do you want to know?'

'How you come to be working here at Maggie Mayer's will do for a start.'

He skilfully questioned her, listening attentively as she told him about her childhood, and how after her father had died her mother had become housekeeper to Stanley Jones. He nodded understandingly when she told him that when her mother had died she'd moved in with the Flanagans.

'And then came the fracas outside the Cotton Exchange,' he mused.

She nodded, biting down on her lower lip.

'Do you like being here?'

Lucy shrugged her shoulders. 'I like Maggie. She has been very kind to me and I . . . I haven't . . . I haven't actually started work yet,' she stuttered.

Richard Thomas shifted in his chair, and stretched out his long legs. 'So this really is your first night, is it?' He looked amused. 'Does that mean I am going to be your very first client?'

Lucy bit her lip and looked away nervously.

'Speak up!' His tone became more assertive. 'I want to know.'

Lucy nodded, unable to bring herself to speak.

'What about this fellow Jones? Wasn't he ever your lover?'

'Good gracious, no!'

Richard Thomas smiled superciliously. 'I hope you are telling me the truth. It certainly bears out what Maggie told me about you, but time will tell. If either of you have been lying I shall soon know.'

Lucy felt outraged. He had seemed so kind and understanding so why did he have to spoil it all with such hateful questions. It made it all seem so sordid. 'Of course I'm telling the truth, why would I lie?' she asked heatedly.

He shrugged, then his face softened in a smile that made her senses spin, and made her feel she would do almost anything he asked to please him.

Almost before she knew what was happening he'd risen from the armchair, and was taking her in his arms. She stiffened as she felt his long lean fingers slipping the straps of her new blue dress from her shoulders. Then it was slithering down over her white satin slip to lie in a heap at her feet. Her slip followed and suddenly she found herself on the bed, and Richard, divested of his business suit, lying there beside her.

From the first, perhaps because he knew Lucy was new to this, it seemed that Richard was treating her as a lover rather than a prostitute, taking his pleasure slowly and soothing her with his touch. He kissed her very gently at first, his lips caressing her eyes, her cheeks and her throat until her fears melted away. Then his mouth found hers, and his kisses built up in intensity, arousing spirals of desire in her that masked her inhibitions. She found herself responding instinctively, oblivious to the fact that she considered what she was doing was wrong, or that this encounter was the result of a business deal struck with Maggie Mayer.

He caressed her gently, making love to her so expertly that she offered no resistance when he removed the rest of her underclothes, or when his hands began exploring the more secret crevices of her body.

His own desires mounted until his need was so great that he took her fiercely, and her agonised scream as he entered her served only to incite him to a greater frenzy.

'Maggie was right about you, Lucy, it really was your first time!' he panted.

He stroked her hair back from her brow and kissed her eyelids. 'Don't cry, it won't hurt next time!' he promised as he flopped beside her, utterly exhausted.

After he left she lay awake for a long time reliving the events of the evening, unable to relax either her body or her mind.

Her own physical response frightened her. She had been shocked at her loss of control over her senses, and appalled that she had offered no resistance, but had let him invade her body without any protest.

Was this the reason why her mother had been afraid for her to be alone with Stanley Jones, Lucy wondered. Had her mother's strict insistence on modesty been because she suspected that left to my own devices I'd do anything he asked of me, she thought guiltily.

Immediately after they'd made love and he'd moved away from her, Lucy had resolved that there wouldn't be a next time. She never wanted to see him again, but now that she was lying there on her own she ached to feel his arms around her once again.

She shuddered, and rolling over buried her face in the pillow. Coming to Maggie Mayer's had revealed a side of her character she'd never imagined existed.

Even though she felt bruised and sore she drifted off into a dreamless sleep.

When she woke it was with a feeling of relief that her initiation was over. Sleep seemed to have eliminated all recollection of pain, fear and revulsion, as well as all the doubts about her new way of life. She remembered their encounter with sensual pleasure. She ran her hands over her body, amazed at how they were able to arouse memories of where Richard's hands and lips had touched her.

She felt a little ashamed of her reactions and throughout the day her thoughts were so chaotic and mixed that more than once she was on the verge of telling Maggie that she was leaving because it wasn't the sort of life she wanted.

That evening, though, when Richard arrived at the salon, she found every nerve in her body tingling with desire as she accompanied him upstairs to her bedroom.

Richard visited her most evenings and little by little, as she lay in his arms after they had satiated their needs, she began to learn something of his background.

Babs had described him as handsome, selfish and ruthless. Lucy found he was all of these things but he was also intelligent, demanding and ambitious. He had trained to be an accountant, and was now the assistant manager of Bunney's, one of the largest department stores in Liverpool. She learned from their conversations that he had his own flat, an expensive car, and that he played golf regularly because of the benefits of mixing on the same social level as Liverpool's most wealthy businessmen.

'Don't you want to get married?' Lucy asked dreamily.

'Oh yes!' He rolled over on to his side and kissed her. 'That is a very important part of my plan!' He ran his fingers over one of her exposed breasts. 'I want a magnificent house on the Wirral, looking out over the sea, and a beautiful wife to run it for me so that I can entertain my business colleagues and friends.'

'And children?'

Richard's hand caressed her spine, sending tiny tingling shocks radiating through her. 'Children? Yes! Three I think is a good number, don't you? Two boys and one girl.'

'Why not two girls and one boy?' she teased.

Maggie watched their growing closeness with mixed feelings. Richard Thomas had paid her well for allowing him to initiate Lucy. Afterwards he had insisted that she should be kept exclusively for him.

At first Maggie had been happy enough to comply, but recently there had been growing unrest amongst the other girls. On those nights when Richard Thomas didn't come to the salon, Lucy could spend her time as she pleased. The others were often expected to take on more than one client in the course of the evening.

Maggie talked to Selina about it, and asked if she had heard any rumblings of discontent.

'Of course they feel disgruntled,' Selina told her. 'I don't blame them! She's the newest one here, she's been given one of the best clients, and she does the least work.'

'It's not her fault,' Maggie pointed out. 'Richard has asked me to keep her exclusively for him. And he does pay well.'

'He's never here at the weekends, though, so surely she could entertain some of the other clients then? He need never know!'

Maggie frowned. 'Lucy would be bound to tell him.'

Selina rubbed her thumb and forefinger together. 'Offer her some of this,' she smirked. 'That should help her to keep her trap shut.'

Lucy's feelings for Richard were far too strong for her to cheat on him in any way. In confidence she told him about Maggie's plans for her. Richard was furious.

'You mustn't let this happen,' he told her. 'I won't share you with anyone else. Do you understand?'

Lucy's eyes misted with tears. She knew she'd taken a terrible risk in mentioning it to him, particularly when Maggie had told her not to do so. 'So what do I do if she tells me to entertain someone else?' she asked.

'Refuse, of course!' he told her irritably.

'That sounds easy, but it's impossible. If I did

that Maggie would probably throw me out and I've nowhere to go, no family or friends to take me in.'

'Rubbish! If you got a proper job you'd be able to afford a bedsit. A girl of your calibre shouldn't be working in a place like this anyway,' he told her brusquely.

'I'd like to think that,' she smiled, 'but I know how hard it is to get a job, and unless I have one I wouldn't be able to pay for a room.'

Richard's face darkened; frowning, he concentrated on her problem. Then his face lightened, and holding her in his arms he whirled around the room. 'The answer is so simple I can't believe I didn't think of it before,' he exclaimed.

'And the solution is?' she prompted.

'You leave here and come and work at Bunney's, of course.'

'Doing what?'

'You said you'd trained as a telephonist at the Cotton Exchange. Well, if you could work their switchboard you can cope with ours.'

'It sounds a wonderful idea,' Lucy breathed, her eyes glowing. Then her face fell. 'I'd have to find somewhere to live . . .'

'I'll take care of all that. I'll set you up in a flat, and I'll be able to see you there whenever I wish. It's a perfect solution.'

A place of her own, even if it was only one room, would be one of her dreams coming true. A job at Bunney's, working under the same roof as Richard, even if she never saw him, would be sheer bliss. Except she'd be under an obligation to him instead of Maggie, a niggling voice inside her head reminded her.

'You mean you'll give me a job if I'll become your mistress?' she asked, feeling uneasy about the arrangement.

'What's wrong with that?' he asked huffily. 'It's no worse than what you're doing now. The only difference is you'll be earning money to spend on yourself instead of lining Maggie Mayer's coffers.'

Lucy still felt it was demeaning. 'It's a big step for me to take, can I think about it?' she demurred.

'Think about it? If you care for me as much as you say you do then I would have thought you'd jump at my offer.'

She smiled, wondering if this was perhaps the moment to tell him that she didn't only care for him, she was crazily in love with him. 'I do care about you, more than you know, but let me think about it overnight, please Richard,' she said cautiously.

'All right, providing you promise not to let Maggie talk you into sleeping with anyone else.'

Chapter Twenty-Four

It was a dull, drizzly November day when Lucy left Maggie Mayer's house, a day as downcast as Lucy's spirits.

Maggie was livid when Lucy told her about the arrangement she'd made with Richard Thomas. Maggie's shapely chest heaved, her handsome features contorted with rage, her emerald-green eyes grew icy.

Maggie's imperious manner and refined way of speaking that Lucy admired so much vanished. It might have been Selina standing there bawling her out.

'You ungrateful little bitch! After all I've done for you is this the way you repay me?' she stormed. 'You can leave now, right now. I won't have you under my roof another minute. What's more, you can go in what you arrived here in. Don't you dare take a single thing I've bought you. Do you understand? The old sack you brought your stuff in is down with the rest of the rubbish in the basement. Ask Ada to get it for you, not that there's anything worthwhile in it, only the clothes you stood up in. You arrived penniless, and that's the way you can leave.'

'Look, I'm very sorry ... it was Richard's idea ...'

'Richard's idea!' Maggie mocked. 'Why would he want to go to the expense of setting you up in a flat, and go to the trouble of finding you a job, when he can come here and have you, or any other whore he chooses, any time he pleases? Tell me that?'

'He didn't like the idea that I would be seeing other men, he wanted me for himself,' Lucy whispered, tears trickling down her cheeks.

'You stupid little cow! I had no intention of keeping to that arrangement, I only told him that to keep him keen.'

'He believed you! And so did I.'

'So rather than do your fair share like the other girls, you wheedled your way round him, and persuaded him to set you up in a place of your own,' Maggie said scathingly. 'With never a word to me, you two-timing little bitch! Get out. Get out of my sight!'

Tears streamed down Lucy's cheeks as she packed her scant belongings into the old sack. Maggie was so determined that she should take only the things she'd arrived with that she sent Ada to collect everything from Lucy's wardrobe, and to check what was in the sack.

'She said everything you had on that she'd bought you was to take off and leave behind,' Ada told her. 'Even your dress and your slip.'

'So what can I wear, I can't go out into the street naked.'

Ada shrugged. 'The things you came in, I suppose.'

'You mean this!' Lucy held up the thin cotton dress that she'd been wearing the day she arrived.

Ada grimaced. 'You won't be very warm in that, chuck. Is that really all you've got to put on?'

'That and a skirt and a blouse is all that's here,' Lucy said, taking them out of the sack. 'I haven't even got a coat!'

'Then you'd best wear the dress as a petticoat, and put the blouse and skirt on top,' Ada advised. 'That will give you a bit of warmth, and you won't need to cart that old sack around with you. I'll find you an old shopping bag for the bits and pieces from your dressing-table.'

None of the other girls, not even Babs, came to say goodbye, or wish her well as Ada chivvied her out of the back door in the middle of the afternoon. She was anxious to get her out of the house before clients began to arrive, or Maggie scolded her for not carrying out her orders more efficiently.

Lucy stood on the pavement, clutching the faded canvas shopping bag, trying to think what to do. The only way to make sure Richard didn't walk into a first-class row with Maggie Mayer was to let him know what had happened. She had no money so she couldn't telephone him, and if she turned up at Bunney's looking so shabby she was afraid the doorman might turn her away.

She shivered as the raw November wind coming off the river whistled down the street, whipping dust and paper into the air. The only alternative was to wait somewhere nearby so that she could stop him going into Maggie's place.

She'd have to make sure that Daisy couldn't see her when she opened the door to clients.

Although the gusts had died down, a freezing mist was falling, and the waiting seemed interminable to Lucy. Her feet and hands ached with the cold and even the tip of her nose felt frozen.

Every time a car pulled up she hoped it would be Richard. When it wasn't she had the sickening fear that this might be one of the nights when he didn't come. If that happened she didn't know what she could do. She had no idea where his flat was, and even if she had she didn't have the courage to go there.

Her relief when he eventually pulled up was so great that she could barely speak coherently.

He looked astounded to see her standing in the roadway. 'What's going on? Why are you out here? And why on earth are you dressed like that?'

'Can I get into your car please, Richard, I'm frozen,' she begged, her teeth chattering.

He hesitated, distaste on his face as he looked at her shabby appearance. Then he unlocked the passenger door and bundled her inside.

The warmth was a soothing balm to Lucy. She huddled down in the passenger seat, shivering, and with tears trickling down her face.

Richard slid back into the driving seat and turned to face her. 'Now, what's going on?'

'Not here, Richard,' she snuffled. 'Drive down the road, away from Maggie's place.'

His jaw jutted angrily, but he complied with her request. He drove to the end of the road, turned up a side street and stopped. 'Come on then, tell me what all this is about.'

His face was dark with fury by the time she had finished.

'What the hell did you think you were doing, blabbing the whole thing to Maggie Mayer?' he asked angrily. 'All you had to do was say you were leaving. There was no need to tell her where you were going, or to involve me in any way.'

'You don't understand, Richard. It wasn't as easy as that. Maggie wouldn't let me walk out. She'd helped me so much, bought me clothes, and provided me with a home, so she felt she owned me almost.'

Richard frowned, but made no further comment. 'What are you going to do now?' he asked. 'Do you want me to drive you somewhere?'

'You said you were finding me somewhere to live,' she reminded him.

'Well, yes, but I haven't done anything about it . . . not yet. It was more an idea for the future than a definite plan.'

'What!' Lucy's face blanched, and her tears started again. 'I thought you already had somewhere. I've nowhere else I can go,' she sobbed.

'Hell!' He looked uncomfortable. 'Nowhere at all? Haven't you any friends? What about that cousin of yours, Selina?'

'She's a friend of Maggie's so she's not likely to take me in. Anyway, my uncle said I was never to go back to their place again.'

Richard pulled out his cigarette case and

selected one. 'Give me a minute to think,' he said irritably, lighting it and inhaling deeply.

'Couldn't I stay at your flat for a few days?' Lucy asked tentatively.

'Heavens, no! That's quite out of the question,' he scowled. He stubbed out his cigarette. 'I think I have the answer but I'll have to make a telephone call first.'

They drove to Exchange station, and Lucy waited apprehensively as Richard went to find a telephone. She couldn't stop shivering, not with the cold, but with anxiety. From the car she watched him make the call. He looked anxious, then he was talking animatedly and the expression on his face changed.

He was whistling as he came back to the car. 'That's fixed then. A furnished bedsitter in Rodney Street, right in the city centre, which will be perfect for you.'

'Isn't that where all the specialists and surgeons have their consulting rooms?'

'That's right. There's a caretaker on the premises, and he has a key so we'll go straight there and get you settled in.'

Lucy didn't know whether to feel elated or not, but it was comforting to know she wouldn't have to spend the night on the streets. She'd started to think that she might have to ask the police to find her somewhere to sleep, like she'd had to do when Brenda's mother had refused to let her stay with them.

Rodney Street did sound rather grand. And a bedsitter of her own was something she'd been dreaming about ever since she'd left Belgrave Road. Even so, she felt a little bit nervous about living completely alone.

She shot a sideways glance at Richard, wondering if she dare tell him of her qualms, but he looked so grim as he concentrated on driving through the city traffic that she kept quiet.

The imposing four-storey houses in Rodney Street looked very austere as they drew up outside. Because it was evening, most of them were in darkness, and the brass name-plates on each door shone eerily in the street lighting.

Richard cruised slowly down the street, peering at the numbers. 'Here we are.' He braked so sharply that Lucy almost hit the dashboard. 'Out you get then. Bring your belongings with you. This way.'

He hurried her towards one of the houses, and then propelled her down a flight of steps to the basement. There were two doors and he rang the bell above the one marked 'Caretaker' and stood tapping his foot impatiently until it was answered.

Lucy caught a glimpse of a wizened old man who handed Richard a key. Then the door slammed, and Richard was fumbling to put the key in the lock of the other door.

It was like entering a dark tunnel; the only light came from the street lamps outside. Richard struck a match and blundered forward to light the gas mantle fixed on the wall of the passageway. It took several moments before it flared up enough to cast a dim yellow light on their surroundings.

Ahead of them was a half-open door leading into a room. Richard pushed it wide open and struck another match to locate the gas lamp, and they waited for that one to splutter into life so that they could look round.

The room was of medium size, smelled musty, and appeared to be very dingy with drab wall-paper and dark curtains. There was only one small window, and that looked out on to a brick wall.

A single bed was pushed up against one wall and a narrow table and two chairs stood facing it. At the far end was a curtained-off doorway that led down a step into a tiny scullery with a brown stone sink and a cupboard for storing food. A door opened out on to a paved area, and facing it was a small brick lavatory.

'Well. This looks quite good, doesn't it,' Richard enthused, his normal good humour restored. 'Everything you need. Look, there's even a kettle on the gas stove!' He pulled her close and kissed her on the mouth, then looked at his gold wristwatch. 'I won't be able to stay very long as I have an important meeting I must attend.' He patted her shoulder. 'Don't worry, though, I'll pop along some time tomorrow, and make sure everything is all right.'

Lucy pulled away from his embrace. 'What do I do about food?'

He frowned. 'Haven't you any money to get some?'

She shook her head. 'Maggie never paid us. She provided our meals and bought all our clothes.'

'Good God! I had no idea.' He fumbled in his trouser pocket and pulled out a handful of change and thrust it towards her. 'Here, this should be enough to buy whatever you need for tonight. I'll sort everything out tomorrow.'

The next minute he was gone. Lucy sat down on the narrow bed and looked around her in utter despair. This was worse than anything she'd ever known, worse even than the Flanagans' place in Anfield Road.

She thought of all the wonderful plans Richard had talked over with her. When he'd said he would find her a job, and somewhere to live, she'd thought he was taking her to a proper flat. Somewhere warm and cosy that she could turn into a love nest for them both.

What had she done! This place was little more than a hovel. If she could think of anywhere else to go she'd leave right now, she told herself. Only there was nowhere else for her to go so she'd have to make the best of it.

Pulling herself together she went out into the scullery to make herself a cup of tea. She filled the kettle, put it on the gas ring, and then realised she needed a match to light the gas. She searched in the cupboards and drawers but couldn't find a box of matches anywhere. All she found was a piece of mouldy cheese, and a hunk of stale bread. There wasn't even a packet of tea so she couldn't make a drink even if she found some matches.

She counted out the money Richard had given her. There was enough to buy bread, tea and milk, but it was now so dark outside that she felt too scared to go out. The shops would probably be closed by now anyway. It meant going to bed hungry, but she felt so depressed that it didn't seem to matter.

Lucy went over to the bed and pulled back the top cover. A bedbug scuttled from under the soiled pillow and disappeared down the side. She pulled the bed away from the wall to try and catch it, only to discover a mass of rubbish and a network of spiders' webs.

She dragged the bed into the middle of the room and as she stripped off the musty sheets, so that she could remake it, the room was suddenly plunged into darkness. She felt paralysed with fear. She knew there was a shilling amongst the money Richard had given her, but she had no idea where the gas meter was.

She tried to pluck up courage to go outside and ring the caretaker's bell, but by the time she'd groped her way as far as the door her nerve had gone. He'd looked so wizened that she'd felt frightened of him even when Richard was there, so how could she face him on her own?

Fully clothed, she lay down on the bed and curled into a ball, but she couldn't sleep, she needed to use the lavatory.

She groped her way back into the scullery. The key in the door leading out into the yard was difficult to turn, but she finally managed it. Easing the door open she looked outside. Fear of the unknown raised goose bumps on her arms and made her tremble. Dark shadows almost obscured the little brick building, but her need was so great that she nervously ran across the strip of yard.

The smell from inside, when she pushed open the door, was so vile that she gagged, but it was too dark to discover the cause. Afraid to sit down, she crouched over the gaping hole. A scuttling sound sent her pulses racing. She froze as something warm and furry crossed her foot. She sensed it sniffing at her legs, and she retched as bitter bile rose in her throat.

Panic-stricken, she dived for the safety of the scullery. She plunged into the gloom, slamming the door behind her. The horrifying thought that she had left it wide open when she went across to the lavatory, and that a rat or something could have come in from outside, flashed through her mind.

She curled up on the bed, straining her ears, and trembling at the slightest sound. She felt cold and hungry and desperately unhappy. She went over and over in her mind all the plans Richard had shared with her, and the dreams she'd built up.

Away from Maggie's place he seemed to be almost a stranger. The disparaging way he'd looked at her, and his unconcealed disgust about the way she was dressed, had been unnerving.

Tears of self-pity streamed down her cheeks as she contemplated her future. At that moment she would have given anything to be safely back in Belgrave Road. She should have listened to Stanley and accepted his offer, but it was too late for that now. She should never have handed back her keys. She could at least have taken refuge there while he was in prison, until she had somewhere else to go.

She lay for what seemed to be hours in the darkness, her heart racing as she went over and over her many problems, such a jumble of troubled thoughts raging through her brain she feared her head would burst.

Finally she fell asleep from sheer exhaustion.

Chapter Twenty-Five

The bedsitter in Rodney Street seemed even grimmer by daylight. Lucy found it hard to believe that such squalor lay behind the neatly painted black door, or that eminent surgeons and specialists had their consulting rooms on the floors above.

It was a grey overcast day, but she was so hungry that she forced herself to put a comb through her hair and venture out in search of food. The raw wind coming off the Mersey blew straight through her thin blouse and skirt, and she wrapped her arms round herself to try and keep warm as she hurried along the streets.

Lucy bought only the bare necessities of bread, tea, milk, margarine, sausages and a box of matches. She carefully sorted out the shillings from her change, and put them aside for the gas meter, determined that she'd never again end up in darkness like she had the previous night.

She counted up the little that was left to see if there was enough to buy soap, a cheap bottle of disinfectant and a scrubbing brush, but she was a few coppers short so reluctantly she left the disinfectant on the shelf.

By the time she'd found out where the gas meter was located, fed some of the shillings into it, boiled the kettle, and cooked two of the sausages she was ravenous.

The food restored her energy, and as she drank her third cup of tea she began planning how she could make the room more clean and comfortable.

It took her the rest of the morning. She stripped the grubby sheets off the bed, washed them, wrung them out as much as she could, and then hung them out in the small back yard hoping they would dry.

She saved the soapy water to wipe down the paintwork, the insides of the kitchen cupboards, scrub the floor, and to scour every inch of the lavatory after she had cleared out all the old rubbish that was stored there. She piled that up in the far corner of the small yard as tidily as possible.

Richard didn't put in an appearance until after six o'clock that evening. She was sitting in the dark, afraid to put the gaslight on because she had no more money for the meter.

'I thought you were out on the town when there was no light on,' he commented. 'Don't you know how to light the gas mantle?'

'I know how to light it, but I can't afford to waste it,' she told him tartly. 'The meter gobbles up money.'

'Surely I left you enough last night to last you for days?'

'I used that to buy some food, and a scrubbing brush. The place was absolutely filthy. I've spent all day cleaning it.'

He looked put out. 'You don't sound very

286

pleased with the arrangement,' he said in a disgruntled voice.

'I'll get used to it. It will be better when I have a job, and can afford to make it more comfortable. I'll have to buy some clothes first, of course, since I've only got what I stand up in because Maggie wouldn't let me bring away any of the things she'd bought me.'

'Yes, I thought about that. I've brought you some things from the store,' Richard told her. 'They're out in my car, I'll bring them in before I leave.'

'What about the job you promised me? You said you could get me taken on as a telephonist at Bunney's, remember.'

He frowned. 'It's not a very good idea. You'll have to try somewhere else.'

'Please, Richard! It's important. I need a job, so if you can get me one at your store then why not?'

'Because it wouldn't be a good idea for you to be working at the same place as I do. It might start unpleasant rumours.'

'It needn't! We need never talk to each other . . .'

'I said *no*, Lucy, and that's final!'

He moved towards her, taking her in his arms, his mouth hot against her cool skin. She tried to respond, knowing it was expected of her, but her entire body ached after her strenuous bout of cleaning.

Richard was quick to notice that she was not receptive, and because he felt affronted he treated her with unaccustomed roughness. He made love

287

savagely with complete disregard for her feelings, leaving her bruised and disillusioned.

Once again he made the excuse that he had a meeting to attend so he couldn't stay. 'Slip your coat on, and come out to the car and collect the parcel of things I've brought for you,' he said as he prepared to leave.

'I haven't got a coat,' Lucy snapped. 'Have you forgotten? I've only got the clothes I stand up in, so can you bring the parcel in for me?'

Richard stared at her in disbelief. 'Please yourself,' he said impatiently, then shrugged and walked towards the door.

Lucy felt engulfed in despair, not sure if he was going to come back. She knew she ought to go after him, and apologise for being so snappy, but she couldn't bring herself to do so. Yet if she didn't, and he never came back again, how would she manage? She had no money left to buy any food, and only a few coins which she knew she must keep for the gas meter.

She felt weak with relief when she heard his footsteps returning, and so grateful when he handed her the brown paper parcel that she flung her arms round his neck.

He held her briefly, then pushed her away. Pulling out his wallet he extracted three pound notes, and tossed them down on the rumpled bed. 'That should keep you in food and gas for a while,' he said abruptly. 'I may not be able to call in every day.'

Lucy stared at him in dismay. 'Don't say that, Richard,' she protested. 'I'm so frightened being here on my own. Please try and come,' she pleaded, gritting her teeth.

'We're not joined at the hip, you know,' he said sardonically.

Lucy felt crushed. 'I thought this was what you wanted? For us to have somewhere where we could be together.'

He shrugged. 'I do have a life of my own!'

'You came to see me nearly every night when I was at Maggie's,' she reminded him.

He smiled with deliberate indifference. 'That was then, this is now.'

'What do you mean by that?'

'You work it out, I must go!'

He left abruptly without even kissing her goodbye. It was as if he couldn't get out of the basement room quickly enough.

After he'd left, Lucy sat for a long time with her head in her hands wondering what was happening to her. Was it her fault she was in this terrible situation? Things seemed to have gone in a downward spiral ever since her mother died. If only she hadn't promised that she would leave Stanley Jones's house and go and live with the Flanagans.

There were so many 'if only' regrets, she thought miserably. She'd tried so hard to make her own way, and stand on her own feet, but events turned all her efforts to dust. Every time she tried to rise up in the world, better herself in any way, she seemed to land face down in the mud.

The cold dankness of the room penetrated her

thin clothing and forced her into action. As she moved she caught her leg against the brown paper parcel and her spirits lifted as she started to unwrap it, eager to see what Richard had brought her.

The contents dismayed her. Her indignation increased as she unwrapped an ugly brown tweed skirt that was far too big for her, a gaudy multi-striped jumper, a drab dark grey blouse, a clumpy pair of boots, and a black shawl like the one Aunt Flo had sometimes worn, only this one had a huge hole in it.

Lucy couldn't believe her eyes. Surely Richard didn't expect her to wear any of this? None of it was remotely suitable for someone of her age.

She studied the labels on them; they indicated that the items had come from his store, but she couldn't believe they'd ever been on sale there. Bunney's was one of Liverpool's top stores, and yet these things looked second-hand, as though he'd got them from a pawnbroker's bargain stall.

A piece of card dropped to the floor and she picked it up. It read 'Sale Rejects' and a moment's shame pulsed through her. They had come from his store all right. They were rejects! Sale items that hadn't sold because they were so horrible, or because they were damaged. Her anger flared. How could he do this to her? She couldn't even go after a factory job dressed in these.

She hunched up on the bed, the black shawl wrapped round her shoulders for warmth, while she tried to reason out what to do. The money he'd given her wasn't very much, but it might buy her something decent to wear as long as she didn't eat, or use any gas for heating or cooking. So much depended on how long it was before Richard came again.

She hated to feel obliged to him for money. It was worse than being expected to hand over her pay packet unopened and receive a few shillings pocket money.

Once she had a job, and was independent, things would be different, she told herself. The next time Richard called, if he was in a better mood, she'd remind him of his promise to get her a job. The sooner she was earning her own money the better.

She slept fitfully and awoke feeling queasy. She boiled the kettle, fried the remaining two sausages, and scraped margarine on to the one remaining piece of bread. Before she could take a mouthful she was violently sick.

The upset passed quite quickly, and by midday she felt well enough to go out. It was quite mild, and there was a faint glimmer of weak sunshine, so she felt warm enough with the striped jumper on underneath her own blouse.

Lucy wondered if it would be any good going over to New Brighton to ask Brenda if she would lend her some warm clothes. Remembering how Mrs Green had reacted last time, however, she decided it might only be wasting her precious money to do so.

She wandered round the city centre, looking in the shop windows and planning what clothes she would buy once she was earning and had some money. As it began to get dark she bought some bread and milk, and hurried back to her room in Rodney Street, hoping that perhaps Richard might come to see her after all.

The evening seemed endless with nothing to do and no one to talk to. She missed Babs and the other girls, and all their chatter and laughter as they sat around in the salon waiting for clients to arrive. She hadn't appreciated how lucky she was, she thought, her mind whirling with memories of all the warmth, good food and comfort Maggie had provided.

She was worse off than Frank and Stanley were in prison, she thought. She was completely isolated, but at least they saw other people at meal times, and the warders spoke to them. She had seen no one since she'd come back, and she hadn't even seen the caretaker since the night she'd moved in. She didn't even know his name.

The next morning she had another bout of sickness.

It was three days before Richard called again, and each morning she felt ill. On two occasions she retched so much that she needed to lie down afterwards. The strange thing was that by the middle of the day she felt quite all right again. She wondered if she ought to see a doctor, but knew she couldn't afford to do so.

When Richard eventually turned up she told him about her problem. 'I've only had the plainest of food, so it can't be anything I've eaten,' she said.

He looked at her strangely, his eyes narrowing.

'Are you trying to tell me something?'

'What do you mean?'

His face hardened. 'You're trying to trap me, Lucy, aren't you? Well, let me tell you it won't work.'

She shook her head, bewildered by his tone and his belligerent attitude.

'I don't know what you mean, Richard.'

'You're trying to make me think you're pregnant, aren't you?'

Stunned, Lucy gaped at him in silence.

'If you are then you'd better get rid of it, pretty damn quickly,' he went on harshly.

She stared at him wide-eyed, the colour draining away from her face. 'Oh no, don't say that!' she whispered horrified.

'Why? Does it ruin all your plans?'

'Please, Richard, don't talk like that.' She tried to put her arms round him, but he pushed her away.

'It won't work, Lucy. You'll get nothing out of me by trying to blackmail me.'

'Blackmail you? I don't know what you are talking about! If I am pregnant, then it must be your baby. I have never been with another man.'

His lips curled. 'Pull the other one!'

'That's the truth and you know it is,' she protested hotly. 'Maggie Mayer will back me up.'

'I bet she will! A nice little scam the two of you have pulled. You prove I'm the father of your little bastard, and then she can make me pay so that I'm not disgraced.'

'How can you be disgraced because we are

expecting a baby? You told me it was your ambition, to start a family once you had a nice house in the Wirral. Well,' she blushed shyly, 'this is your chance, isn't it?'

'Are you mad?' Anger made the veins on his forehead stand out. His dark eyes flared and his jaw jutted aggressively.

'It's what you told me,' Lucy repeated stubbornly. She was remembering the blissful session at Maggie Mayer's when after they'd made love they lay in each other's arms, and he had told her of his dreams and ambitions for the future. He'd said that one day, when he was in charge of Bunney's, he would have a house out in the Wirral, looking out over the sea, with a lovely garden, and that he wanted two or maybe even three children. It had all sounded so idyllic at the time, and she'd happily shared his dreams with him.

'I may have told you that, but you surely don't think I would marry a little trollop like you!' he told her scornfully. 'When I marry it will be to someone like Marguerite Bannerman, my boss's daughter. Someone of my own social standing, who can help me advance my career.'

Lucy stared at him appalled. Her dreams were crashing by the minute. All the plans and promises that he'd shared with her were for him alone. He'd never intended that she would remain in his life. Babs's warnings about not becoming emotionally involved with a client drummed inside her head. She'd been an utter idiot. She'd let Selina fool her, let Maggie treat her like a chattel, and let Richard use her body as though she was a whore.

'So what happens to me?'

'I've already told you. Get rid of it!'

She stared at him bewildered. 'How do I do that?'

'Here.' He reached for his wallet, took out a handful of notes and carefully counted them. 'Fifty pounds, that's a fortune to someone like you. Enough for an abortion and to find you somewhere else to live. I brought you some clothes the last time I came.'

Tears scalded her eyes as she heard the door slam behind him. How dare he insult her in this way? He'd brought her a bundle of old things that Bunney's hadn't even been able to get rid of in their sale, and now he was offering her money to get rid of their baby.

Chapter Twenty-Six

In sheer desperation Lucy resolved to go and see Selina since she knew no one else who could help her. She hated the idea of having to ask her, but since Richard had only rented the basement room until the end of December, and refused to pay out any more, she was so disheartened that she felt she had no alternative.

It had become much colder and in an attempt to keep warm she was wearing all the clothes she possessed, even the ugly tweed skirt that Richard had brought, on top of her own skirt. Despite all the layers, she still felt chilled to the bone.

She knew she looked ridiculous walking around in the middle of December wearing only a blouse and skirt, but she had no coat and she couldn't bring herself to use the black shawl. Becoming a shawlie really would have reduced her to the lowest form of life in Liverpool, she thought defiantly.

As she set out to walk to the H & Y Foods factory, the brightly decorated shops, full of people buying Christmas presents for their loved ones, brought back memories of the Christmases she had known in Belgrave Road when her mother had been alive.

Stanley Jones had enjoyed Christmas, and he'd

always doubled the housekeeping money so that her mother could buy extra food and decorations. For weeks beforehand her mother had been busy making the Christmas cake and puddings in readiness for the great day.

Even Stanley had stirred the pudding mixture, and made a secret wish. On Christmas Day he would sit at the head of the table and carve the big juicy chicken, with its savoury stuffing and slices of streaky bacon over the breast to keep it moist, that her mother had roasted. Served up with cranberry jelly, roast potatoes and roast parsnips, as well as an assortment of other vegetables, it was always a veritable feast.

They'd always left enough room for the Christmas pudding. Her mother would bring it into the dining-room, rich brown and with an appetising steam rising from it. Stanley would pour a tablespoonful of brandy over the top, light it and they'd watch with satisfaction as the blue flame flickered into life, flared up and then slowly died away. There was always a silver threepenny bit inside, and by some magical luck, Lucy recalled she'd always been the one to find it in her helping of pudding.

And there'd been presents, too. She and her mother exchanged gifts; things they each knew the other wanted. Their present to Stanley was usually a tie, cufflinks or, occasionally, a book they thought he would like. His presents to them were always generous, especially to her, Lucy recollected.

When she'd been small it had usually been a

toy or a doll, and always a book or annual of some kind. As she grew older he gave her more grown-up presents. The last Christmas she'd spent at Belgrave Road he had given her a beautiful brown leather handbag. It was one of the many items that had been missing when she'd opened up the sack containing her belongings after she'd been turned out of Anfield Road.

She arrived at the factory gates as the girls were all coming out. Emma spotted her and came rushing over to talk to her.

'What's up, what are you doing here?' she gasped, her eyes wide with surprise. 'I never expected to see you ever again. What are you doin' with yerself?' she gabbled excitedly. 'Where are you living? Selina said her old man chucked you out!'

'He did, that's why I've come to see Selina,' Lucy told her.

'Yer hoping to get your job back now she's the one in charge of us girls?' Emma giggled.

'Selina is in charge? I didn't know that!'

'Yeah, she and Jack Carter have made it up, and he put her in charge of our shift. We daren't say a word against him these days,' Emma laughed. 'For a time, though, after they'd split up, she didn't half have a cob on, and she slagged him off worse than any of us have ever done. Now they're back together again she's all over him.'

'Are there any jobs going?'

Emma shrugged. 'Don't think so. Have you tried shop work, they sometimes take on a few more people around Christmas time when they're extra busy.'

Lucy sighed. 'I've tried, but they all say they want someone with experience.'

Emma nodded. 'That's true. I must run or I'll miss my tram. Good luck, I hope Selina is able to wangle it for you.'

It was another half an hour before Selina came out of the factory. Lucy had almost given up waiting. Then she saw her cousin, the fur collar of her winter coat pulled up around her ears, coming through the gate and calling good-night to the night watchman.

'Selina.' Lucy caught her by the arm, afraid she was going to walk right past her.

'What do you want?' Selina's tone was sharp, her manner unfriendly.

'I need some help. I don't know who else to turn to.'

'Try Frank. He's out of prison, out of work and his life's a bloody mess, thanks to you!' Selina snapped.

'Frank's out! What ... what about Stanley Jones?'

'Your lover boy is still in the nick. He had a longer sentence than our kid, or have you forgotten?'

Lucy shivered. 'How could I ever forget? Never a day goes by that I don't remember that awful night.'

'So what you doing hanging around here then? You want to be careful, you might really get raped next time,' Selina said callously.

'I need help and you were the only person I could think to ask,' Lucy told her. 'I ... I'm pregnant.'

'Flippin' 'eck! You're what?' Selina's blue eyes widened in surprise. 'Well, you can't blame that on me,' she sniggered. 'Nor on our Frank,' she added, her eyes sweeping down over Lucy, 'he's been inside for too long.'

'It's Richard Thomas's,' Lucy said.

'Gerroff! You mean the feller who talked you into leaving Maggie's place?

Lucy nodded, tears welling up in her eyes.

'Then go and ask him for help. Maggie said he was loaded. Assistant manager at Bunney's, isn't he?'

Lucy bit down on her lower lip, too choked to answer. From Selina's attitude it was obvious she'd been wasting her time coming to see her, but she'd been the only person Lucy could think to turn to for help.

'I thought you told Maggie that he was setting you up in a flat and getting you a job as telephonist at Bunney's?' Selina went on when Lucy didn't answer.

'That's what he promised to do. Then he said it wasn't a good idea for me to work at the same place as he did.'

'He found you somewhere to live, though?'

Lucy shivered. 'Yes, a basement flat in Rodney Street. It's horrible. There's rats, cockroaches and bedbugs, and it's dank and smells horrible.'

'It's a roof over your head. Mistresses can't be choosers,' Selina jibed.

'You probably know all about that,' Lucy flared, goaded by her cousin's attitude. 'I've heard you've made it up with Jack Carter.'

'Oh, you have, have you? I suppose you thought I could get you your job back. Well, nothing doing. You ruined our relationship once so I'm not going to risk it happening again.'

'I'm not looking for a job,' Lucy said quickly.

'Gerroff!' Selina looked sceptical. 'What do you want then?'

Lucy chewed on her lower lip uneasily. 'I want to know how to get an abortion.'

Selina looked taken aback. 'You're living in Rodney Street. There are plenty of doctors and surgeons who do that sort of thing right on your doorstep, or right above your room,' she smirked. 'Ask one of them. It will cost a packet, but I'm sure Richard Thomas will pay rather than lose his good name, especially now that he's announced his engagement.'

Lucy frowned. 'What are you talking about?'

'He hasn't told you? Haven't you seen it splashed all across the *Echo*? He's engaged to Marguerite Bannerman. She's the daughter of the chairman of Bunney's.'

'I didn't know. I can't afford a newspaper,' Lucy said dully.

'Finished with you, has he? Can't say I blame him,' she sneered. 'You've let yourself go. You look a right Murry-Ann in that get-up!'

'So would you if you had nothing decent to wear,' Lucy said bitterly. 'Did you know that Uncle Fred had taken all my things out of that sack, and stuffed it full of old straw and news-papers?'

Selina's mouth gaped. 'Oh, my God! I thought the old bugger was more flush than usual, he must have flogged them!'

'So now you know why I look a mess. I don't feel well, either. I'm sick all the time,' Lucy added.

'Well, you will be if you're preggers! You should've stayed at Maggie's place. She'd have seen you were OK if you got duffed up. It happens all the time with the girls, but she looks after them.'

'Then would she help me?' Lucy asked eagerly.

Selina looked doubtful. 'She could, but I don't know whether she will or not. She was bloody livid when you walked out on her and took one of her best clients with you.'

'I made a mistake. I know that now,' Lucy admitted.

'Seems to me that you're pretty good at making mistakes,' Selina said contemptuously.

'Would you come with me ... to see Maggie,' Lucy pleaded. 'I'm too scared to go on my own.'

Selina stared at her for several moments, as if silently debating what to do. Then she shook her head.

'Please, Selina!' Lucy begged.

She doubted if Maggie would speak to her if she went there on her own, but she'd seen the empathy between Selina and Maggie and was sure that if Selina asked her then Maggie would do whatever was necessary to help her.

Selina shook her head even more emphatically,

her long wavy hair bouncing on her shoulders. 'Lemme be, I don't want any part of it. You're on your own, Lucy. You'd better try somewhere else. As I said before, you're living in the right neck of the woods to find a quack who'll do it. Get Richard to pay; it's his fault you're in the club. Don't leave it too long, though, or you may find it's too late.'

'Please help me, Selina,' Lucy pleaded, brushing away the tears that were trickling down her cheeks. 'I don't know anyone else to ask.'

'God! You're a silly cow,' Selina said irritably.

Lucy said nothing, but stood shivering, biting down on her lower lip, and looking pleadingly at Selina.

As Selina started to move away she clutched at her arm. 'Why won't you help me, Selina?' she implored. 'What have I done to make you hate me so much?'

'Hate you?' Selina looked taken aback. 'What makes you think I hate you?'

'You've made it obvious from the first day I arrived at Anfield Road.'

Selina looked shamefaced. 'Gerroff! You imagined it!' she blustered.

'No, you made it clear,' Lucy told her. 'You accused me of leading Frank on, and of causing trouble between you and Jack Carter, yet you knew quite well it wasn't true. Why? You can't have been jealous of me!'

Selina laughed harshly. 'I hated your guts, kiddo.'

Lucy looked bemused. 'I don't understand? I wasn't a rival.'

'Of course you were, you daft bint! You're young, pretty, well spoken and you were smartly dressed,' Selina reminded her.

'And you hated me because of that?'

'I loathed your prim and prissy manner. The way you tried to be so nice to us all. You let my old man mouth off at you and still smiled sweetly at him.'

'I was scared stiff of him.' Lucy shivered. 'And I was scared of Frank.'

Selina snorted. 'Our Frank was besotted by you. He probably still is, silly bugger that he is.'

'And yet you still hate me?'

'Not really, not now. Look, I tell you what, I'll ask Maggie when I see her if she'll help you. Don't build your hopes up, though, not after the way you did the dirty on her. Maggie doesn't forgive or forget very easily.'

Lucy smiled in relief. 'Thanks! When will you let me know?' she asked as Selina started to walk away.

'Tomorrow morning. Meet me here before eight,' she said over her shoulder.

Lucy felt confused as she trudged back to the city centre. She wasn't too sure Selina would ask Maggie, and if she did it was quite possible that Maggie would refuse.

Tomorrow she'd know, but as a precaution, she resolved, she would study the brass plates outside the houses in Rodney Street, and see if she could find out which doctor to approach if Maggie wouldn't help. She knew an abortion was illegal, but she still had the fifty pounds Richard had given her to pay for it. She sighed. To her it was a small fortune, but would it be enough to make one of them break the law?

She paused as she reached Bunney's to stare at the brightly lit windows. There was a Christmas tree in the main one, decorated with cotton-wool snow and pretty baubles. Presents were piled up in fancy boxes underneath it. If the money Richard had given her wasn't enough then she'd march right in there and up to his office, and ask him for more, she thought rebelliously.

At that moment Richard himself came out of the store, and walked across the pavement to where his car was parked, its bodywork gleaming in the bright street lighting. Lucy hesitated, wondering whether she dare go and speak to him, or whether it might only make matters worse between them if she did.

Before she could decide what to do, a woman came out of the store and walked towards his car, and Lucy saw he was holding the passenger door open for her.

The woman was tall and slim with delicate features and swept-back blonde hair. She was elegantly dressed in a cream coat trimmed with a huge fur collar, and very high-heeled shoes that made her look both fashionable and fragile. Lucy knew instinctively that it was Marguerite Bannerman, the woman Richard had become engaged to.

Her voice, when she spoke to Richard, was clear and beautifully modulated, but she sounded supercilious, and the smile she gave him was almost regal.

Lucy walked on. She'd lost him, there was no doubt about that. She couldn't compete for his affections against a woman who looked so glamorous.

She trudged despondently back to her basement room in Rodney Street, feeling the whole world had turned against her. Her only hope was that Selina could persuade Maggie to arrange for an abortion, but she wasn't too optimistic.

There were only four days until Christmas, and she'd be spending that on her own. And once Christmas was over it was only a matter of a week before she'd be completely homeless.

Chapter Twenty-Seven

'Maggie refuses to help you, she doesn't even want to hear your name mentioned,' Selina told Lucy the next morning. She thrust a bundle at her. 'Here, you may as well have this, you look as though you can make use of it.'

'What is it?' Lucy undid the string and brown paper, then gasped in surprise. Inside was the grey tweed coat her mother used to wear when she went shopping.

'The woman who bought it asked for her money back because the moths have been at it,' Selina told her, 'so you may as well wear it.'

'Thank you!' Lucy struggled into it. Her mother had not been as tall as her so it barely reached her knees, but it was thick and warm so it would keep out the wind.

'I've got to go,' Selina told her abruptly. 'Nothing more I can do for you. Hope you make out OK. Stanley Jones should be out of prison in about a month, so then you can move back in with him.'

'I can't do that! I can't break my promise to my mother,' Lucy said stubbornly.

'Then it's the streets, or your friend Brenda Green! You don't have enough stamps on your card to go on the dole.'

Lucy shuddered. After their last encounter,

when Brenda's mother had refused even to give her a bed for the night, Lucy thought it highly unlikely that Brenda would help her.

'It's worth a try,' Selina told her. 'She was asking how you were when she came over to see Frank the day he got out.'

Lucy's heart lightened. Optimistically, she pulled her mother's old grey coat tighter round her, and battling her way against the howling wind set off for the pier head before her courage deserted her.

It was not yet nine in the morning, and the ferry boats were packed to capacity with workers coming over to Liverpool. Compared to her, even the shop girls and office workers were smart and well dressed. Lucy felt so bedraggled with her unwashed hair and mishmash of clothes that she almost turned round and walked away.

This is your last chance, Lucy Patterson, she told herself firmly. You've got to do something soon or, as Selina warned you, it will be too late to have an abortion, and you'll end up in the workhouse.

Once on the boat, huddled in the warmth of the inner deck, she managed to summon up some of her optimism.

Brenda can only say no, she told herself. I'm not asking her for money, only to tell me where I can get an abortion. I'm sure she knows all about things like that. She'll probably lecture me on what a fool I've been, but I can stand that as long as she tells me how to put things right again.

Everything in New Brighton was closed and silent, the pier deserted and barred. All the amusements, and most of the shops selling seaside gifts and rock, had closed up for the winter. The air of desolation was pierced every now and again by the shriek of a ship's siren, or the blast of a foghorn as tugboats guided a large boat or liner cautiously up the Mersey to dock at Liverpool.

Brenda might not even be out of bed yet, Lucy thought as she stood outside the pub, looking at the shuttered windows. She tried the door, but it was locked, and when she peered in through the frosted glass panel to see if there was anyone cleaning the floor, or polishing the tables, there wasn't even a light showing anywhere.

She turned away, fighting back tears of frustration, undecided whether to walk around for a bit and wait until there was some sign of life, or to get a bus to Seacombe and catch the next boat back to Liverpool.

She had used up almost all her money to come over, so it seemed madness to waste the journey. It was too cold to stand still, so she decided she would walk along the promenade while she thought about what to do.

The incoming tide was savage, lashing against Perch Rock and slapping against the shore. She leaned on the railings and stared down mesmerised as it churned the wide strip of water between Liverpool and New Brighton into a murky foam.

How easy it would be to solve all her problems by jumping into it. Soon the tide would be on the turn, so if she did it now her body would be carried out beyond the Bar and into the Irish Sea in a matter of minutes.

She pulled back, refusing to give in to the temptation, and began to walk back towards the pub. She mustn't give up hope, she told herself. There was still the possibility that Brenda would help her.

Back at the pub there was still no sign of activity, no lights, no cleaning in progress. The temptation to return to Rodney Street was strong, but some faint spark of hope still burned at the back of Lucy's mind.

I'll walk to the top of Victoria Road, up one side and down the other, she resolved. By that time there must be someone about.

She felt exhausted when she reached the top of the hill at the junction with Rowson Street. Turning, she began to make her way back down. Halfway she spotted a newsagents that was also a café opening for business. The proprietor was stacking a wire rack outside the door with papers.

Lucy paused to check on the remaining coppers in her purse, then went inside and ordered a pot of tea and an egg on toast. She'd left home so early in order to meet up with Selina before she went to work that she'd had nothing to eat, and she was so hungry that she finished it in no time at all.

She was pouring herself a second cup of tea when Brenda walked in. She was warmly dressed in a smart tweed skirt, green woollen pullover and over it a three-quarter-length beaver lamb coat. She was holding a copy of the *Liverpool Daily Post* that she'd taken from the rack outside. They gaped at each other in astonishment.

'What on earth are you doing here?' Brenda asked in astonishment.

'I could ask you the same thing.'

'I live here. I've just popped out for a newspaper.' She walked over to the counter and paid for it before joining Lucy at the little table where she was sitting.

'So? What are you really doing here?' she asked again. She undid her fur coat before pulling out a chair and sitting down.

'I . . . I was hoping to see you.'

Brenda bristled. 'You mean you were going to come to the pub? Flippin' heck, Lucy, you know how that would get me into trouble!'

'I was going to be discreet. I was hoping you might be in the pub helping with the cleaning or something.'

'We employ a woman to do that!'

'Yes, I know, but if I asked her to tell you I was outside I was sure you'd try and get away.'

'Possibly!' Brenda patted her red hair, and smoothed her green jumper down over her skirt. 'Anyway, what did you want to see me about that was so important? I can't find you work, you know what my mother said.'

'I know. I'm not looking for work, not at present, anyway. I do need some help though.'

Brenda's eyes raked over her as if seeing her

clearly for the first time. 'You hard up or something? You look like a bag of rags! You always used to look so smart, now you look a mess. What's happened to all your clothes?'

'It's a long story.'

Brenda stared at her for a moment. 'If we're going to sit here while you tell me about it then we'd better have a pot of tea.' She turned and signalled to the man who was stacking the shelves behind the counter.

Lucy waited until the fresh pot of tea and an extra cup arrived before beginning to tell Brenda why she was so desperate to see her.

Brenda's green eyes became wider and wider as Lucy related what had happened since she'd lost her job at the Cotton Exchange and her Uncle Fred had turned her out of Anfield Road.

'You didn't fit in, that was the trouble,' Brenda told her. 'You were so different from them. Selina hated you because you were all the things she wasn't.'

Lucy shook her head. 'Selina is stunning. Alongside her I felt like a drab little mouse.'

'Selina's flash and brash and she's always been a bit of a tart,' Brenda retorted.

'I suppose that was her excuse for diddling me out of the money she got for selling all my mother's clothes and some of my things, was it?' Lucy asked bitterly. 'My Uncle Fred was no better. He stole the rest of my things. That sack I had to leave behind the night he turned me out was full of straw and old newspapers when I came to open it.'

Brenda looked shocked. 'Didn't you do anything about it?'

Lucy shook her head. 'What could I do? When I told Selina she said he was flush for weeks on what he got for my stuff.'

'That's terrible!'

'Another thing, I'm pretty sure that Frank had something to do with my being attacked,' Lucy stated. 'For one thing, he knew Doug Baldwin. For another, what was Frank doing hanging round the Cotton Exchange at that time of night? It was almost as though he was there waiting to see what would happen.'

Brenda looked angry. 'Lucy! I'm sure it was no such thing. Anyway, what was Stanley Jones doing there?'

'Leaving off work, the same as I was. It was a good thing he was there.'

'What's happened is all in the past,' Brenda muttered, as if anxious to forget the whole matter.

'I lost my job at the Cotton Exchange because of all the bad publicity when I was attacked. The trouble is, I haven't managed to find another one,' Lucy stated.

'So what you been living on then?'

'This and that!' Lucy blushed furiously, then in a rush added, 'I had nowhere to live, and no job, so Selina introduced me to Maggie Mayer.' She stopped as she saw the look of incredulity in Brenda's eyes.

'Selina took you to Maggie Mayer's place? And you've been working there! You mean ... you mean you've become a prossy?'

Lucy bristled at her derisory tone, colour burning her cheeks. 'I'm not there any more,' she said quickly.

'Flippin' heck! You of all people working at Maggie Mayer's,' Brenda gasped. 'I can't believe it!'

Lucy bit down on her lower lip as she stirred her tea, too choked to go on.

'You may as well tell me the rest,' Brenda said. 'Come on, spill the beans.'

Haltingly Lucy told her the whole story. About how kind Maggie Mayer had been to her, giving her a room, buying her lovely clothes, and then introducing her to Richard Thomas. She wiped away her tears as she told Brenda all about the way Richard had promised her a flat and a job.

'And then dumped you in a basement flat in Rodney Street when Maggie turned you out?'

Lucy nodded. 'He even said I was trying to blackmail him when I told him I was pregnant,' she sniffed.

'So what are you going to do now?' Brenda asked.

'I don't know. If I have a baby I'll be in an even worse dilemma than the one I'm already in. I won't be able to work even if I could find a job, and I haven't enough stamps on my card to qualify for the dole so I'll be means tested if I apply for any sort of help. Either that or I'll have to go to the Salvation Army, or some other institution that helps the down-and-outs. I came over to see you, Brenda, because I thought you might be able to tell me how to go about getting an abortion.'

'Gerroff!' Brenda looked shocked. 'Your Aunt Flo won't like the sound of that, Lucy, if she ever gets to hear about it. Surely you know that abortion is considered to be a mortal sin by Catholics.'

'Maybe, but it would be even more wicked to bring an unwanted child into the world.'

'There must be some other way out of your trouble,' Brenda insisted.

'None that I can think of,' Lucy said huffily.

'The best thing you can do for the moment is to go and live back in Belgrave Road,' Brenda told her. 'I'm sure Stanley Jones won't mind.'

'I can't, I don't have a door key any longer,' Lucy reminded her.

'We can soon sort that one out,' Brenda said briskly. 'I'll see if I can persuade Frank to go and ask Stanley for his.'

Lucy shook her head. 'I don't think it would be right for me to live there even if he agreed. It would start too many rumours,' she said lamely. 'And I doubt if he would give Frank the key anyway.'

'Oh, blow what people think,' Brenda exploded. 'Look at the state of you,' she went on crossly. 'Here we are, it's almost Christmas, and you're looking like a tramp! In about ten days' time you'll be out on the street anyway, from what you've told me.'

Lucy sighed. 'I know. I'm sure, though, that if I

could get back on my feet, and manage to find a job, I could start again without having to involve Stanley Jones.' She blushed furiously, 'It means getting rid of the baby, of course.'

Brenda shook her head. 'I can't help you there,' she stated firmly. 'Anyway, wouldn't it be better to go through with having it, and then get it adopted? Probably be much safer than going to a back-street abortionist.'

'How am I going to live until then?'

'By staying in the Belgrave Road house, of course.'

'No!' Lucy said determinedly. 'I can't possibly do that, Brenda.'

'For God's sake, stop being so stupid and pigheaded. There's enough room in that house in Belgrave Road for the two of you to live completely separate lives if that's what you really want.'

'I made a promise to my mother, you know that!'

'Promises are made to be broken, and I'm damn sure that if your mother knew how you've ended up, and the trouble you're in, then she'd understand. In fact, she'd probably tell you that you should have gone back there to live a long time ago. If you had, then he and Frank would never have ended up in jail,' Brenda added tartly.

'Brenda!' For a moment Lucy felt resentful but she managed to overcome it.

'I'm the first to admit that the Flanagans have been pretty hard on you, Lucy, one way or

316

another,' Brenda went on. 'But I can't ask you stay with me, even though I'd like to, because my mother wouldn't stand for it.'

'So it's back to my basement in Rodney Street,' Lucy said, tears filling her eyes.

'Only for a few days until I get hold of Stanley's keys and then you can move back into Belgrave Road, at least until he comes out of prison. That will give you time to think about what you want to do.'

'If I don't know what I want to do now, how will a couple of weeks make any difference?' Lucy muttered.

Brenda shrugged. 'It's either that or go yourself and ask Maggie Mayer to help you.'

Lucy looked dubious. 'Selina said she wouldn't!'

'You don't know if Selina really asked her, so unless you go and see her yourself you'll never know whether she'll help you or not,' Brenda told her. 'They are friends, you know, and it was that cow Selina who introduced you to her in the first place, and got you into this mess.'

'She was trying to be kind,' Lucy defended.

'Don't kid yourself. I bet Selina got something out of it. Think about it,' she went on when she saw the shock on Lucy's face. 'You were young, pretty and attractive, exactly the sort of fresh face Maggie Mayer's punters would go for, and you were naive enough to fall for it. Selina would get a pay-off all right!'

Chapter Twenty-Eight

Lucy couldn't believe her eyes when she opened the door of her basement flat late on Christmas afternoon and found Brenda standing there.

When she'd first heard the shrill ping of the bell her heart raced, hoping against hope that it was Richard.

'What are you doing here, on Christmas Day?' she gasped.

'Happy Christmas to you, too,' Brenda grinned. She pulled the collar of her brown beaver lamb fur coat higher round her neck. 'Aren't you going to ask me in, or do I have to stand here and freeze to death?'

'Come on in.' Lucy pulled the door wider. 'You'd better keep your coat on,' she said quickly as Brenda was about to slip it off. 'There's only a gas fire and it doesn't give out much heat.'

She indicated for Brenda to sit down in the only armchair, wrapped the black shawl she'd been wearing before she went to answer the door around her shoulders again, and perched on the edge of the bed.

'Flippin' heck, this is grim!' Brenda commented as the drab surroundings registered.

'I did tell you! Would you like a cup of tea or some Camp coffee?'

Brenda pulled a face. 'If you've got any glasses we'll have some of this,' she grinned, pulling a half bottle of port out of her handbag.

Lucy shook her head. 'I haven't any glasses, only cups, I'm afraid.'

'They'll do! Any port in a storm,' Brenda quipped. 'I took it for Frank, but changed my mind about giving it to him,' she added by way of explanation, as she poured out a generous amount for each of them.

'You've been to Anfield Road to see Frank?'

'Yeah! I asked him to try to sort things out with Stanley about the keys to Belgrave Road, but he said now he's out of the Walton Waldorf Astoria wild horses wouldn't get him back there, not even as a visitor.'

'It's probably not meant to be,' Lucy muttered.

Brenda shrugged. 'I don't know about that. Anyway, I saw Selina, and she said she'd had another word with Maggie Mayer!' She held out the bottle of port towards Lucy. 'D'you want a top-up?' she asked.

Lucy bit down on her lower lip. 'Is it meant to console me because Maggie said she wouldn't help?'

'No, not at all. Maggie will help you, but there are certain conditions.'

Lucy stiffened. 'Go on. What are they?' she asked dully.

'Maggie will arrange an abortion, but you've

got to agree to go back there to work after it's over.'

There was a stunned silence. They avoided looking at each other as Brenda waited for Lucy to say something.

Brenda could stand it no longer. 'What you going to do then, Lucy?' she prompted.

Lucy looked deflated. 'I've no choice, have I?' she said sheepishly.

'Of course you have, luv!' Brenda exclaimed with some exasperation. 'You can do what Maggie wants, or you can go and stay at Stanley's place and carry on having the baby.'

'And how do I bring it up, and feed it, and clothe it? Do I teach it to beg at the pier head or to do juggling tricks at the Tivoli?' Lucy asked cynically.

'No need to get lippy with me,' Brenda snapped. 'I'm only trying to help you.'

Lucy covered her face with her hands. Her shoulders shook. 'I know,' she sobbed contritely.

Brenda put an arm around her shoulders. 'Don't take on so, Lucy. We'll sort something out. Why don't you take a couple of days to think things over? Maggie said she couldn't do anything until after Christmas.'

'I have to be out of here by the end of December!'

'That's a week away,' Brenda told her. 'Plenty of time to make up your mind about what you want to do.'

Lucy drained her cup; the port sent warmth radiating through her, and for a brief moment she even thought that perhaps her troubles were over.

'I've got to go,' Brenda told her, standing up and tightening her coat. 'My mum and dad weren't very happy about me going to see Frank, especially as it's Christmas Day and we've friends coming tonight for Christmas dinner. Look, I'll leave the rest of the port with you, there's still half the bottle left.'

Lucy felt her head was spinning as she let Brenda out of the door. She had never had port in her life before, but it had tasted so delicious, and warmed her up so much, that she had been unable to refuse when Brenda topped up her cup the second time. Now she felt as if the room was spinning, and all she wanted to do was lie down and sleep.

When she woke it was pitch dark, and she had no idea what time it was. How long she lay there in a semi-trance, thinking back over the past year, she had no idea.

She found it increasingly hard to believe that her life could have gone downhill so rapidly. She was grateful to Brenda for her help. But at what a price! She shivered at the very thought of working for Maggie Mayer again, knowing that this time it wouldn't be Richard, but absolutely anyone at all.

Thinking of Richard brought back all the old longing. They'd been so good together, she really had loved him, and she'd been so sure that he felt the same way about her.

When she'd lain in his arms, and he'd confided

in her about his career plans, and the wonderful house he intended buying in the Wirral, she really had thought that he was talking about her future as well as his own.

When she told him she was pregnant, she had expected him to be surprised, but pleasantly so, and to make a fuss of her, and make plans for their future together.

Instead, it had been the beginning of the end of their relationship. She didn't know which had saddened her the most, the terrible basement room he'd rented for her, or the bundle of ill-assorted clothes he'd brought her.

It had certainly made her realise exactly what he thought of her, and where she stood in his order of priorities, she thought bitterly.

Once the child she was carrying was aborted, that would sever her final link with Richard, so perhaps then she'd be able to put him out of her mind completely.

She tried to convince herself that her feelings for him were over. Next time she saw a picture of him and Marguerite Bannerman in the *Echo*, instead of her pulses racing she'd be able to turn the page without a tremor. When eventually their wedding photographs were plastered across the *Liverpool Post*, or *Liverpool Echo*, they'd have no more effect on her than if they were the photos of a stranger.

She forced herself upright, groping around trying to find the matches so that she could light the gas mantle.

Perhaps returning to Maggie Mayer's place, and working as a prostitute, was the right career for her, she thought, recklessly tipping the remains of the port into her cup. All her relations and friends had turned away from her so she couldn't sink much lower.

Perhaps she should have had the courage to climb over the railings on New Brighton promenade, and jumped into the murky, swirling waters. Would Richard, or anyone else, have missed her if she'd disappeared into the Mersey?

Would there have been headlines blazoned across the evening paper, or merely a three-line comment tucked away at the bottom of an inside page?

Aunt Flo might light a candle, and say a prayer for her, but no one else would care. Gone and forgotten by everyone, except perhaps Stanley.

Stanley was still in prison, she reminded herself, and they probably didn't get a chance to read the *Echo* in there so he might never know. When he came out he'd either think that she was avoiding him, or that she'd gone off and started a new life for herself. There would be no one to tell him any different. Not unless he bumped into Brenda, or Aunt Flo. And would they bother to tell him the details?

Her head ached with the strain of thinking about it. Depression gripped her like an iron clamp. Her life must surely have touched bottom by now, she told herself, so there was only one way for it to go, and that was up.

She'd let Maggie arrange an abortion, and afterwards stay and work for Maggie, but only because that was what she had to promise to do.

She wouldn't give up hope, though, and if ever she had an opportunity to better herself she'd remember what Brenda had said – promises were sometimes meant to be broken.

Chapter Twenty-Nine

December ended with gale-force winds, snow and rain. People huddled indoors unless they were absolutely forced to go out and face the elements.

The only person in the whole of Merseyside who didn't complain about the weather was Stanley Jones. Newly released from Walton Jail, he welcomed the sight of the winter landscape, and enjoyed the feel of the lashing rain and biting winds.

He hadn't realised what claustrophobia was until he found himself incarcerated in a cell along with three other men. He had hated every second of it. The stinking latrine in one corner of the cell, and the stench of other men's body odours, turned his stomach. The habits of his cellmates, and their coarse foul language, sickened him. The brutality of the screws unnerved him, and the petty regulations that governed his every action turned him from a reasonable law-abiding person into a man who spent every waking hour scheming how to dodge or dupe those in charge.

He'd ached for freedom, to see stars in the sky at night, and the sun and clouds by day. He'd longed to be back in his normal routine, sleeping in his own bed, enjoying the luxury of eating the food he wanted at his own dining table, and getting up in the morning, and going to bed at night, when he felt like doing so.

Even the prospect of crossing by ferry from Seacombe to Liverpool seemed like a holiday trip in comparison with the prison routine. He hadn't realised what a pleasure it could be to walk round on the top deck, and feel the wind on his face, to watch the gulls veering overhead, and to listen to the klaxons and hooters from the shipping on the Mersey.

He'd missed the daily thrill of seeing a magnificent passenger liner berthed at Liverpool pier head. Or seeing a huge ship, that had been waiting out at the Bar, being towed upstream by fussy little tugboats so that it could dock and let its passengers disembark or unload its cargo.

Not being able to smoke, drink, gamble or chase women was no hardship to Stanley, because he'd never indulged in such pursuits. It did offend him, however, to hear his cellmates continually talking about these things. Especially when they spoke about women in vulgar or derogatory terms. It repelled him when he had to listen to them detailing what they wanted from a woman, or describing how they treated their girlfriend or wife.

Frequently they ridiculed him because he refused to take part in their discussions, calling him a nancy, or asking him if he was 'one of them sort', names he found offensive. Most of the time he ignored them, listening in silence, trying to disregard both their innuendoes and their personal anecdotes.

When they passed round grubby thumb-marked snaps of their women he made no comment, nor did he reciprocate. He had no pictures of Lucy, nor did he need any. Her sweet gamine face was etched permanently on his mind.

He thought about her constantly. Lying in his narrow bunk bed, unable to sleep because of the snores and grunts going on all around him, he would relive the halcyon days from when he had first known her, when she was a mere child, and he'd been able to guide her and teach her things. Now she was a grown woman with a mind of her own.

It had broken his heart when she'd insisted on leaving Belgrave Road. He knew it was because of a promise made to her mother, but Mrs Patterson had been dying at the time, and he was sure she'd not been in full control of all her faculties. If she had been could she possibly have made Lucy make such a promise? She must have known how much he cared for Lucy, known he would never harm her in any way. On the contrary, he would have done everything in his power to make her happy.

He'd been dismayed when he learned she was working in a factory, and even more shocked when he'd visited the Flanagans' house in Anfield Road. The cramped conditions there must have filled her with the same feeling of claustrophobia as he was experiencing in prison. The rough, uncouth ways of the Flanagans were on a par with those of his cellmates.

It had given him tremendous pleasure to be

327

able to use his influence to arrange a job for her at the Cotton Exchange. Although they were in completely different parts of the building he'd felt that he was keeping an eye on her, ensuring that she was safe.

Sometimes he wished she would come to visit him, on other days he prayed she wouldn't. He would have felt it was so degrading for her to see him in prison garb, and in such dire surroundings.

Yet to be able to see her with his own eyes would have reassured him that she was all right, and that she had not suffered any ill effects after Doug Baldwin's attack on her.

Whenever Brenda Green came in to see Frank Flanagan he begged him to ask her how Lucy was, but apart from learning that she'd lost her job at the Cotton Exchange, because of what had happened, there had never been any other news. Frank told him that Brenda never saw Lucy, they'd lost touch, and that Brenda didn't want to talk about her because she blamed Lucy for them both being in prison.

Frank didn't hold with this premise any more than he did. Lucy was being attacked, she'd needed help, and rushing to help her had only been what any man would do in such circumstances. The fact that he knew Doug Baldwin was pure coincidence, Frank maintained.

The two men had talked about it a number of times since they'd been in jail and agreed they'd done the right thing. They came from such different backgrounds that they had very little in common and yet, because of this link, they tolerated each other, and occasionally even sought each other's company.

When they did it was usually because Stanley was asking after Lucy. And, inevitably, their talk turned to the episode that had brought them both to Walton.

'It was a sheer fluke that the blow you aimed at Doug Baldwin was the one that floored him,' Frank would comment. 'After all, the bugger was twice your size, and he'd been in that many fights he knew bloody well how to take care of himself. If he had fallen differently, not caught his head against anything, then he'd probably be alive today,' Frank would insist.

'Given it was my punch then you should never have been locked up as well,' Stanley would add, his voice full of regret.

'Try telling the judge that!'

'I did when we were in court, but no one would listen,' Stanley would remind him.

'Yer right! As far as they were concerned it was a drunken brawl over a judy and we were both involved.'

Stanley hated it when Frank spoke about Lucy like that. A judy, indeed! She had been so protected all her life that she was as pure as a babe in arms!

If only her mother hadn't extracted that foolish promise from her none of this would have happened, he thought angrily. She would have gone on living at his house in Belgrave Road, probably even working at the Cotton Exchange.

If later on, when she was a few years older, she had decided she would marry him then that would have made him blissfully happy. He would never have pressurised her, though, he loved her too deeply for that. Lucy's welfare and happiness were all that mattered to him, and always would be.

As a result of his exemplary behaviour, Stanley was released from prison several weeks earlier than he had expected and he felt it was a wonderful start for the new year.

He was shocked by how utterly desolate the house in Belgrave Road seemed to be when he arrived home. It was the first time the front door had been opened for months, and there was a pile of bills and letters on the mat. He collected them up, then went round opening the windows, letting the icy winds rip through, stirring the dust and sweetening the air. When he had done that, he sorted the letters, circulars and bills into separate piles.

He stood for a minute holding the typed envelope with the Cotton Exchange address stamped on the outside, turning it over and over in his hands, almost afraid to open it. He knew they'd sacked Lucy, and since he'd received no communication whatsoever from his boss, or anyone else for that matter, while he'd been in Walton, he was afraid this might be his dismissal notice.

'If it is then I must accept it,' he muttered aloud as he slit the envelope.

The typed words danced in front of his eyes in a

crazy fashion. He sat down, took a deep breath and concentrated. His eyes were moist with relief when he'd finished reading it. They weren't sacking him. His job was still there for him. They'd been informed of the date of his release, and were inviting him to start back at work the following Monday.

Life took on a new meaning. It had purpose. In a few days' time he'd be back into his normal routine. He was suddenly full of energy. He must make sure he had clean shirts, press his suit, shop for food, clean the house; most important of all, he must find out if Lucy was all right.

As he began to organise himself and his surroundings, he tried to think of the best way to find out about Lucy. He knew it was no good going to the Flanagans' house in Liverpool, because Frank had told him during their first week in jail that his father had thrown Lucy out and warned her never to come back.

The only person Stanley could think of asking was Brenda Green. He'd have to do it diplomatically. He'd drop in at the pub for a drink, and ask her quite casually if she knew where he could find Lucy.

Like most carefully laid plans it didn't happen as smoothly as Stanley had intended. Brenda served him, but she seemed neither surprised nor pleased to see him.

Stanley took a sip of his beer. 'I was hoping to see you, Brenda, to ask if you'd seen Lucy or if either you or Frank had any news of her. She's not living in Anfield Road, or so Frank said.'

331

'Frank's old man kicked her out and now Frank's cleared off to America,' Brenda told him curtly. 'Went without a word to me even though I've stuck by him all the time he's been in prison,' she said bitterly.

Stanley looked taken aback. 'I'm sorry to hear that. Have you any idea why?'

He took a long drink of his beer, almost afraid of what Brenda might say next. He knew Frank was besotted by Lucy, because he'd told him often enough when they'd both been inside, so supposing he'd run off with her?

'I don't know why Frank's gone to America, but I know exactly where Lucy is, and how she is. She's up the duff!'

Stanley looked shocked. 'Do you mean Lucy is pregnant?'

'She's not the innocent little thing you've always thought her to be, you know,' Brenda told him smugly as she saw the concern on Stanley's face.

Stanley looked angry but he said nothing.

'She lost her job at the Cotton Exchange after you were sent to jail, but I suppose you know that because I told Frank to tell you?' Brenda said as she turned away to serve another customer.

Stanley stayed at the bar, his fists clenched, waiting for her to come back and tell him more.

'Couldn't you have helped her? Couldn't she have stayed here? Worked here even?'

Brenda pursed her mouth. 'Not up to me, was it? My mum and dad told me I was to stop seeing her. They wouldn't have Lucy anywhere near, said it would give the place a bad name.'

Stanley was becoming more and more agitated. His spectacles became misted, and beads of sweat glistened on his smooth white forehead.

'So what is she doing now?'

'She asked Selina to help her, and Selina introduced her to a friend who gave her a job and a room to stay in.'

'Thank God for that!' Stanley mopped his brow in relief. 'And is she still there?'

'Funny thing is, she is still there. She's just returned after a month or so away.'

'She's been away on holiday?'

Brenda shook her head and giggled. 'Not exactly a holiday. She's certainly glad to be back again with Maggie Mayer, though, I can tell you.'

'Maggie Mayer!' Stanley looked aghast. 'Did you say Maggie Mayer?'

'That's right.' Brenda's carefully plucked eyebrows lifted questioningly. 'D'you know her then? I wouldn't have thought she was your type, Stanley.'

'If it's the Maggie Mayer I think you mean then of course I know of her! Everyone in Liverpool, in the whole of Merseyside, in fact, knows all about Maggie Mayer. You're not telling me that Lucy is at her place?'

'I'm afraid so! She went there almost as soon as you went into jail. She was one of Maggie's star attractions, apparently. She kept her exclusively for a very special customer. Then the pair of them did the dirty on Maggie. Lucy scarpered because he promised to set her up in a nice little love nest, find her a cushy little job, and keep her as his bit on the side.'

Stanley's face contorted. 'What happened?' he croaked.

'Let me see to the customer who's waiting and then I'll tell you the rest.'

Once again Stanley was left fuming with impatience while Brenda went to the other end of the bar to serve beer.

'Now where was I?' Brenda prevaricated when she came back. 'Oh, I remember, I was telling you about Lucy leaving Maggie Mayer's place. Well, it didn't work out too well, I gather. This chap found her somewhere to live, but it was a basement bedsit in Rodney Street. Filthy dirty and full of rats, bedbugs, and cockroaches. You name it and it was there. The job he'd promised her never came to anything, and she had no decent clothes so she couldn't go looking for work. She was more or less his prisoner, and then when she told him she was pregnant, that was that.'

'You mean she went back to Maggie's place?'

'Not right away. She came over here to see if I could help her. She wanted an abortion, but of course I don't know anyone who does things like that,' Brenda said piously. 'I did suggest to Lucy that she should stay at your place . . .'

'Why on earth didn't she do that! Lucy needn't even have asked, she could have gone there anyway.'

'She didn't have a key, did she? I tried to see you in prison when I was visiting Frank, but they refused to let me even speak to you. Didn't Frank tell you?'

Stanley shook his head. 'And now she's back at Maggie Mayer's?' he murmured sadly.

'Well, the only thing I could think of doing to help her, was to tell Selina, and ask her to persuade Maggie to help Lucy with an abortion.'

'And she agreed?'

'Eventually, but there were certain conditions though. Lucy had to promise that after it was all over she'd stay and work for Maggie. She won't be a "special" any more, of course! Maggie doesn't make the same mistake twice. She probably wouldn't have taken Lucy back, but she is so young and pretty that Maggie knows she's got plenty of customers who will still fancy her.'

Stanley looked taken aback. 'She can't do that,' he stormed. 'That's no sort of life for Lucy!'

'I don't reckon she's got much choice,' Brenda told him bluntly. 'She either settles for Maggie's terms or there's no abortion.'

'So she hasn't had the abortion yet?' Stanley latched on to this piece of news like a drowning man clinging to a piece of flotsam.

Brenda shrugged. 'I don't think so. What with all the Christmas and New Year celebrations, Maggie's had too much on her plate to get it organised. It'll have to be soon, though, or Lucy will have left it too late.'

Chapter Thirty

Maggie Mayer allowed Lucy to move back in the day she had to leave the bedsit in Rodney Street, and told her she'd make all the necessary arrangements for her to have an abortion.

Lucy didn't know which she dreaded most, the idea of having an abortion or the knowledge that once it was over she would be working for Maggie Mayer again.

'This time,' Maggie warned her, 'it will be a very different set-up. There'll be no special privileges like before. You'll be on the general rota, which means I expect you to be available seven nights a week for any man who wants you.'

The idea of killing the baby that could have been hers and Richard's broke Lucy's heart, but she couldn't see any alternative. She had nowhere to live and no job so she had no means of supporting the child after it was born.

Her entire life, Lucy reflected, seemed doomed from the moment her mother died. In some ways she knew she was responsible for much of what had happened. She'd been weak and far too trusting, and she blamed that on the sheltered life she'd led.

After this, once she could get away from Maggie's clutches, she'd make sure she was never taken in by anyone ever again. Starting a decent life for herself wouldn't be easy, but she was determined to try.

The other girls at Maggie's place were surprised to see her again, and amused by what had happened to her. Some of them even went as far as to say she deserved everything that had come her way because she thought herself better than they were. They hinted at dark doings and abortions that had gone wrong, and nodded knowingly to each other about what she would have to endure. Lucy was more confused and worried than ever.

'Old Jinny Jenkins is doing it so you're in for a right treat,' Dora, one of the older girls, told her. 'She's a right old bag! Scruffy, dirty and as rough as any horse whacker. She'll take no notice of your screams, so you might as well clench your teeth and let her get on with it.'

'What do you mean?' Lucy asked fearfully. 'What will she do to me?'

Dora shrugged. 'You'll find out soon enough. Don't want to spoil all your fun, do we, girls?'

'Expect the worst and you might be pleasantly surprised,' one of the others sniggered.

'You'll feel as if you've been kicked in the guts for a few days afterwards,' another cautioned.

'It's very risky leaving it as late as this,' Dora warned her. 'Don't be surprised if you hear it yelping like a puppy.'

Their talk frightened and sickened Lucy. Now that her body had accepted the foetus growing inside her, and she no longer felt sick and queasy each morning, she spent more and more time thinking about the baby as a real little person. The desire to get rid of it diminished a little more each day.

Bringing an unwanted child into the world might be a sin, but she was now not at all sure that this was an unwanted child. It would have been wonderful to have someone of her own to love and care for, someone who would love her unconditionally in return.

Perhaps this was her punishment, she thought sadly. The memory of this baby she was about to sacrifice would be with her always, and she would feel guilty about what she was doing for the rest of her life.

As soon as the New Year celebrations were over, Maggie wasted no more time. First and foremost she was a businesswoman, and keeping a girl who was not working and making her money went against the grain, so arranging Lucy's abortion was top of her agenda.

'Jinny Jenkins will be here at three o'clock. Be ready for her,' she informed Lucy coldly.

'What do I have to do?' Lucy asked timidly.

'Stay in your room. Strip your bed and cover the mattress with old newspapers and an old blanket. Ada will bring them up to you. Leave the rest to Jinny, but do exactly what she tells you. Do you understand?'

Lucy nodded, too frightened to ask any more questions.

'Oh, and make sure you clear up any mess afterwards. Daisy will bring you up a cup of tea when it's all over, and, if you're lucky, either she or Ada will give you a hand to clean the place. If they're too busy, then you'll have to do it yourself.'

'And my baby ... what will happen to that?'

'Baby? It'll be nothing but bits and pieces after Jinny's finished,' Maggie told her callously. 'Don't worry about it. She'll wrap the scraps up in newspaper and we'll get rid of it, along with all the other rubbish, in the boiler down in the basement.'

Even as Maggie spoke, Lucy was sure she felt a tiny fluttering movement under her heart, as if the child inside her was protesting about its fate.

'I don't feel too well, can I go up to my room now?' Lucy asked.

Maggie nodded. 'If you must. Don't start getting hysterical or thinking you can change your mind,' she warned. 'I must want my brain seeing to, arranging this for you and agreeing to have you back working here again after the trouble you've caused me.'

Lucy went to her room, but there were so many terrible thoughts going round and round in her head she was afraid she was going mad.

She looked out of the window at the swirling snow that almost obliterated the street and felt trapped. She decided to slip out for some air.

She pulled on the old grey coat that had been her mother's; it was the only one she had. Maggie had provided her with some dresses, but not a coat. 'You won't be needing one,' she'd said, 'because you won't be putting a foot outside this house for quite a long time!'

The cold was intense. The icy snow lashed against her face and for one moment she was tempted to turn round and go back indoors. Then the sense of freedom overcame her discomfort and she pressed on, pulling the collar of the coat up over her mouth almost to her eyes, so that she could barely see where she was going.

She was almost at the end of the road, leaning against the gale-force wind, when she collided with someone coming the other way. Someone short, stout and solid, and Lucy was winded by the impact.

'I'm sorry, luv. I'm afraid I didn't spot you in this blizzard. Are you all right, chook?'

Lucy gasped. She recognised the voice even though she hadn't heard it for months.

'Aunt Flo!'

The grip on her arm tightened, and Lucy's heart pounded as she waited for the other person to speak again. Was this dumpy figure shrouded in a black shawl really her Aunt Flo, or was she imagining things?

'Lucy! Mother of God, is it really you?'

Tears streamed from Lucy's eyes, as she gave a sob of relief. She wasn't dreaming or hallucinating. Her heart raced; it was her aunt's voice.

'Lucy, my dear!' Aunt Flo's arms went round her, hugging her close to her rotund figure. 'What on earth are you doing out in this terrible weather?'

Lucy stiffened. 'I needed some fresh air.' She

snuffled back her tears. 'What are you doing here?'

'I was coming to Maggie Mayer's place to see you.'

'You knew I was there?'

'Brenda told me. She told me all about what had happened; everything in fact,' Aunt Flo said grimly.

Lucy pulled away. 'She shouldn't have done that,' she said angrily. 'It was none of her business.'

'I'm glad she did! I was terribly upset when I heard what you'd been through. Why on earth didn't you come and see me? I'm sure I could've helped you in some way.'

'How could I, after Uncle Fred threw me out and told me never to come back?'

Aunt Flo sighed. 'He's never forgiven my family for saying he wasn't good enough for me. He shouldn't have taken it out on you, though, and he certainly shouldn't have sold your few bits and pieces.'

'You know about that? I didn't think Selina would have told you,' Lucy gasped.

'She didn't. It was Brenda. She came round to see our Frank but he was out and we got talking. She told me a good many other things as well. To think our Selina not only diddled you over your mother's few clothes, but then took you along to Maggie Mayer's place, makes me sick to my soul. May God forgive her, it was a terrible thing to do.'

'I think she was trying to help me . . .'

'You should've gone back to Belgrave Road. That's where I thought you were.'

'I'd given back my keys. I did ask Brenda to ask Stanley for them when she was visiting Frank, but the prison people wouldn't let her see him,' Lucy mumbled.

'You could have gone yourself and asked him for them.'

Lucy bit down on her lower lip. 'Yes, I know, but I didn't think he'd want me visiting him in prison. I thought he'd be ashamed.'

'No,' Flo Flanagan sighed. 'That's true enough. A man like Stanley Jones would probably have been terribly ashamed for you to see him in that sort of setting. Even so, you knew he wouldn't mind you living at Belgrave Road so there was nothing to stop you getting in through a window, or breaking down the door, now was there?'

Lucy looked at her aunt in astonishment, then giggled hysterically. 'If I'd been caught doing that I would have been accused of burglary, or of breaking and entering, and sent to prison as well!'

'I suppose so,' Aunt Flo agreed half-heartedly. 'Well, never mind, you don't have to do anything like that now because I've got your keys for you.'

Lucy looked bewildered. 'I don't understand, how do you come by them?'

'It's far too long a story, to tell you standing here in this blizzard, chook. We'd better get inside somewhere out of this bitter wind or we'll both end up with pneumonia.'

She took hold of Lucy's arm. 'St Cuthbert's church isn't far from here, we'll go there. It's

342

where I told Fred and the others that I was going anyway, so come along.'

Heads bent against the blinding sleet, buffeted by the wind until they were almost breathless, they clung to each other as they struggled to make their way to St Cuthbert's.

Chapter Thirty-One

'Heaven help us, what are the pair of you doing out in this weather?' Father O'Reilly's elderly housekeeper greeted them. 'Come along in with you both! Give me your wet things and I'll take them through to the kitchen and dry them out for you.'

She took Lucy's coat and Flo's black shawl, handling them gingerly because melting snow-flakes were dripping from them all over the polished parquet floor of the hall.

'Go on through into the parlour, Mrs Flanagan, there's a fire in there. Dry out and warm your-selves while I brew up a pot of tea.'

As they huddled in front of a roaring fire, Aunt Flo fumbled in the pocket of her black skirt. 'Here, Lucy, you'd better take these keys.'

Lucy shook her head and moved away from her.

'What's the matter?' There was alarm in her aunt's voice. 'I'm not too late, am I? You haven't gone through with the abortion yet, have you?'

Aunt Flo placed a hand under Lucy's chin, tilting her face up so that she could look into her eyes. 'I told you I know everything,' she said gently. 'Brenda's explained all about it, and told me about Maggie Mayer's conditions. It's all nonsense, though. You mustn't agree to such an arrangement. She can't make you do anything of the sort.'

'I don't want to go through with any of it!' Lucy whimpered. 'Yet is it right to have a baby when I have nothing to offer it? I've no home, no job, so how could I possibly look after it?'

'There are ways, Lucy,' Aunt Flo insisted. 'You can go back to Belgrave Road for a start.'

Lucy breathed deeply, too overwhelmed to speak in case she said the wrong thing. At that moment she wanted nothing more than to be back there. It was where she'd spent a happy childhood and where she'd grown up knowing nothing but love and kindness.

If only she'd never left Belgrave Road none of this would ever have happened. If she'd never gone to live with the Flanagans there would have been no fight outside the Cotton Exchange, and neither Frank nor Stanley would have ended up in prison. She would probably never have known that such places as Maggie Mayer's existed.

Her promise to her mother rang in her ears, but suddenly it was a hollow sound. Her mother had had no idea what the future would hold when she'd extracted that promise, Lucy thought bitterly. If she could see the sort of life I'm leading now because she forced me to make it, she would be absolutely horrified.

Lucy had never understood why her mother had harboured any distrust about Stanley. He was always so kind and considerate, and cared deeply about her welfare.

345

Richard had professed to love her, but all he had wanted was to use her body for his own pleasure. She remembered the angry spark in his eyes, and the look of outrage on his face, when she admitted that she'd let Maggie know about their plans to live together. And she'd never forget the revulsion in his eyes when she'd told him she was pregnant.

When she'd lain in his arms, listening to his dreams for the future, she'd been stupid enough to think he was making plans for both of them. She'd been under his spell, taken in by his glib words and the magic of the moment. She'd succumbed to his flattery and charm, and let him use her for his own base purposes. And he'd dumped her the moment he thought she might be a liability, she thought resentfully. He'd given her money for an abortion and then completely blanked her out of his life. Paid her off like an overdue bill, wiped the slate clean and then forgotten her.

Stanley had risked his life and reputation defending her when she'd been attacked, yet she'd never once visited him while he had been in jail, or even written him a letter. She hadn't even taken the trouble to find out the exact date when he was being released.

Despite the fact that he was almost a recluse, shy to the point of being bashful, Stanley was so dependable. He'd worked at the Cotton Exchange all his life and yet, until the skirmish with Doug Baldwin, half the people there had never heard of him. She couldn't remember him taking a holiday the whole time she'd known him. His time in Walton Jail was probably the longest spell he'd ever been away from Belgrave Road.

If she went back to Belgrave Road, then surely she'd be using him for her own selfish purposes, just as Richard had used her?

The housekeeper's return with a tray of tea and a plate of cakes, followed by Father O'Reilly, momentarily saved Lucy from reaching a decision.

'So this is young Lucy,' the priest smiled kindly. 'A terrible day for the pair of you to be out. Now eat and drink while we talk. Has your aunt told you about Frank then, Lucy?'

She frowned. 'About Frank? What about him?'

Father O'Reilly shook his head. 'Gone off to America, so he has, and says he's never coming back. Broken-hearted, so she is, poor woman.'

'Oh, Aunt Flo! And you're worrying about my problems when you've got worries of your own! Does Brenda know?'

Her aunt nodded. 'Yes, she came over to see him last night, and it was left to me to tell her he'd gone. She was so upset that she began blaming me not only for her troubles, but for yours as well. That's when I learned for the first time what had happened to you, my dear. She told me every detail, held nothing at all back.'

Father O'Reilly patted Aunt Flo's shoulder. 'Ah now, don't be worrying your heart out over something you can do nothing about,' he warned. 'The Good Lord and the Blessed Virgin are

347

watching over you, and it will all be sorted out in due time.'

Aunt Flo crossed herself. 'Yes, Father,' she agreed meekly.

'Your aunt has told me all about your dilemma, my dear,' he said, turning to Lucy. 'The good nuns will be able to help you. They'll put a roof over your head until your child is born. Afterwards, if you wish to have the child adopted, they'll find a good Catholic home for it.'

Lucy stared at him wide-eyed. She knew she ought to be grateful that he was saving her from the unknown horrors she would have to face at the hands of Jinny Jenkins, but his words sounded so cold, so inhuman. It was almost as if he was talking about finding a home for a stray kitten or a puppy.

'Take your time, Lucy, and think things over,' Aunt Flo advised. She held out the keys. 'Go back to Belgrave Road until you've made your mind up about what you want to do.'

'Perhaps you're right, Aunt Flo. It seems like Fate somehow, Brenda bringing these over to you,' Lucy murmured, holding out her hand for them.

'They didn't come from Brenda! I went over to see Stanley Jones first thing this morning after Brenda told me that you were in trouble, and that you'd gone back to Maggie Mayer's place,' Aunt Flo explained.

The colour drained from Lucy's cheeks. 'You mean you told Stanley about me being pregnant?' she said angrily.

348

Flo Flanagan crossed herself. 'Mother of God, what have I done wrong now? Of course I told Stanley Jones everything. I wanted to get you out of Maggie Mayer's clutches. I knew I couldn't take you back to Anfield Road, not with my Fred feeling as he does. He even thinks our Frank has cleared off to America because of you.'

Lucy's eyes widened. 'What do you mean?'

'Our Frank was in love with you, surely you know that?' Aunt Flo said wearily.

'No, he wasn't! He was in love with Brenda. I thought that now he was out of prison they were going to be married.'

'Poor cow! He'd tell her anything just to get his way with her,' Aunt Flo said bitterly. She looked guiltily at Father O'Reilly. 'Begging your pardon, Father.'

He patted her on the shoulder, but said nothing.

'No,' Aunt Flo repeated, 'he was in love with you, Lucy, and he knew you had no time for him, so no doubt Fred's right and that's why he cleared off. Poor Brenda guessed the truth, and she's heart-broken about it.'

'She must really hate me,' Lucy whispered. 'Yet I swear I knew nothing about his feelings. I always thought he disliked me.' She jangled the keys in her hand. 'It looks as though I've no alternative but to use these,' she said sadly.

'It's for the best for the time being, my child,' Father O'Reilly advised. 'Rest, get yourself strong, and pray for forgiveness and guidance. We'll be offering up prayers for you. Come back here in, say, a week or so's time, and tell me what you intend to do. If you want the nuns to take care of you, then I'll make the necessary arrangements. Your Aunt Flo will be allowed to visit you, but no one else need know anything at all about it.'

'There's no one else who would care,' Lucy said bitterly.

'Except Stanley Jones,' Aunt Flo reminded her. 'He cares about you, Lucy. He is one of the kindest and most compassionate men I've ever known. My Karen loves him. She's a wonderful judge of people!'

Lucy's eyes filled with tears. 'Apart from you, Aunt Flo, Karen was the only one who really made me welcome when I arrived at your place,' she murmured. 'I'd like to see her again.'

'Perhaps you will, one day. Wait until all the furore has died down. Time's a great healer, isn't it, Father?'

'That and prayer!' he agreed. 'You must pray for God's forgiveness, my child, and thank him and the Holy Mother for answering your aunt's prayers and ensuring that love and kindness surround you in your time of trouble.'

'Could I have my coat, please, and I'll be off,' Lucy said.

'And I'll have my shawl at the same time, Father. I'd better be getting back or Fred and the girls will think I'm lost.'

As Father O'Reilly's housekeeper was fetching them, they heard her say, 'Yes, Mrs Flanagan is here. You'd better come on through,' and she showed a man wearing a heavy black overcoat into the room.

350

Flo Flanagan crossed herself. 'The Holy Mother's listened to my prayers and answered them already,' she murmured in awe.

Colour rushed into Lucy's cheeks. 'Stanley, what are you doing here?' she gasped.

'I was trying to find your Aunt Flo to ask where you were. I went to Anfield Road and they said I'd find her here at St Cuthbert's, but it was you I was looking for, Lucy.'

Flo Flanagan looked flustered. 'And now you've found her so you won't be wanting words with me so I'll be on my way, or my family'll be sending the scuffers to find me!'

Father O'Reilly also looked nonplussed for a moment, but then taking Flo firmly by the arm he guided her from the room.

'I'll see you out then,' he said tactfully. As they left the room he shut the door discreetly behind them.

'What are you doing here?' Lucy asked again the moment she and Stanley were on their own.

'I wanted to make sure you were coming back to Belgrave Road to have your baby.'

'Stanley, do you really know what you're saying?' Lucy asked wistfully. 'Think what it will do to your reputation, having an unmarried mother and her bastard child living under your roof. No one will ever speak to you again.'

'That won't matter,' he stated curtly. 'As long as you're there I don't need anyone else.'

She looked dubious. 'There's the baby to think about when it grows older. It would probably get called names when it went to school.'

351

'Not if you married me and it took my name.'

'What!' Lucy's head jerked back, and she stared at Stanley dumbfounded. She couldn't believe she was hearing right. She studied him in disbelief. He'd changed in so many ways that he was like a stranger. He'd lost weight and looked leaner and fitter. His whole manner, even his voice, seemed to be more assertive, and his grey eyes were shrewder and more piercing.

'Marry me, Lucy. I won't make any demands on you,' he promised. 'It will be on your terms. You can have your own rooms and live completely separate from me if you wish. Marry me and I'll claim the baby as mine.'

She wanted to accept, not simply because it would save her from the imminent threat of abortion at the hands of Jinny Jenkins, but because she wanted to give the child she was carrying not only a chance of life but a worthwhile future in happy, loving surroundings.

She studied Stanley more closely. He hadn't only changed physically; there was something deeper. She sensed the difference. He was so much more manly. The shy, self-effacing manner had been replaced by a confident self-assurance; it was as if he had matured while he'd been in prison.

In the past she'd liked him well enough, been appreciative of his generosity at Christmas and the presents he gave her for her birthday, but only treated him with deference because he was her mother's employer.

She'd accepted his help in finding her a job at

the Cotton Exchange because she'd told herself that he felt responsible for her welfare, because his home had been her home for as long as she could remember.

This was the first time, however, that she'd actually thought of him as a real friend and as someone she could confide in and trust implicitly.

But was that enough? A child needed love as well as compassion and financial security. Could they build a happy home for it based on tolerance and respect for each other alone? And what of her promise to her mother that she would leave Belgrave Road and live with her father's sister in Liverpool?

A shudder went through her as the memories of all that had happened as a result of trying to keep that promise crowded her mind. Her mother had meant well but she'd had no idea of the sort of family the Flanagans were. If she had, then their behaviour, and the way they spoke, would have horrified her.

The very last thing she would have wanted would have been for me to have anything at all to do with them, Lucy decided. Mother had been such a stickler for proper behaviour and decorum. This was no doubt the reason why she had been so insistent that I should go and live with the Flanagans, Lucy thought wryly. She would have thought it highly improper for an unmarried girl and an unmarried man to live under the same roof without a chaperon.

Her mother was dead, she was the one now who had to take decisions about what lay ahead.

And it wasn't only her future that was at stake, it was also that of her unborn baby.

She was so overwhelmed by the generosity of Stanley's offer that she felt tears threatening. To go back to Belgrave Road, to enjoy once again the comfortable lifestyle she'd known throughout her childhood, was tempting, but would it be fair on Stanley?

'You can't possibly make yourself responsible for bringing up another man's child!' she protested.

'I want to,' he assured her decisively. 'It would make me extremely happy. You must know how much I love you, Lucy. I always have. At first, when you were a child, I cared for you because of your brightness and gentleness. Then when you became a woman, my feelings changed and grew deeper, and I knew I wanted to be with you always. It was agony to me when you left. But I kept on hoping that one day you might feel the same way about me and come back. Have your baby, Lucy, and let me provide a home for both of you. It will mean I have the family I've always dreamed about.'

Lucy ached to accept his offer, but she was afraid that yet again she might be walking into a trap.

'Lucy,' his tone was a mixture of pleading and weariness, 'you want this baby, you know you do. You can't bear the thought of an abortion. Isn't that right?'

She felt herself weakening. Stanley might not set her heart racing or her pulse tingling as Richard Thomas had done, but she cared a great deal for him and knew he would always treat her with consideration and respect.

Perhaps that was love, true love, she reasoned. Could it be that her feelings for Richard had been nothing more than an adolescent crush?

'Come on, Lucy,' Stanley urged, 'make up your mind. You'll be completely free to live your life exactly as you choose. I won't make any demands, I promise.'

She offered no resistance when Stanley took her hands, cradling them between his own. 'You know how deeply I love you, Lucy. Don't turn me down. You may not feel the same at this moment, but I'm confident that given time your feelings for me will grow into love,' he insisted.

He raised her hand to his lips. 'Until then, my dearest, I can promise you that my love is great enough to encompass all three of us,' he affirmed, his grey eyes brimming with the love he felt for her.

Shyly, Lucy reached out and pulled his face closer. Her lips were warm and trusting as they met his. 'Let's go home,' she whispered.

To find out more about Rosie Harris and other fantastic Arrow authors why not read *The Inside Story* – our newsletter featuring all of our saga authors.

To join our mailing list to receive the newsletter and other information* write with your name and address to:

The Inside Story
The Marketing Department
Arrow Books
20 Vauxhall Bridge Road
London
SW1V 2SA

Patsy of Paradise Place
Rosie Harris

After years of neglect by her mother, when her father comes home from sea and sets up as a carrier at the Liverpool Docks, Patsy dreams of being a proper family again.

But when her father is killed in an accident and her mother returns to her errant ways, Patsy must keep the business going with the help of her childhood friend, Billy Grant.

And when Patsy falls passionately in love with fairground showman Bruno Alvarez, who leaves her pregnant and heartbroken, only loyal Billy stands by her in her troubles.

But when he is badly injured at work Patsy is left friendless and without a home . . .

arrow books

At Sixes & Sevens

Rosie Harris

Living in the shadow of their domineering father, Rhianon and Sabrina Webster plan two very different futures. Edwin dotes on his youngest daughter, beautiful, flighty Sabrina, but it is homely, steady Rhianon who holds their little family together. Until one fateful day when Pryce Pritchard, the man Rhianon loves, gets into a fight and all their worlds are thrown into turmoil. Pryce is arrested – and Sabrina disappears . . .

Months later Rhianon chances upon her sister and is shocked to find her pregnant, living in squalid lodgings in the poorest part of Cardiff. When Davyn is born Sabrina will have nothing to do with him, and kind-hearted Rhianon looks after the little boy, patiently awaiting Pryce's release. But when Pryce is finally set free, he brings with him secrets that will devastate them all.

arrow books

Looking for Love

Rosie Harris

Abbie Martin has grown up in squalor in one of Liverpool's most deprived areas. The youngest of three, she longs to be loved by her mother, but Ellen spends all her time with her eldest son, while Abbie and her brother, Sam, take refuge with their neighbours, Sandra Lewis and Peter Ryan.

Although vibrant and attractive, Abbie pushes people away with her constant need for reassurance. Infatuated with Peter, she longs for the day when he tells her that he loves her. And Sam is courting Sandra. But Peter and Sandra have a secret – one that will destroy the friends' relationship should it become known.

Will Abbie finally find the security and affection she has been searching for all her life, or will she always be looking for love . . . ?

arrow books